"I'll get some fresh water from the stream and then we..." He paused and stared at her as though deciding whether or not to finish his words.

"And then?" Sheena prodded.

"And then we can talk about our betrothal and forthcoming marriage."

Her stomach tightened as he turned and walked out. "Better now than later," she whispered, trying to make herself believe it. From the time he'd found her in Anna's garden and then during their ride, Robbie had been almost...caring.

Sheena watched him fill the bucket. Before he turned back, she studied him closely, though there was not much to see other than his tall, muscular figure and the strength in him as he held the heavy bucket out into the strong current. As he stood, she hurried to the cupboard to find cups.

His steps behind her told her he was there and it was time.

Time to make him realize she could not marry him.

Time to gain his help in forcing their parents to see the truth of their betrothal.

Time to confess her truth?

Author Note

Back in 2005 when I was writing the book that would become *Taming the Highlander*, I had no idea that it would be the first in a series that stretched over nine medieval and two Regency romances! Or that the story about Connor MacLerie, the Beast of the Highlands and quintessential alpha hero, would become my bestselling book and the start of my most popular series. When brainstorming this book and comparing timelines and stories yet untold, I was thrilled to see a possible connection between my MacLeries series and my current A Highland Feuding one.

Sheena MacLerie, Connor and Jocelyn's youngest daughter, had yet to meet her match, and when looking for a heroine for Robbie Cameron, the heir to the Cameron Clan, I thought she was the perfect woman for him. That doesn't mean that their path to love is easy or without challenges—I could never resist making things difficult for my heroes and their heroines. And it doesn't mean that her powerful father won't muck things up for the couple as they seek their happy ever after!

I hope you enjoy this "crossover" story between my two Highland series. By the end of it, you'll decide for yourself whether Connor is a nightmare father-in-law or the best one!

TERRI BRISBIN

The Highlander's Inconvenient Bride

HARLEQUIN®
HISTORICAL™

Recycling programs
for this product may
not exist in your area.

ISBN-13: 978-1-335-40725-2

The Highlander's Inconvenient Bride

Copyright © 2021 by Theresa S. Brisbin

All rights reserved. No part of this book may be used or reproduced in
any manner whatsoever without written permission except in the case of
brief quotations embodied in critical articles and reviews.

This is a work of fiction. Names, characters, places and incidents
are either the product of the author's imagination or are used fictitiously.
Any resemblance to actual persons, living or dead, businesses,
companies, events or locales is entirely coincidental.

This edition published by arrangement with Harlequin Books S.A.

For questions and comments about the quality of this book,
please contact us at CustomerService@Harlequin.com.

Harlequin Enterprises ULC
22 Adelaide St. West, 40th Floor
Toronto, Ontario M5H 4E3, Canada
www.Harlequin.com

Printed in U.S.A.

When *USA TODAY* bestselling author **Terri Brisbin** is not being a glamorous romance author or in a deadline-writing-binge-o-mania, she's a wife, mom, grandmom and dental hygienist in the southern New Jersey area. A three-time RWA RITA® Award finalist, Terri has had more than forty-five historical and paranormal romance novels, novellas and short stories published since 1998. You can visit her website, www.terribrisbin.com, to learn more about her.

Books by Terri Brisbin

Harlequin Historical

A Highland Feuding

The MacLerie Clan

Visit the Author Profile page at Harlequin.com for more titles.

Prologue

Lairig Dubh, Scotland, home of the MacLerie Clan,
the Year of Our Lord 1367

Sheena MacLerie stared at the tapestry hanging on the wall and tried to admire her sister's accomplishment in finishing it herself. But the whistling sound of the belt sweeping towards its target forced her eyes closed with each stroke. She could not help herself.

As she watched her father punish the boy who'd pushed her into the river, she winced and gasped with each stroke of his belt. The boy receiving the whipping did not make a sound, other than a soft exhalation with each stroke.

She wanted to cry out to stop it, but she'd brought this about and could not utter a word now. If she had just stayed away from them, none of this would have happened. If she had played with her sister as her mother had asked, Robbie Cameron would not be suffering through this.

Oh, he had not begun by shoving her off the edge into

the water. Nay, that had been the third or fourth time he'd tried to keep her away from his and her brother's plans.

First, he'd managed to slip away after sending her on a wayward and non-existent errand for her mother. They'd got away while Sheena had spent a tedious morning inside the dull and gloomy keep, sorting the colours of thread in her mother's sewing box.

Then, when she grew better at following them, Robbie had locked her in a cupboard and got away for an entire day without her. Remembering it now, she realised that she'd not been frightened at all and spent the few hours in it asleep, the dark and warm space more a comfort than not.

But neither of those had been in her father's view. Sheena had complained to her mother, so at least she was aware of this pattern of his of excluding her. This time though, Connor MacLerie, chieftain of the powerful MacLerie Clan, could not ignore it.

Tears were streaming down her face now as her father stepped away and nodded to the men holding Robbie's arms.

Robbie straightened his garments before turning around and bowing to her father. As clan chief and Robbie's foster father, it was her father's right and duty to see to the discipline of those he fostered. She just did not remember seeing him do this to another in his care. Twinges of an unwelcome feeling grew within her.

Guilt.

'You do not mistreat a lass, Robbie. Even…' he paused and looked over to meet her own gaze '…when you think it might be warranted. Do you understand?'

'Aye, my lord,' Robbie whispered.

'I canna hear you, lad. Speak up and look at me.'

This time, he did raise his head and meet her father's gaze. Nodding, Robbie spoke up. 'Aye, my lord. I understand.'

'She is still but a child and can be annoying. But a man must have a care.'

Robbie's gaze now flitted over to hers for a scant moment before speaking. And in that single moment she saw such hatred that she gasped again. 'Aye, my lord.'

Robbie waited until her father dismissed him with a curt tilt of his head and he walked out. If his first step or two were a bit shaky, it was to be expected. But he held his head high as he left the solar, where the man known as the Beast of the Highlands had gathered his closest kith and kin to see to this matter. Sheena wanted to follow Robbie and beg his forgiveness, but her father's next words held her in her place.

'Sheena MacLerie, you are not blameless in this misbehaviour. You have been told to leave the lads to their tasks before.'

That inkling of guilt disappeared as tremors of fear and the grip of shame held her so tightly she could not draw breath. When her father used that tone of voice, nothing good would come of it. She nodded quickly and looked away from his harsh amber gaze.

'Jocelyn, see to the lass.' Her mother rose from her chair and walked to the door, waiting for Sheena to follow her.

'Come with me, Sheena.'

If her father's tone scared her, her mother's broke her heart, for it was filled with disappointment. And she hated those moments when she knew she'd disappointed her parents.

Her mother climbed the stairs to the floor where the

family's bedchambers were and led Sheena to a small one that was unused. Opening the door, she motioned for Sheena to go in.

'You will remain here until I call for you, Sheena. You might want to spend some of this time praying for forgiveness for your own part in what just happened to a lad who is here as a foster brother to you and Aidan and Lilidh. One who has just been shamed before those of importance to him and for no reason other than your own wilfulness.'

Sheena cried aloud now, unable to keep in her guilt and shame. Because she wanted his attention. Because he would not give it. Because...

'Mother, I—'

'Nay, Sheena. Speak not to me now or I will say things I will regret. Go in now. You will get no supper this night, so do not ask for it.'

Sheena could not make her feet move.

'Go. In. Now.'

She ran, throwing herself on the small pallet in the corner of the chamber and sobbing as she heard the door slam closed and locked. When her tears ran dry and her stomach hurt from sobbing so hard, Sheena sat up and pushed her now messy hair out of her face. Using the edge of her sleeve, even knowing she should not, Sheena wiped the remains of her tears from her cheeks and chin.

Sitting in silence, she thought on her mother's words, but more, she thought about the look of hatred in Robbie's eyes. That fiery glance told her he would never have anything to do with her again. He would probably not have a word to say, nice or cross, for the rest of her life.

And the worst of it was that she truly liked Robbie. Most of the time, when she was not pestering him, he was nice. Tall and growing taller, serious about learning from her father and always courteous and respectful of her mother, he would become the warrior his clan expected of him. While she would just continue as the unwanted child she was.

The sun, shining in through the lone window in this chamber, taunted her. She'd finished her tasks earlier and should be out playing with her friends. Sheena climbed up on the pallet and onto the storage cupboard and peered out of that window.

Below in the yard, life went on without her. Her father's warriors trained. Her father's servants carried out their chores and duties. Her father's orders being followed every moment of the day. And she had no doubt that her father had, with her mother's consent and approval, determined her punishment too.

Just when she would have turned away, she saw Robbie.

He stood alone in the shadows next to the stable. Though one or another called out to him or waved, he did not wave back. She could feel his pain as he shifted from foot to foot. For a moment he leaned back against the rough stone wall behind him, but then he stiffened and moved away.

And she gasped as he did it, knowing the pain was caused by the whipping she'd brought about. She must come up with a way to make this better. To beg his pardon and to make him not hate her.

Three days later, she was allowed to leave the chamber. Sheena was permitted to eat supper with the family and, as she glanced around the hall, she noticed that Robbie was not present. She was stubborn like her father and so she waited and watched for her opportunity to speak to him. It took her two more days to finally find him and, even then, he would not meet her gaze. The door to the stables opened and Robbie entered. Sheena was seeing to her favourite horse when he walked slowly past her without uttering a word.

'Robbie,' she whispered, 'I would speak to you.' When he took another step, she moved to the wooden gate at the end of the stall. 'I beg you to hear my words.'

'I must see to my duties,' he said without turning to her. 'Leave me be.'

'Robbie, I did not mean for you to be punished.'

At first, he did not reply. But he turned to face her.

'I just asked you to leave me be. And, like before, you could not. Now, word will be sent to my father and my uncle of my transgression and punishment, Sheena, and I will be called home. I will pay another price to them.' He wiped his hand across his eyes and shook his head. 'A disgrace. A failure.'

The slump of his shoulders as he turned away broke her heart. And the words pierced her, for she understood being a failure in her father's eyes.

'But it was my fault, Robbie. Not yers.'

'It matters not now, Sheena. For your father took action to punish me and my uncle and father will consider me guilty just on that.'

She watched him walk through the stables and said nothing else. For what else could she say?

Over the next few years while he lived with them, Sheena convinced herself that disliking him would make it easier for her to keep her distance. So she made the dislike a habit and soon she'd convinced even herself that she believed it. She turned her devotion to horses and conquered her old fear of the huge beasts. In a short time the experienced stablemaster was praising her skills of handling, care and riding horses to her father.

As they grew older, the space between her and Robbie grew greater and greater until she never wanted anything to do with him and had little chance to. Sheena avoided him during the times when they were both at gatherings and sat as far away as she could when at table. By the time Robbie was called home to visit some years later, she could not have changed how she felt about him if she'd wanted to. Not that she wanted to. And for his part Robbie continued to meet her gaze any time he happened upon her with the expression of one smelling something rancid and disgusting.

When the day came for him to return to Achnacarry, their feelings towards each other had not changed. But instead of him leaving Lairig Dubh and their days of loathing ceasing, a surprise was announced.

At an appropriate time, to be decided by their parents, she would marry Robbie. Truth be told, Sheena had never expected to have any part in the decision about whom she married. As the daughter of a mighty chieftain, her value lay in the connections her marriage would make and the alliances forged or strengthened by it. With a deep sadness in her heart, this action by her parents just reinforced her comprehension of their total disregard for her.

The only part of it that saved her from true despair was knowing she would never be called to serve as her mother did. With her weaknesses and lack of abilities to oversee a clan and a keep and village, Sheena would not have to since Robbie was the nephew to the chieftain and would never rise to the high seat of power. Even with all that was between them, Sheena resigned herself to the fact that she would do her duty and accept her place as the wife of a man who did not love her.

Then word came from Achnacarry that Robbie's father had claimed the high seat of the Cameron Clan and her marriage would see her as the wife of the heir of his clan. Terrified by such a prospect, she prayed nightly for an escape from such a life and from the shame of her secrets when they would inevitably be exposed. She prayed that Robbie's father would want a higher connection for his son and heir. She prayed...and prayed.

The Good Lord Above had listened to someone else's prayers for, in far too little time, Sheena MacLerie found herself officially betrothed to Robbie Cameron. Two years after her sister Lilidh married, Sheena received word summoning her to Robbie's home in preparation for their marriage.

Aye, the Almighty's attentions were elsewhere when Sheena MacLerie truly needed them.

Chapter One

*Achnacarry, Scotland, home of the Cameron Clan,
the Year of Our Lord 1377*

'The MacLerie and I wish this marriage to be accomplished soon.'

Words Robbie Cameron had dreaded hearing, even if they were not unexpected, echoed in his head. He'd avoided even thinking on the betrothal since the day it had been made, without his approval or knowledge. The MacLerie had told him of it one day, during the time Robbie had lived at Lairig Dubh as Connor's foster son. The day when he was called home by the order of his chieftain, his uncle, to attend the man's third wedding, or was it his fourth? Though it had not been official at that time, but by the time his father had replaced his uncle it had been made so. He had been in his minority so he'd not even attended the ceremony that would have been held.

'Must it?' he asked.

His mother's quick inhalation drew his attention. Since he'd never once spoken of the arrangement, his parents most likely thought he favoured it. And nothing could be further from his true feelings.

'Do you have some concern over it?' Robert Cameron, chieftain of the Cameron Clan, asked quietly. His father rarely raised his voice and Robbie knew that if he grew any quieter hell was about to rain down on earth. A shiver ran down his spine at the soft tone of his voice now. 'Son?'

He had many concerns about the betrothal and the suitability of the two of them to marry. Since the incident that had brought him shame and a whipping all those years ago, Robbie had avoided her—he did not speak or even look at her if he did not have to. The last woman on earth he wanted to marry was, indeed, his betrothed, Sheena MacLerie.

'I have grave concerns over it, over her, Father,' he said. 'But none serious enough to break the agreement and jeopardise the concessions you won from The MacLerie.'

Now his mother approached, worry in her gaze, and stood before him. 'Robbie, why is this girl not acceptable to you?' she asked.

'The MacLerie spoke of some youthful mischief between the two of you, but he never suggested a more serious issue,' his father said. Robbie could feel his mouth drop open. The MacLerie had not revealed Robbie's disgrace and humiliation before the chieftain's closest advisors and kin? His father frowned. 'Did something else cause strife between the two of you?'

Youthful mischief? That was how Connor MacLerie had described it to his father? Had he never revealed the rest? Robbie could not remember much of that first visit home after the punishment. His clan had been in upheaval for a number of years as their feud with the Mackintoshes ebbed and flowed. A whipping for misbehaviour would have been a minor thing in the face of the challenges and changes at that time.

'Nay, Father,' he said, even as so much more swirled through his thoughts.

'Robbie, we would not have you unhappy in your marriage,' his mother said. 'Do you have some concern or something…?' He had never spoken ill of the lass to his parents before and, from their hopeful and happy expressions, he would not begin now.

'I will fulfil my duty to the clan,' Robbie said. He drew his shoulders back and exhaled.

Though his mother hugged him and murmured good wishes and words of joy in this arrangement, her gaze studied him as if she did not quite believe his acceptance. Strategic marriages were expected of those in his position—tanist, heir to the high seat of his clan. It was the story of her life as well, so his acquiescence should not surprise her. He was, after all, her son and she'd raised him to know his duty and the cost of betraying it.

Marrying Sheena MacLerie would be just that—a marriage of allies, lands and power. For he'd seen the grievous damage done when his father had allowed his feelings for his mother to affect his decisions and Robbie had sworn never to follow that same path. For the good of the clan.

Nodding at his father, he waited for any other questions. 'Do you wish anything else of me, Father?'

'The lass will arrive soon to live here awhile and become familiar with us and our ways before the marriage.'

'And to reacquaint herself with you, Robbie,' his

mother added. A soft gleam in her gaze revealed her hopes for this union.

His father cleared his throat. 'The MacLerie will follow in some weeks to finalise the agreement and witness the wedding.' Standing tall with his shoulders thrown back and a serious, stern expression on his face, The Cameron asked the fateful question once more. 'Do you agree to marry Sheena MacLerie?'

Robbie knew this was the last time he could reveal his true feelings on the coming match and marriage. But, seeing his father's resolve and understanding what his duty was in this matter, Robbie did and said the only thing his conscience and loyalty would allow...

'Aye, sir. I will marry The MacLerie daughter.'

Having got the response he wanted, his father clapped him on the shoulders and shook him. 'Good! I am gladdened by your consent. Now we can move forward to strengthen the clan, expand our holdings and ally ourselves with The MacLerie.' His father released him and walked to face his wife. 'Elizabeth, you have everything prepared for her arrival?' Before she could speak, he laughed. 'I am certain you do, love. Do you have need of more servants or anything else?'

'Nay, husband, I have things in hand.'

Something had gone unsaid here and Robbie tried to sort through what had been spoken to work out what was missing. A tremor of unease trickled down his spine.

'Father?' He waited for his father to face him. 'When is Sheena expected to arrive?'

He thought he had time to truly accustom himself to the idea of marrying the one woman he could not abide. He thought he could ease into the decision and ready himself to be, at the least, tolerant of her. From the broad smile that spread over his father's face, Robbie knew that his hopes in this were for naught.

'On the morrow.'

'Pardon?'

'I said she arrives on the morrow. A messenger arrived about an hour ago with word of her approach.'

Time was up for him and any thoughts he had of avoiding this. Though he'd been raised with the expectation of being a minor member of the clan hierarchy, his father's unexpected rise to chieftain had changed all of that. When his uncle would have pushed both Robbie and his brother aside and out of sight, now his father's position brought them both into prominence and increased the necessity of carrying out their duty of loyalty to their clan.

Robbie nodded to his parents and walked away. So many thoughts and questions filled his mind that he simply left the keep and headed to the yard next to the stables. The last time he'd seen Sheena she'd been training her father's newest colt. Unmindful of the danger, she had mounted the horse before it would tolerate a saddle or bridle of any kind and she rode the almost wild horse through the village and back to the keep, with her hair flowing out behind her, loose and wild, making her look like some heathen goddess of old. Incandescent with joy, she'd faltered when their gazes met and he'd seen her eyes were filled with only loathing.

And, as in every moment he'd ever shared with her or any time he'd watched her, she never did as she'd been told to do. She broke her father's rules, damn the consequences, when it came to working with the horses, or staying away from the boys in his care. She disregarded her mother's lessons on correct behaviour and her warnings about the proper upbringing for a young woman who would be a wife to and mother of chieftains or their sons.

Soon, too soon, she would ride into Achnacarry and become his problem. The 'wee beastie', as he'd called her more than once, would need to grow up and change to be the wife of the future chieftain. She would need to become a mature woman who understood her place and fulfilled her duties. She could no longer be the hoyden who ran wild and followed her own path, ignoring duty and expectations.

Robbie let out a breath as he watched the horses run loose in the yard. On the morrow she would arrive here and, with his mother's and cousin's help, would learn what was expected of her now.

Surely Sheena MacLerie would try to obey her father and mother by carrying out her duties. Surely even an unruly lass would grow into an honourable, mature woman at some point in her life.

Yet, even as he hoped, he knew differently for he'd seen the true Sheena MacLerie and understood what was heading in their direction. Reckless behaviour. A lack of acceptance of responsibility. Ill prepared for the role of being a laird's wife. Robbie knew all that and more to a certainty and his stomach roiled in anticipation of her arrival.

On the morrow.

From what the guard told her, Sheena understood that they were only an hour or so from the Cameron chieftain's home at Achnacarry Castle. The morning had dawned clear and brisk and the journey was uneventful. No one else seemed to feel the tightening tension that she did as each mile brought them closer and closer to her fate—marriage to the last man on earth who she'd want to marry. Spirals of dread spread through her as she moved mile by mile towards Achnacarry and…him.

After hours on the road at a slow pace, Sheena felt her own restlessness spreading to the strong horse under her. It took more and more concentration to hold him under control. He needed to run. She needed to give him his head and let him. When they came on a more level part of the road as it neared the River Arkaig along the loch, Sheena decided to allow him some freedom. Easing her hold on the reins and waving off the others, she touched the sides of the horse and urged him on.

And the horse took off, leaving the rest of those who escorted her in the dust. Sheena pressed her knees against the horse's sides and lowered her head and body. The horse understood and galloped along the road faster and faster until Sheena could not contain her laughter. A sense of desperation echoed through her as she enjoyed this bit, this last bit, of freedom before becoming someone else. Had she been paying closer attention and not enjoying the feel of the wind against her face, she would have noticed the too-sharp turn in the road sooner. Now, instead of being able to slow or stop in time, she and the horse charged into the bushes and into a large patch of brambles hidden among the undergrowth.

The scream of the horse as the sharp needles scraped his coat and embedded deeper in his skin made her entire being tighten and her stomach roil. The brambles grabbed and tore at her skirts and legs as the horse fought to escape. As quickly as she could, Sheena regained control of the poor creature and guided the horse to a clearing and jumped from his back. Trying to soothe his agitation with whispers and soft touches, she waited as her guards soon arrived at her side and helped her get the giant horse calmed enough for her to examine the injuries. They were deep and bleeding and would need to be tended to quickly.

'The injury is not so grievous that he canna make it the rest of the way, my lady,' her guard said.

'Fergus, we need to make haste to Achnacarry. I must tend to these quickly.' She held her hand up to him and he pulled her up behind him on his mount.

'My lady, remember that ye ken that ye canna do that here. The stablemaster will see to yer mount,' he said, turning to look at her over his shoulder. One of the other guards held her horse's reins and handed them off to her when she reached out for them.

Staring at the poor creature, Sheena comprehended that this situation represented the changes she faced. Aye, she knew things would be different here and a sense of panic flooded her. The thought of accepting those changes made her want to turn back to Lairig Dubh now.

Not only would she no longer have the freedom to tend and train horses as she had in her father's keep, but she would lose other freedoms and bits of control she'd had as the daughter of The MacLerie. She could only hope that Robbie and his father would understand that this was not an ordinary situation and would allow her involvement when it came to her own horse.

'We will see about that when we arrive. For now, let us be on our way.'

It took longer than she'd hoped to make their way across the final miles, but finally they entered the village and approached the gate of the castle. Men, women and children stood watching as they passed by. None waved or acknowledged her. The cool stares simply followed her as she rode past. Did they think she did not know how to treat the injured horse? Did they know who she was? Whatever she'd expected as a welcome, this was not it. Had their messenger not arrived?

When the lead guard would have ridden to the entry-way of the keep, she ordered them to stop as she glanced around the huge yard. Buildings of all sorts lay scattered around the perimeter. Some she could identify by the smells and odours emanating from within them. She turned and searched the rest for one that should be located close to the enclosed yard and found it.

'The stables are over there,' she called out.

Fergus did not argue and, with a nod at the others, he guided the injured mount across the expanse. By the time they arrived a giant of a man stood in front of the wide doors. Without speaking a word to her, he approached her horse and whispered soft sounds as he took control of the bridle to soothe the agitated animal.

'I am…' She began to say her name. He waved her silent before she could finish. She slid down from behind Fergus and followed as the man moved.

With a few hand signals to others watching, he led the horse slowly inside the building, all the while caressing and whispering to him. Doors swung open, a path was cleared and a gate to a stall was unlocked without a word being spoken. Only when the horse was in the stall and tied securely did the man speak.

'My lady, I am Geordie, stablemaster for The Cameron. I will see to yer horse now.'

'Geordie, I will remain to see to his care myself.'

A wave of tension flowed through the place as everyone watching gasped at the challenge to this man's position and responsibilities. Men placed in charge could be prickly when women, especially young women, dared to question them, but Sheena had lived her whole life around that and was not prepared to relent.

'The stitches will need to be deep,' she said, tugging her gloves off and holding them out to her maid, Elen, who now stood at her side. 'There…and there, especially. Some minor scratches would need an unguent applied, but the areas where the brambles tore would have to be stitched.'

'Aye, my lady,' Geordie said. 'Get my box,' he ordered one of the lads watching. 'And two buckets of water—one heated, one cool.'

'I can prepare a potion that will…'

'No need, my lady. I hiv one in my box. When did he last drink?'

'Before the injury,' she replied, moving closer to the stall and the man so boldly making decisions that were hers to make. 'What will you use to make him sleep?' she asked, her curiosity at his confidence forcing the question out.

'This and that, my lady,' the man said. He winked and nodded. 'This and that.' In spite of her initial trepidation, Sheena liked him for his easy manner. She waved off her guard and her maid and moved closer.

Understanding that this was his domain, much as Donal claimed her father's stables as his own, she did not interrupt as he called out to his helpers and prepared a concoction to dose the horse. She watched and took note of the ingredients and how he did it. Grasping the edge of the stall, Sheena held her breath as Geordie approached the horse to give him the potion.

'My lady, if ye hold his head he will be calmer.'

She lost not a moment entering the enclosure and taking hold of the bridle. And she did not miss the twitch of a smile that tilted the corner of the man's mouth. Whether humouring her or needing her help, she cared not. Once she was in place, the bucket that contained a small amount of water mixed with a larger amount of the liquid was held up to the horse's mouth.

'Urge him to drink,' Geordie said.

'Come now, my strong lad,' she whispered, stroking the horse's head as she did so. 'Drink up.'

It took several minutes of coaxing for the entire amount to be consumed. It took less time for the effects to begin. With Geordie's help, the horse was guided to the floor, his head now across Sheena's lap. This was all her fault and she would not leave until she knew the horse was treated.

With a steady and clearly experienced hand, the stablemaster cleaned and stitched the long and deep scratches and gashes. They could not be bound or bandaged, so he applied a thick unguent to coat them and aid in the healing. Sheena did not realise she was crying until he held out a clean piece of linen to her and helped her ease out from under the horse and stand.

'My thanks, Geordie,' she said, nodding at the man. 'And for your help.'

'Ye are welcome, my lady. He's a fine piece of horseflesh. A bit big for ye, I would think.'

'I have had him since he was born. Trained him myself,' she said, smiling through watery eyes.

'Weel, then, ye must have a way wi' horses to do that.'

'Aye, Geordie, the lady has a way with *beasts* and creatures.' Sheena recognised the voice before he came out of the shadows and into view. She closed her eyes for a moment, knowing more was coming and waiting for it.

''Tis people she does not ken how to treat well.'

Though spoken mildly, the insult in the words was clear to everyone who heard them and soft gasps echoed in the stable. She stiffened in response while she ignored the many retorts that pushed against her control and shook out the hay from her skirts as she turned to face him.

'Robbie.'

'Sheena.'

'Come,' he said, holding out his arm to her. 'My father, The Cameron, waits inside his hall to greet my betrothed.'

Before she accepted, Sheena turned back to Geordie. 'My thanks for your able and excellent care. I will be back later to check on him.'

'Nay, you will not.' Robbie's words felt like the lash of a belt. Undaunted, she smiled at Geordie. 'You have duties to see to.'

'Again, my thanks.'

She did not dispute or argue his order. That would waste her effort. Sheena nodded to the others who had helped and reluctantly placed her hand on Robbie's arm. She walked at his side, never slowing, never speaking, until they reached the entry to his father's hall.

As they stepped within, she let out a breath. 'Still the same insufferable prig you've always been, I see.'

Sheena almost laughed when he stumbled at her words. Only his need to answer the chieftain's call prevented him from replying. But she knew he would indeed have time enough to offer a retort later.

Too much time.

Chapter Two

After the insult, which he should have expected considering their last several encounters had not gone well, Sheena walked at his side in silence. Her hand lay on his arm in a way that suggested she would bolt at any moment.

'Welcome to Achnacarry, Sheena,' he said, fighting the words he truly wanted to say. Her blatant disrespect for his parents should be expected and yet he'd hoped her behaviour would have reflected some maturing since their last interactions.

During his last visit to Lairig Dubh, after he'd returned here for his uncle's planned wedding, she'd avoided him, disappearing from the hall when she was expected to stay at his side. And when she could not, she had whispered angry little insults that only he heard. She must have hoped, as he had, that his father's elevation to chieftain would nullify their betrothal. Instead, The MacLerie and The Cameron had confirmed the arrangements already made and Robbie and Sheena continued as betrothed to each other.

'How was the rest of your journey?' he asked. That

was when she pulled her hand from his arm and stopped without facing him.

'Do not pretend that you care, Robbie.' She tugged the sleeves of her gown and shook out the front of it as she avoided facing him. 'Do not.'

'I care about the disrespect you show my parents and the rest of my family, who wait on you within.' He nodded at the keep nearby and faced her, standing with his hands on his hips. 'Instead, you choose to see to that horse.' He let out an angry breath.

'He could yet die.' Her hands balled into fists at her side. 'I am certain your parents would not deny him the care he needed.'

He ignored the hint of worry in her voice. 'But you did not ask them, did you, Sheena? Once again, you do as you wish and others be damned.' The words were out before he could stop them. His accusation was too close to the truth, too close to what had happened all those years ago.

He'd tried to purge all the leftover anger as soon as his father had said the betrothal would stand. Yet the way he'd reacted to the sight of her in the stall and even now revealed his failure. Robbie wanted no more reminders of his failures with Sheena MacLerie. He could not stop himself as he pushed her once more.

'And how did the horse get injured, Sheena?' Her stricken expression told him his suspicions were correct— she'd been responsible somehow, another bearing the consequences of her actions—misguided or apurpose. 'So you have not changed after all.' He turned away and held out his arm. 'Come. My parents wait on you in the hall.'

'And you have not stopped blaming me for your disobedience, have you?' She placed her hand on his arm and turned away. 'Nothing but duty to fill your life?'

Robbie clenched his teeth and, for the first time, successfully kept his tongue behind them as he took the first step and waited for her to resist. When she did not, he walked up the steps of the keep, where the guards opened the doors to them.

''Twould seem nothing has changed between us then.'

'Insufferable prig,' she whispered again, just as they stepped inside.

Nay, nothing had changed between them.

They made their way through the assembled tables and people towards the dais, where his parents and others sat. Only when the feeling of her hand trembling on his arm finally got his attention did he look down at his betrothed.

Panic had replaced anger in her gaze and that startled him. He'd never seen the brave, stubborn and, aye, pain in the arse daughter of the mighty Beast of the Highlands falter before in all the years he'd known her. Oh, she'd trembled when her father directed his ire at her—who would not?—but never in other situations. Even their angry exchange just now did not surprise him. But this did.

As quickly as that emotion appeared, it was gone. Her head tilted a bit and her chin jutted forward and her resolve showed in the way her lips pressed together into a straight line.

Robbie drew them to a pause at the steps leading up to the dais and waited for her to curtsy before his parents. He noticed changes that had happened in the years since he'd seen her on a regular basis. He'd ignored her as much as possible during those last few years when he'd fostered with her family. Now, though, she presented not the awkward lowering of a child, but the flowing and graceful obeisance of a lady.

'Lady Sheena, welcome to our home and our family,' his mother said. Standing as she spoke, she motioned them forward as his father nodded. 'Come, join us at table.'

Robbie guided Sheena up the steps and around the table and waited for some gesture of acceptance or pleasure from her, but none came. He would not describe her as, well, as anything, for her face carried no expression at all right now.

'Sheena,' he whispered as he climbed the first step. 'What is it?'

She startled for a moment and presented a weak smile as they made their way around the table to the two empty seats. When they reached his mother's side, Sheena proved once again she could surprise him. She lifted her hand from his arm and offered a curtsy to his mother. It surprised him because it was one that befitted someone of much higher rank. For, in spite of her marriage to the chieftain, his mother should be the one showing respect for the daughter of a very powerful and titled nobleman who stood high in the King's honour.

'I beg your forgiveness, Lady Elizabeth,' she said, bowing her head. 'I have been rude to keep you and your company waiting on my arrival here.' Tucking her soiled gown to make it less obvious, she continued. 'I should not come to your table in this condition either. I'll understand if you wish me to retire.'

For one brief, so brief, moment his mother was stunned into silence, a sight or occurrence that rarely happened. Lady Elizabeth MacSorley was hardly ever without a word to say. Even Robbie's father was startled at the situation, until his mother shook her head.

'Nay, Sheena. You are welcome here now. You must be exhausted and famished after your journey and the accident.'

The tension at the table was broken and, after a nod of welcome from his father, his mother pointed to their places. When Robbie would have guided Sheena to the open seat next to his, his mother said otherwise.

'Robbie, seat her here so we can refresh our acquaintance.'

Once they were all in their places, the servants brought out platters of roasted meats and accompaniments and the aromas filled the hall and the soft grumble of Sheena's stomach made him smile. Though they'd switched seats, Robbie knew what was expected of him and he filled Sheena's plate with some of the roasted quail and thinly sliced beef and other offerings. Though she nodded in acknowledgement of his actions, she would not meet his gaze.

His mother managed to ask a series of questions without seeming overbearing or intrusive throughout the meal. Robbie listened and watched, now a bit uncertain of what he thought he knew about the young woman who sat at his side—the woman he was betrothed to marry.

When the meal drew to a close, once again his mother spoke up. 'Sheena?' Sheena looked over at his mother. 'I have invited our cousin, Lady Glynnis MacLachlan, to be a companion to you. You are both of an age and you will find her an asset as you settle here with us.'

Glynnis, with her soft manner and ladylike behaviour, was the perfect choice of companion for Sheena, who might learn much from his cousin if she tried. His mother smiled as Glynnis bowed her head in Sheena's direction. And though at one time Robbie had thought she was under consideration as a match for him, he felt nothing but admiration for the young woman who would make some nobleman a fine wife. Glynnis chanced to look in his direction and he smiled in appreciation of her grace and welcoming manner.

He began to stand to escort Sheena to her chambers when his mother placed her hand on his arm to stop him and spoke once more. 'Glynnis, would you please show Lady Sheena to the chambers we selected for her? Sheena, I pray you will speak up if they are not to your liking or if you are in need of anything to make you more comfortable here?'

Speak up? Was his mother wishing for the Beast's daughter to show her true nature? Sheena stood and turned to his parents and Robbie clenched his jaw, awaiting her words, which would prove either inappropriate or ungrateful. Sheena tended to speak first and think on the words later.

'I thank you again, my lady, for your welcome and your attention to my comfort. I am certain that my chambers will be perfect and that Lady Glynnis will suit me well as a companion.' Sheena curtsied to his mother and nodded at his father before turning to follow Glynnis from the dais and out of the hall.

Robbie, along with everyone else in the hall, watched as the two walked side by side to the doorway and corridor that led to the stairs and above. When those present turned back to their interrupted conversations, he found himself lost in thought.

He'd grown up with the lass. He'd spent years fostering with her family and knew her. *Knew* her. He'd seen the good—limited though it was—along with the bad. Yet the Sheena MacLerie who'd just left the hall was a very different one.

Oh, she certainly was not the girl of his memories, although he had expected that she would have matured physically since the last time he'd seen her a few years ago. Even then, he'd tried not to pay too much attention to her. After his humiliation because of her actions, he'd forced his steps to go widely around her. If they were in a chamber or gathering together, Robbie would seek out a place as far from her as possible. If that place kept her out of his sight as well, all the better.

For some time after his punishment at the hands of her father, staying away from her had taken some doing. Only with practice had it become a natural thing for him. When their parents had gathered to make their betrothal official, he'd forced himself to accept that she'd grown up, and then returned to deliberate ignorance of her.

It mattered not that she had been a wilful child. It mattered not that she was now a young woman. All that mattered was that he was at peace with carrying out his duty for the good of the Clan Cameron. Well, if he was not yet at peace, he would be soon. He needed to be. Duty mattered. Honour mattered.

'She has grown much since we saw her last,' his father said quietly. 'She has the look of her mother at that age.'

'You knew her mother?' Robbie leaned forward to meet his father's gaze as he asked.

'Jocelyn MacCallum was a noble-born lady of marriageable age and status when my father sought a bride for me,' his father replied. Glancing at his wife first and then Robbie, The Cameron continued. 'A fine prospect, though a bit poor for my father's standards. Not what a man would call beautiful, but something in her eyes that was...'

'Special?' his mother offered. 'Intelligent?'

For a moment Robbie considered the surreal nature of this discussion between his parents. But marriages were business arrangements, securing lands, cattle, gold and protection among allies or settling feuds or disagreements between enemies. That was how the negotiations for his parents' marriage had started out.

'Something,' his father repeated. With a glance in the direction where Sheena and Glynnis had walked, he nodded. 'It's in her daughter as well.'

Before his mother spoke the words that gathered behind her tongue, a word slipped out of his own mouth. 'Hellion?'

'Hush!' his mother warned. ''Twill not do for others to hear you speak of her with disrespect, Robbie.' She smoothed her hands on her lap and shook her head. 'No matter what happened before, you agreed to the betrothal with her. Am I correct?'

Suddenly he felt like the six-year-old Robbie Cameron who'd been caught misbehaving by his mother. Her tone turned him from a man grown to that helpless child in no longer than a moment.

'Aye, Mother. Father. I agreed to marry Sheena Mac-Lerie.'

'Let go of your old resentments and begin anew. Give her a day or two to settle in and see to her horse's recovery. She clearly worries over the creature's welfare. Things will grow to be more at ease between you.'

'I told her not to return to the stables and to leave the care of her horse to Geordie.'

'And others heard you give this order?' His mother's voice lowered to almost a whisper and that feeling of being a six-year-old flooded back through him. He could not work out what mistake he'd made. Before he could say anything, his mother stood. 'Robert, I leave this to you.'

And she was gone. He stared as she and her maid moved as though a herd of cattle, angry cattle, were nipping at their heels. So quickly in fact that none of those yet seated at table could stand out of respect for the ladies' departure.

When his father called for a flask of *uisge beatha* rather than more ale, Robbie waited. After his father had swallowed a large amount of the potent drink and Robbie himself had taken a mouthful or two, The Cameron slapped him on the back and leaned in closer.

'Mayhap I should have had this talk with you a while ago…'

Robbie wondered if the flask would be enough as his father began speaking.

As it turned out, it was not.

'Shall we unpack your trunks or would you like to retire after travelling so far, my lady?' Glynnis asked. 'Or would you like to refresh yourself?'

The beautiful, soft-spoken young woman had guided her up the stairway and along the hallways to this chamber and now waited to do her bidding. Another woman, a maidservant selected to help her until Elen found her way in this new place, stood near the doorway also waiting for her orders.

Sadly, she'd ruined the dress her mother had ordered for her arrival here by tending to her horse's injury. The front of the dress, already stiff from the drying blood and other debris, would never shed the stains…or the smell. How Lady Elizabeth had permitted her to sit at table, she would never know. And yet the lady had barely glanced at the muck and refrained from any comments about it at all. Sheena let out a breath, knowing she would never be as gracious as either Lady Elizabeth or Lady Glynnis.

'Isabel, bring hot water and fresh bath linens,' Glynnis said to the servant. 'I will find something for you to change into and after that you can decide how you feel about working on the trunks or tumbling into bed.'

Without waiting for her consent, they fell into their tasks and soon Sheena found herself sitting on the edge of the bed, divested of the gory gown and boots, washed of the day's dust and wearing a fresh shift and robe. Without being asked, the maid brushed Sheena's hair and braided it for bed. Sheena did not correct the lass about her preference to let it loose, knowing she would free it from its bounds before she slept.

Glynnis was organised and thoughtful, pushing her along but not too much, as she guided Sheena from one task to another. After dismissing Isabel to see to the ruined gown, the young woman stopped and waited by the door.

'I can leave you, if you'd like to retire,' she offered.

Sheena gazed at the wide dark brown eyes set in a heart-shaped face and wondered at the source of this woman's patience and graciousness. Surely Sheena had missed receiving those qualities when the good Lord gave them out!

'I am not ready to sleep,' she said, sliding off the bed. 'Too restless, I fear.'

'You have so much to be excited about, my lady. Moving here. Marrying Robbie. So many new things to do. I swear 'twould keep me awake!'

Sheena did not have the desire or the will to disabuse the young woman of her incorrect assessment of how things were for Sheena. And she had neither the time nor the interest at this moment to delve into what the lady knew or did not know.

'Would you help me with the trunks?'

Several shelves and cupboards lined the far wall of the large chamber. It took little time for them to pull out boots and shoes and garments that needed airing and arrange them. Elen would see to any other washing or mending, though Sheena doubted the gown worn this day would be saved from the rag bin. Soon her cloaks hung on pegs by the door, her clothes remaining in the trunks were sorted and Sheena knew she could find whichever piece of clothing she needed.

Only when she paused to look around the chamber did she feel the weight of exhaustion pressing down on her. Glancing at Glynnis, she smiled and nodded.

'My thanks for all your help with this. I know the servants could have seen to it, but I appreciate that you did.'

'It was my pleasure, my lady.' Glynnis dipped into a curtsy.

'Sheena. Please call me by my given name since we are to be cousins.'

'Very well, Sheena. I will take my leave of you. Lady Elizabeth said you are to be at your leisure on the morrow, so no one will disturb your rest. Isabel will bring a tray when you are up and about.'

Everything that could be done for her comfort and welcome had been done. Just as her mother did for their guests. Just as her sister Lilidh did for her husband's household. How would she ever manage to do that? To oversee such a massive household as this one when she could not even…

'Have you need of anything else, Sheena?' Glynnis interrupted her thoughts and Sheena shook her head. 'I will seek you out on the morrow and show you the rest of the keep and grounds when you are ready. I think you will grow to love it as much as I do.'

Without another sound, the woman was gone. Sheena could only hear the sound of her own breathing in the silence of the chamber now. She put out all of the candles and lanterns except for the one closest the bed before removing her robe and laying it over the end of the bed. Just as she pulled the tie off her braid and climbed up onto the bed, listening as the ropes stretched beneath her, a soft knock on her door stopped her.

Tugging the door open a crack, she expected to find either Glynnis or Isabel with some forgotten item or message. So the sight of Robbie in the corridor surprised her. More so, the sight of a slightly drunken and wobbly Robbie was quite unexpected.

'Sheena…' he said. He slurred the beginning of her name and put his hand on the doorframe to support himself. 'I do not wish to bother you, but…'

She only now took a good look at him and noticed that he wore his hair longer than when he'd lived at Lairig Dubh. It touched his shoulders when he did not have it pulled away from his face as he had at supper. He smiled at her and his bright blue eyes reflected back the flickering light of the flames behind her. He was handsome when he smiled. She shook her head at such a fanciful thought.

Robbie had rarely smiled in her presence since that

long-ago day, so she could not be held responsible for not knowing of it. He'd grown taller now too, and towered over her by several inches.

After some moments passed without another word, Sheena eased the door open a bit more and nodded.

'Do you have need of something, Robbie? 'Tis late, you know.'

The strangest expression covered his face and Sheena could not find the words to describe it. He swallowed several times, swayed again before regaining his balance with his hand on the doorframe. As she watched, his gaze moved over her from head to toe, not once but twice and again. When his eyes met hers once again, he stammered a few words before making any sense.

'As an honoured guest…er…as the betrothed of the tanist of the Clan Cameron…er…there is no place in the keep or village where you are forbidden to go.' His words made sense and yet they did not.

'Robbie? What are you saying?'

He cleared his throat three times before he spoke again. Being in his cups was either something he did not do often or something he did not do well. She must remember that for later.

'I have sent word to Geordie to consult with you about the care of your horse, Sheena.'

And without another word he walked off down the corridor towards where Glynnis had mentioned the other chambers were, for the chieftain and his family. She stepped into the hallway and watched as he made his way in the flickering shadows thrown by the torches, wondering if he would need help to find his bedchamber. A muffled curse echoed off the stone walls before she heard a door slam and believed him successful in his search.

Confused by him and utterly exhausted, Sheena returned to her chamber and climbed into bed. The warmth of the layers of heavy woollen blankets and the comfort of the thick feather mattress pulled her quickly towards sleep. But her thoughts, muddled as they were by fatigue and worry, kept her awake for hours as she turned the day's events over and over in her mind. And thoughts about the changes to the young man to whom she was betrothed stirred up questions and memories she'd rather not have stirred.

He'd been a headstrong boy, always seeking a thrill in adventures around Lairig Dubh and keeping up with her older brother Aidan as they frolicked and played and grew up. They'd taken lessons together from the good brother whom her father had brought in from the abbey to teach them reading and writing and their numbers. They'd learned to fight, with their hands and weapons of all sorts. They had been inseparable.

Her biggest sin had been in liking him more than she should and wanting to be part of his circle.

Her sister, Lilidh, had been busy learning to be a lady. Her mother's attentions had always been divided between family and overseeing the huge estate and people of the Clan MacLerie, leaving Sheena with little of it for herself. So she'd chased her brother and Robbie, hoping to be accepted as one of them.

Though the incident between them had brought her father's long-desired attention, it had not been the kind of attention she'd always wanted. Worse, it had resulted in Robbie's punishment and shame and turned him from her completely. His hatred had made clear to her something she'd known for a long time—she was unworthy.

Unworthy of trust. Unworthy of love. Unworthy to be alive when her very birth had nearly taken her own mother's life. For forcing her to face that truth, she'd hated Robbie too.

It had been easier after that to ignore him and to detest him and to never wish to tell him another thing. But her sins had come back to haunt her when her parents told her of the planned betrothal, one she could not naysay.

One that would expose the rest of her shame and make her father once more regret that she'd lived at all.

Chapter Three

'The wee laddie is off his feed, but he's a strong 'un and will be better soon, my lady.' Sheena watched as Geordie walked to her, where she stood looking into the large stall. 'In no time at all he'll be carrying ye hither and yon.'

The part of her that had always been in charge of Wee Dubh warred with the part that urged her to respect this man's pride and place. When he lifted the latch and opened the gate, she smiled. Sheena slipped inside and heard the latch lock behind her, tucking the small jar of unguent deeper into the folds of her gown.

'How did you know what I named him?' she asked, taking one slow step and then another towards her horse. He nickered and sought her hand as soon as she drew close enough to him. Glancing at Geordie, she asked, 'Wee?'

'I didna, my lady!' Geordie laughed and shook his head. ''Tis his name, in truth?'

'Wee Dubh. For his size and colour as well.'

It had been meant as a jest for she'd known this horse would grow to be a huge animal when he was a colt. And his colouring was like the straw on which he lay—the palest shade of brown possible.

Her words made Geordie laugh even louder. 'Good on ye, lass!' he said. 'I mean, my lady.' He nodded in respect, but his smile never wavered. She liked this man. 'Weel, small or large, dark or light, he will heal soon.'

Her movement to hide the liniment she'd brought caught his attention.

'Did ye bring him a treat?' He nodded at her hand.

'Begging your pardon, Geordie,' she said, lifting her hand up to show him the jar. ''Tis what I use on injuries.'

The stablemaster took the jar and lifted the thick cloth over it to smell the ointment within. 'The Young Laird said ye might bring it by. I was wondering at it.'

The Young Laird? Robbie?

'Did he?'

'Aye. He wanted me to ken that ye should be consulted about the wee laddie here.' He inhaled once more and his brow gathered in a deep furrow above his kind blue eyes. Geordie shook his head and shrugged. 'Smells close to my own, but something else...' Another intake of breath before a smile broke out on his whiskered face. 'I wouldna hiv thought to add feverfew, lass.' He coughed and smiled at her. 'My lady.'

'My cousin's wife sees to our herb garden and suggested it. I think it helps.'

'Weel, my lady,' Geordie said as he nodded at her. 'If ye havna met our healer yet, 'twould be something to discuss with her. Ye might want to ask her to concoct some for my use too. Seek out Anna Mackenzie in the village.'

The next hour or so passed in companionable quiet as they saw to her horse's injuries. Geordie had decades of experience in working with and caring for the Clan

Cameron's horses and yet he never seemed to belittle her lack of it. When Glynnis discreetly made herself known, Sheena realised she'd learned so much in such a short time with the old man.

Brushing the bits of hay and dirt from her gown, Sheena stood and thanked him for his time and his care and followed Glynnis out into the yard. The bright sun this morn was truly a blessing, for most of her journey had been accomplished in either the dense misty rain that cloaked the hills and lochs in floating clouds or the heavy downpours that had them seeking shelter for fear the pathways they rode on would flood out from beneath them. Sheena tossed her braid over her shoulder and followed Glynnis's constant soft chatter towards the gates.

The one thing she could not ignore was the size of the keep and the village that surrounded the road leading into it. She'd paid little heed to it on her arrival yesterday but now noticed how large it actually was. Glynnis chatted on, giving details and descriptions about the place and the family that Sheena barely heard. Wave after wave of fear grew within her until she fought to draw in a breath. A vice of terror closed around her chest.

It was one thing to marry Robbie, in spite of how she felt about him, when he'd been the eldest son of the chieftain's brother, destined to a smaller role in his clan. But now he was tanist and expected to inherit the high chair of the mighty Clan Cameron after his father. As his wife… As his wife, Sheena would… Sheena would…

The darkness closed around her vision, making it impossible to see and she lost control over her body. Everything grew darker and tighter and tighter until…

'Sheena!' A hard tap on her cheek and another finally broke through the panic that was overtaking her.

'Sheena, look at me!' Glynnis's face changed from blurry to sharp before her as Sheena grabbed the woman's hand before she could slap once more.

'I...' What could she say?

'Are you well? Do you need to return to your chamber and rest?' Glynnis asked. She placed her hand against Sheena's forehead and then her cheek. 'You lost all the colour in your face and I feared you would faint.'

''Tis just exhaustion from the journey here,' Sheena said, gaining her balance and stepping back from the woman. 'I am well.'

'We can put this off until you have rested. We should go back to the keep.' Glynnis was studying her closely, so Sheena shook her head and forced a smile.

'Nay. Truly, I thank you for your concern.' She smoothed her palms down the skirt of her gown and stood a bit straighter.

She would have assured Glynnis once more, had not a tall, very handsome young man, with a smile that was appealing in a wicked sort of way, approached and stood before them. She blinked, not believing that a man could be this beautiful, but he did not change. Indeed, if anything, he was even handsomer on second glance.

Clearly a Cameron, but not even the tell-tale prominent nose that so many in their clan shared detracted from his rugged beauty. And, like some dumbstruck fool, she could only stare at him, for words and most thoughts had deserted her.

'Have ye need of help, Glynnis?' he asked.

His deep voice sent tremors through Sheena's very bones and yet she noticed in her stupor that his voice had somehow softened when he spoke the lady's name. Sheena forced off the remnants of the panic that had taken over her and answered his question in spite of him directing it to her companion.

'I am well,' she said to both. 'Glynnis, I am well.'

'Ye look a bit peaked, if ye ask me,' the gorgeous man said in that voice.

'Iain,' Glynnis interrupted, 'Lady Sheena says she is well.'

'Lady Sheena?' this Iain asked, his brow raised and his head tilted. 'Forgive me for not kenning, my lady. I missed yer arrival yesterday and supper last evening.' He narrowed his gaze—his striking blue gaze—at her. 'Mayhap I should see ye to my mother, for ye still look ready to faint?'

'Sheena, this is Iain Mackenzie, cousin to your *betrothed* and son of our healer, Anna Mackenzie.' She heard the way Glynnis spoke the word *betrothed*, as though to remind one of them, or both, that she was committed to another.

'Geordie spoke of your mother, Iain. I would like to meet her, but I have no need of her talents right now.'

Some unspoken message passed between this man and her companion and Sheena found herself being guided, gently but firmly, down a path towards a stone dwelling. It was much larger than the other cottages around it, she noticed, and set a bit apart. As they reached it, the door swung open and a woman greeted them, wiping her hands on a sturdy apron as she did so. From the resemblance to Iain, Sheena recognised that this was Anna Mackenzie.

'Are you well?' she asked as she pushed the door open wider and motioned them to enter. 'You look pale. Sit. Here.'

Before Sheena could say a word, she found herself

guided once more, this time to a chair next to a large table. The woman moved around the chamber, to the hearth, back to the table, and reached up and tugged some leaves from baskets and plants hanging overhead. Glynnis and Iain had taken up positions behind her, standing as the fiercest guards might in a dangerous situation. Although she'd only just met them, she could not help it when a smile tugged at the edges of her mouth.

One of her biggest fears, among the many that lived in her heart, was the fear that she would have no friends here. And, knowing the situation with Robbie, she had worried that she would be alone. A glance over her shoulder gave her the tiniest bit of hope that she might have found two.

Finally, Anna stood and placed a cup before her on the table. 'I saw you arrive yesterday, lady, and know you must be exhausted. I am glad you came to see me.' Sliding the cup closer when Sheena did not lift it, she continued. 'This should refresh you for now.'

Sheena picked up the cup and tried to sniff it before taking a mouthful.

Anna laughed as she tipped the cup up. ''Tis just a mix of some herbs and berries. Nothing to harm you.'

'Of course not, Mistress Mackenzie. I thank you for making it.'

Her first sip spread the warm tea over her tongue. Although she did not usually imbibe warm drinks like this one, it was sweet and smooth, smoother even than her father's *uisge beatha*, and it soothed her as it coursed its way to her belly. Another swallow simply confirmed her first opinion. Soon, the cup was empty.

'Iain, have you no duties this day? I thought you were

heeding Davidh's message and going to the keep when you left?' Anna asked her son.

Looking back at him, Sheena noticed how the handsome young man seemed only a lad when his mother addressed him. She knew that feeling well, being the youngest daughter of the feared Beast of the Highlands, a man rumoured to have killed with his bare hands and to destroy those who stood against him. One glance or harsh word from him and Sheena was like a bairn once more. She'd confessed to sins she had not committed under his unnerving stare.

Without another word, Iain nodded to his mother and Sheena. He'd reached the door before he turned back and looked at her companion.

'Good day, Lady Glynnis.'

He was gone with the click of the latch on the door. Everyone remained unmoving and silent for several moments until Anna let out a rather loud breath and spoke. ''Twould seem he is not my little lad who loved to carve wooden animals for me any longer.'

'I think not,' Sheena said. Her little lad was now a strikingly attractive young man who clearly had the Lady Glynnis on his mind now.

'He yet carves animals,' Glynnis added softly.

When Sheena glanced at her, Glynnis would not meet her gaze. Sheena looked at Anna to see her reaction and watched as a strange mix of concern and sadness entered her eyes. As the woman picked up the empty cup before Sheena and took it over to the wash bucket, she nodded.

'He is old enough to ken his own mind,' she admitted in a soft voice. 'And already too old to pay heed to his mother's counsel, whether he needs to hear it or not.'

Looking back at Glynnis, Sheena saw that her expression mirrored Anna's.

'I thank you again for your hospitality, Mistress Mackenzie. I am feeling much recovered. I would like to speak to you about the unguent I make for my horse's injuries at some time soon. Come, Glynnis, we are expected…by Lady Elizabeth. We cannot be late.'

Sheena did not wait for Glynnis to consent. She simply dragged her the first few steps until she acquiesced and came along more willingly. When they reached the main path through the village, Glynnis tugged her hand away and stopped.

'Lady Elizabeth does not expect us,' she said. 'Indeed, the lady said to be at your leisure this day.'

Sheena crossed her arms over her chest and narrowed her gaze at her companion. Clearly, the perfect Lady Glynnis MacLachlan had been born that way. Never raised her voice. Never got into trouble or angered her parents. This Lady Paragon MacVirtue would do what she'd been raised to do without whimper or objection.

Yet that brief conversation with Iain's mother, during which few words were spoken but several meaningful glances had been exchanged, held more import than any of those involved were letting on. Even she could tell something more was happening. But Sheena did not yet know the way of things here.

Why had she not paid more heed when her mother was explaining the connections of kith and kin within the Cameron clan? Sheena tried and failed to remember the intricacies of the line of inheritance and powers within the mighty and large family. Letting out her frustration on a breath, she gave up and dropped her arms.

'Do you wish to speak of it?' she asked. Glynnis's

expressive eyes widened for a moment as though she would, but her only reply was the slightest shake of her head. At least she did not deny that there was more.

'Let us walk and not waste the sun's appearance this day.'

Sheena really did not wish to pry or push. Nay, that was not true. She wanted to ask dozens of questions and yet she held in her unseemly curiosity from this woman who'd been nothing but kind to her. Worse, she was an interloper here—or was for now—and yet she was curious about those with whom she would live the rest of her life. A shudder shook her body and soul at the thought.

'I beg your pardon, Sheena, for being inattentive to your discomfort. This is the second time, or thrice now, that you have shivered like that. Clearly you have not recovered from your journey yet. If you are chilled or tired, we should return to the keep so you can rest.'

'Nay, Glynnis. I am just overwhelmed, and I suspect not even a warm bed before a huge fire will ease that.'

They walked a bit in silence until they reached the main path through the village. Glynnis drew her to a stop and turned to face the direction from which they'd come.

'The smithy is just there.' Glynnis pointed to their left. 'The baker for the village and the healer whom you have met...' she pointed to the other side '... Mistress Mackenzie also tends a garden for Lady Elizabeth and sees to the one above the falls.' With her hand gestures as she spoke, Glynnis helped Sheena get her bearings of the layout of the village and lands surrounding the keep. 'Loch Arkaig and the Disputed Lands of the Mackintoshes are to the west and the other holdings like Tor Castle are to the south and across Loch Lochy to the east.'

'So huge,' Sheena whispered. 'So many people.'

Fighting the fears that lived within her, fears of her inadequacy and of her failures that constantly pushed against her control, she took a breath and another.

This could not happen now. She could not let the terror take hold. Aye, she was in a new and unfamiliar place and those could trigger these attacks. But nay, not now, not here.

Not here. Not now.

Not here. Not now.

The warm hand that slipped into hers shocked her from the panic.

'Come, I will show you the gardens.'

Glynnis did not wait for consent or any word before she slid her arm around Sheena's waist and led her away from the crowded village paths to a sheltered place filled with rows and rows of fragrant green plants. When Sheena looked around, she noticed the healer's house blocked the view from the road.

'Mistress Mackenzie returned to Achnacarry some years ago from her family's lands in the north. Iain's father was a Cameron.' Sheena struggled out of the confusion in her thoughts to follow the soft words. 'His father was the Old Laird's son.'

Soon they were sitting on a wooden bench on the edge of the garden. Sheena gazed at the well-cared-for beds, following their orderly outlines, trying to calm herself.

As Glynnis talked on, ignoring what she'd so obviously seen, Sheena knew that it was only a matter of time before everyone in Achnacarry witnessed her afflictions and knew her shame. What would happen then?

How could she be accepted as the tanist's wife when they knew the secrets she carried?

Chapter Four

By midday the pounding in his head and the roiling burn in his belly had eased and Robbie stopped wincing at every sound or word spoken around him. Several winks and nods told him that others were aware of the cause of his distress. Few Cameron men alive had not suffered the morning of reckoning after a night of overindulgence. Especially not when his father's special *uisge beatha* was involved.

On any other morning he would see to his duties and carry out the day-to-day tasks expected of him, whether overseeing the guards or consulting with his father and the other elders about the plans to rebuild one of the mills. His days had been filled with duty since his father took the chieftain's chair at his uncle's death and Robbie became the heir, the clan's tanist. Years of no expectations followed by almost seven years of preparation and training, here and south in Tor Castle. Though he did not anticipate his father leaving it to him soon, he would be ready to serve his clan. This morn, though, he struggled to accomplish anything useful. He'd avoided the midday meal and had almost reached the stables when his brother fell into step with him.

'Tomas! I had not heard of your return from Tor,' Robbie said, slapping his younger sibling on the back. ''Tis good to see you.'

'Father summoned me back to meet my future sister-by-marriage,' he said. In a lower voice, he continued, 'Though I suspect it was Mother's doing.' Tomas tilted his head and narrowed his gaze. 'Or was it yours?'

'I did not ken that my betrothed was coming until the day before she arrived. So nay, 'twas not my doing.' Robbie nodded at the stables as they approached the large open door. 'But I am glad you are here. Come, let me show you.'

Tomas walked at his side down the row of stalls until Robbie stopped before the one where Sheena's horse stood. His brother let out a long whistle. 'Good God, whose horse is this?' Tomas said, climbing up on the lower slat of the gate. 'He's a beauty!'

'He belongs to my betrothed.' Robbie examined the horse as Tomas did. The animal seemed improved already, which relieved Robbie. He hated to see any creature suffer needlessly.

'Did she bring him as a gift to you?' Tomas whistled again. 'I am jealous.'

'Nay, brother. Not as a gift to me. Sheena rides him.'

Tomas dropped back to the floor and shook his head at Robbie's words. 'A lass rides this brute? How can she?' The horse under discussion let out a snort and stamped his front hooves. Tomas shook his head. 'He would be a handful for even the strongest rider.' The horse shifted in the large stall, turning and exposing the dressing on his other side. 'What happened to him?'

Geordie called out to them as he made his way down the stables to where they stood. 'Milord. Milord,' he said, nodding at each of them. At the sound of his voice the horse nickered and stamped again until Geordie reached his hand out over the gate.

'He's faring well already, milord,' Geordie said as the horse bumped his nose under the stablemaster's hand. 'Ah, my good laddie, I've no treats for ye now.'

'An accident on the journey here left him injured,' Robbie answered his brother's question. Her name sat on the tip of his tongue, but he stopped himself before placing the blame where it belonged.

'Aye, but 'tis mostly a flesh wound that needed stitching and care. Not deep at all. He will be running aboot soon.'

'I cannot imagine a wee lass riding this one,' Tomas said. 'Not even The Beast's daughter!'

Robbie interrupted before Tomas could say anything more about Sheena or her terrifying father. 'Has the lady been here yet this day, Geordie?'

'Oh, aye, first thing this morn. We washed and dressed the laddie's wound and she went on her way with Lady Glynnis. Towards the village.' He turned away from the stalls to face them. 'Are ye well yerself, my lord? Ye look a bit green around the edges,' the man said. When he winked, Tomas burst out laughing and slapped Robbie on the back.

'Just tell me it wasna Father's favoured brew?' Robbie did not confirm or deny his brother's suspicions, which led his brother to look instead at the stablemaster. Geordie's nod and wink were all Tomas needed. 'Should I whisper my words? Would you like to sit in the quiet corner to recover?' he whispered loudly.

Robbie grabbed his brother and shoved him towards the door. 'We will be on our way, Geordie,' he said, nodding as he passed the man.

'Aye, milord,' he replied. After meeting Robbie's gaze, he whispered the words once more. That only served to make Tomas laugh louder and harder as they made their way out of the stables and into the yard.

'So, tell me of your betrothed. Is she as horrid as you described after your last encounter? Is that what made you drink so much last night?'

The few years between them had never got in the way of them being close friends as they'd grown up. Neither of them had expected the turn of events that placed them now in line for the chieftain's seat. At times, in truth, neither of them had expected to survive their uncle's nefarious plans.

As he met his brother's eyes and pondered how to answer his questions, the subject of those impertinent enquiries walked across the yard. He and Tomas were not the only ones who stopped and stared in silence as the lady and their cousin Glynnis made their way to the door of the keep. Just as they reached the edge of the shadow thrown on the ground by the massive stone building, the light of the sun shone from behind Sheena, exposing the shimmering hair around her face and the outline of her feminine curves.

As the fire's light had done last night when he'd knocked on her door…

Her unbound hair had flowed around her body, catching the flickering light of the flames behind her and somehow seeming to come alive. Gold and auburn and white and blonde strands had been lit up by the fire.

He'd wanted to reach out to see if her hair burned with the heat of the hearth.

The flames had outlined her body, and even though her thin chemise had covered her from neck to feet it had hidden almost nothing from his sight. Shadows and light had sketched her curves, dark against the firelight, showing the fullness of her breasts and the flare of her hips and yet not showing.

There had been a tantalising glimpse of the darker place at the junction of her thighs. When she'd turned for a moment he had even been able to see the tips of her breasts and the feminine shape of her belly and her bottom. For a moment he'd forgotten the reason for his visit to her, and he had known that the *uisge beatha* was not the cause…

His brother's low whistle pulled him out of those memories and back to the yard. Robbie shifted, recognising his body's reaction to the memories of seeing her.

'Not so horrid, from that expression on your face?' Tomas shoved his elbow into Robbie's side and jutted his chin out in her direction. 'The Wee Beastie has grown a bit, and in all the right places, eh? This marriage might not be such an ordeal for you after all.'

Unable or unwilling, he knew not which, Robbie did not wish to discuss his growing confusion about Sheena with anyone. He'd responded as any man would when seeing a lovely young lass nearly naked before him. Even her.

Now, he pushed his reaction and Tomas away and straightened himself to his full height. 'It matters not if this marriage is unwanted or unpleasant, 'tis my duty to the clan and to Father and I will honour that.'

Robbie walked towards the keep, not waiting for

Tomas. After a few paces, his brother caught up with him. Any hope for silence was disappointed a moment later.

'Always duty first. Always honour. Always…'

Robbie swivelled in front of his brother and stopped in an instant, blocking Tomas's path and forcing him to look up.

'Aye, my duty is always first. We came back from the brink of destruction and only by accepting his duty did Father manage to reclaim his position and guide the Camerons back into power and into honourable alliances. My duty is to continue his line and his legacy and I have pledged to that. Even if it means marrying a woman I do not want. Even that one.'

'Robbie—'

'And by accepting my duty, you have the freedom to make choices about your own future. So, do you suggest I should choose another path now?'

Tomas swallowed several times and looked ready to argue, until he did not. With a curt shake of his head, he lowered his gaze, accepting the truth of Robbie's words. Tomas would have choices in his life *because* Robbie had accepted his duty and Robbie did not begrudge his brother that. It had taken him a long time to reach that point, but Robbie's life was now for his clan.

'Come. I will renew your acquaintance with my betrothed and you can speak to her about her horse. That's a safe topic of conversation with her.'

He'd begun to turn away when he saw it. Tomas's wince in reaction to his brother's words. Or mayhap his tone? Robbie shrugged and walked away. Duty actually called.

Entering the keep, he climbed the stairs to the entry

of the hall and saw that Sheena, Glynnis and his mother were gathered around something on a table near the dais. With Tomas dogging his steps, he made his way to the place where they stood.

'And this is my husband's third great-grandfather,' his mother was saying, pointing to the parchment on the table. 'The stories are that he began gathering kith and kin into what is now the Clan Cameron.' At his approach, his mother smiled. 'I am showing Sheena your ancestors. Come.'

Robbie nodded at Sheena and met Glynnis's smile with one of his own. Positioned across from the women, he could watch them as his mother explained the story of his ancestors. The huge sheet of parchment, now unrolled across the table's surface, covered the length of it. Each generation included a drawing or sketch of what each ancestor chieftain looked like, though how many were accurate no one knew. As he glanced down where his mother pointed, the only thing he could see that had travelled down the generations was that crooked nose. Lines led to the septs or branches of the clan that spread off in different directions indicating when the family had moved out and married across the great clans of the Highlands.

A frown formed on Sheena's brow as she listened without speaking. Her gaze darted from place to place on the large parchment, never remaining on any one spot for more than a moment or two. There was something in the way she frowned as she tried to follow his mother's explanation. But what seemed to be concentration on her part was something else and she grew more alarmed as his mother named another and another of the Camerons on the chart. Only because he'd been studying her did he notice the small gesture on Glynnis's part—a touch of her hand on Sheena's elbow—as his cousin leaned over and pointed to the chart.

'You met Iain earlier, Sheena. Here he is, tucked away in this side of the clan.'

Glynnis slid her hand over the chart, pointing out and repeating some of the names, explaining Iain's place in the hierarchy of the Camerons. When she told Sheena that he could have been chief if his father had not been killed in the dispute with the Mackintoshes, a chill went up Robbie's spine. Whether it was Glynnis's tone or the boldly spoken explanation, he could not tell. But hearing it so plainly put him on edge. Though his father had two heirs, each ready to follow him, Robbie understood that Iain Mackenzie, son of Malcolm Cameron, had a claim too. If a dispute over their claims ever arose, the elders of the clan—the heads of each sept and branch—would make the decision of which man would succeed Robert.

He'd be damned before he'd let someone else step into his place after he'd agreed to take Sheena as his bride. If he had to go through with this, he would hold onto his own claim and see it through.

Yet the admission did not sit well within him. It bothered him in an inexplicable way, so Robbie pushed those concerns aside and turned his attention back to Sheena. He watched as Glynnis pointed and read the names of various Cameron lairds and chieftains. Sheena's lips moved slightly, as though repeating each name and bit of knowledge to herself after Glynnis read them aloud. Nothing seemed amiss, so why did it feel as though something was?

'This is always in my solar and for your perusal, Sheena. As are all the books I own and use.'

'My thanks, Lady Elizabeth,' Sheena whispered. Strange that, for he heard no warmth or excitement in her acknowledgement. His mother's collection of manuscripts and other books and letters and such was extensive, expensive and highly prized. For someone just given access to such a treasure, his betrothed's tepid response did not seem right.

'If you have recovered from your journey, join me on the morrow and I will begin showing you how we manage things here in the keep and over in the village. After you break your fast, you and Glynnis can come to my solar.'

'Again, my thanks, Lady Elizabeth,' Sheena said, this time nodding respectfully at his mother.

Once more, he saw the gesture only because he was watching closely. Glynnis covered Sheena's hand for a scant moment before dropping hers to her side. Why did his cousin offer such a gesture of comfort to his betrothed? Anyone who knew Sheena knew she was not the kind of person who wanted or needed coddling. She had a way of keeping people at a distance—either by her actions or her attitude—and Robbie did not remember that she'd made friends easily or frequently.

Nay, she'd preferred to follow and bedevil her brother and him. She never did anything that was expected of a lass. Never did anything expected...

'Ah, Sheena, here is my younger son, Tomas,' his mother said, motioning for his brother to approach. 'Tomas, your brother's betrothed and youngest daughter of The MacLerie, Sheena.'

Robbie waited as Tomas moved to her side and held out his hand to her. Sheena never glanced at him as she offered hers to his brother and she smiled at Tomas's gallant gesture of bowing over it.

'My lady,' Tomas said as he stood up, 'if only we had met first, I would have surely laid claim to you.' A blush crept up Sheena's cheeks at Tomas's teasing words, but she did not take her hand from his. Her warm smile at his brother irritated him.

'Aye, Tomas, you two are of a more similar age. If only…' The words were out before he could stop them.

His mother's soft gasp and Sheena's slight startle were the only replies to his rude comment. Well, other than the immediate uncomfortable silence that fell around them. Even Glynnis would not meet his eyes when he looked at her.

'I did not ken that Robbie had such a charming brother,' she said after a few moments' delay. 'But now that we will be brother and sister, you must call me by my given name.'

'I will, *Sheena*,' Tomas said, before releasing her hand. 'I heard that the monstrously huge horse in our stables is yours. Is that true?'

'Aye, 'tis. Wee Dubh is mine.' Joy infused her every word and her expression at the mention of the damned horse. Her face lit and the tension he'd seen on it while she examined the scroll was gone. The blasted horse was the only thing she cared about.

'Geordie told me you'd visited the horse this morn, but I would love for you to show him to me. If you have no further tasks now?' Tomas looked at their mother for approval. Their mother. Not him—her betrothed.

'My lady?' Sheena turned and waited her approval. His mother would never refuse this.

'Go. Enjoy this unexpected good weather while we

have it,' his mother said. 'Glynnis, would you stay for a moment?' His cousin nodded and still would not meet his eyes.

Without a moment's pause or hesitation, Sheena took Tomas's hand and allowed his escort away from the table. By the time they reached the door, their laughter echoed back to everyone listening. And each person in the hall was listening, be they kin or servant.

'You said you accepted this betrothal.' His mother's soft voice at his ear surprised him.

Robbie turned to face her. 'I have.'

One of her eyebrows lifted at his answer. 'Have you truly?' she asked. Her gaze was so intense it was hard to meet it.

'Not here, Mother.' He gave up the truth to her. 'And it matters not, so we need not speak of it again.'

'It matters because it is obvious,' she whispered back. 'And oh, aye, we will speak of it.'

She stepped back and walked away before he could say anything else. Glynnis followed his mother, rushing to keep up. Glancing around, he realised that many had been watching and listening and he'd made a mess of this. Again.

Word of this encounter would spread and everyone would know that he did not want her. That, in spite of his agreement to the betrothal, he did not want to marry the daughter of The MacLerie.

Robbie left the keep and sought out a task or chore that would keep him busy for now as he considered what to do. Duty required him to marry her. Duty required his obedience to his father, his Chieftain. Duty kept them all safe. Somehow, he would have to find a way to carry out his duty to his clan without letting his true feelings get in the way of it. Theirs would not be the first marriage centred on family loyalty. Indeed theirs would be the customary manner of marriages.

But, damn it all to hell, he did not want to marry her.

Chapter Five

Sheena fought the urge to look over her shoulder as she left the hall on the arm of Robbie's brother. Tomas talked constantly as they walked, his long legs covering the distance in far fewer strides than she needed to keep up with him. Well, he chattered until the moment the door closed behind them and they stood on the steps of the keep. A moment of silence passed before she realised he'd stopped talking.

'Did you do that apurpose?' she asked. 'The leave-taking and the chatter?'

'Aye.' Tomas released her arm and smiled. He was not exactly a younger version of Robbie, but their resemblance to their father was clear. 'I thought to avoid the coming bloodshed that would have disturbed my mother.' She faced him. 'Was I wrong?'

'Nay.'

He motioned towards the yard and she walked at his side.

'You have the look of a woman who resorts to anger rather than tears when hurt. Someone who would draw blood with words or swords before she would cry.'

Sheena blinked and blinked to keep the unexpected tears away. Aye, he'd seen the truth of her in only a moment. A stranger in spite of their connection. Although now suffering the unexpected need to cry, she usually reacted as he'd described. Indeed, she *had* been tempted to throw an insult back at Robbie in response to his. Only the presence of so many—and Lady Elizabeth— had given her a reason not to do so. Her kin called her fiery and hot-tempered and compared her to her father and his legendary reputation. She allowed them to believe that, to keep anyone from looking too closely at her to see the reasons behind her actions.

'Here now,' he said, stepping a bit ahead of her so he could glance back at her. 'This is not the way I thought things would happen when I met the woman who is to be my sister-by-marriage. The one who saved me from such a fate. Well, you and Robbie have saved me for now, from such a fate.'

If he was trying to distract her, it worked.

'How did you think it would go?' she asked, unable to resist the lure he'd thrown.

Tomas stopped and pointed out a shady place near the stable. By the time they reached it and stopped, her stomach was tight with worry.

'I thought I would find two people anxious to take their vows. Or, at the least, ready to marry.' He shrugged. 'This has been arranged for years. In all that time I have never heard a word of concern or opposition from my brother.' His gaze narrowed at her. 'And yet his insult and the dangerous gleam I saw in your eyes told me that I must interfere or watch as you two ruin it.'

Sheena let out a sigh, the breath she'd been holding

since they'd stopped. 'I do have a temper,' she admitted to him.

'And my brother has a way of needling you. He did the same to me as we grew up,' he said, holding out his arm once more. 'I will not interfere again if that is your wish.'

'I would suggest that you only do so when you fear for your brother's life or safety.' She smiled up at him and noticed again the similarities between Tomas and Robbie and their father. The same height. The same colouring. The same crooked nose and smile. 'Or you may be too tired to ride Wee Dubh when he has healed.'

They turned into the stables and he caught sight of her horse. When she lifted her arm from his, Tomas raced to the gate of the stall. Wee Dubh stamped his hoofs at the sound of her voice, anticipating a treat from her.

'You would allow me to ride him?' Tomas asked, his glance flitting back and forth between her and the horse. For a moment he seemed more a young lad than the young man he was. His smile widened as he waited on her word.

'Once Geordie gives word, aye,' she said. 'If you wish.' Tomas jumped up and down several times as she laughed.

Drawn to the cheering, Geordie walked from the other end of the line of stalls and his duties to greet her. 'My lady,' he said with a respectful nod. 'Nothing has changed since this morn.'

'I did not intend to disturb your work, Geordie.' And she'd not intended that at all. It was just so nice to have someone else be interested in Wee Dubh that she'd forgotten how much work the stablemaster did in a day.

'Once Lord… Tomas meets him, we will be out of your way and gone.'

'Ye can visit any time ye wish, my lady,' Geordie said. Did he always sound this welcoming to those who interrupted him? 'The young lord knows good horseflesh when he sees it. As ye do, my lady.'

'She said I can ride him, Geordie!' Tomas reached out and rubbed Wee Dubh's nose when the horse approached him. 'We will ride out to the loch, laddie, and I'll give you your head.' The horse nickered and tossed his head as though agreeing. Wee Dubh did like to run, so it was not far-fetched to think he would agree. 'Mayhap take you back to Tor with me.' She knew his words were simply teasing so she worried not over such a threat.

'When you give permission, Geordie.' She turned back to the knowledgeable man. 'When you say he is healed enough to be mounted.'

''Twill not be long, my lady. He's a strong 'un.' They walked closer and the horse pushed Tomas's hand away and came to the place where she stood. But when she and Geordie both reached out, her horse chose Geordie's hand to nuzzle.

'Traitor,' she whispered. 'Such a fickle-hearted beast.'

'Just remember you gave your permission,' Tomas said, stepping away. With a nod to Geordie, they walked back into the yard.

'How far is Tor?' she asked. Sheena remembered that Tor Castle was the ancient seat of the Camerons and now their southernmost holding.

'About ten miles south.'

'And you live at Tor rather than here?' She walked at his side, glancing around the yard as the usual busyness of the day progressed around them.

'Robbie and I both lived there with our parents while my uncle ruled, but they moved back here when my father took the High Seat of the clan and Robbie's circumstances changed.'

Sheena wished again she'd paid more heed to her mother's explanation of clan ties and kin. All she could remember now was that the Camerons had nearly been torn apart, first by their ongoing feud with the Mackintosh Clan and then from betrayal within their own ranks. Their chieftain had betrayed his own, nearly destroying them.

And Robbie's change in status meant that her fears were real about her own fate. If her parents had spoken of it in the last few years at all, she'd either forgotten or ignored it as much as possible—while hoping their arrangement would be severed in light of some better one for him and his new status.

Tempted now to ask for more details, she instead asked a safer question. 'Is Tor larger than Achnacarry?'

'Nay, just older and draughtier,' Tomas said. 'You should ask Robbie to take you for a visit. As wife to the tanist, you should visit all our holdings.'

She swallowed against the immediate and rising fear that threatened when she thought about the expanse of her future duties and responsibilities. This feeling of being overwhelmed was happening more often. Was it the exhaustion of the journey? Was it the uncertainty that filled her every breath and step now? At home, she'd known her place. She'd known her limitations and how to live with them.

Travelling always filled her with trepidation. So many unknowns—people, places, events and more. Though travelling a few miles to their other holding was not as threatening to her as the trip her parents had last tried, she worried over the consequences and possible revelations of her weaknesses on such a trip.

'Was it the thought of my brother that made your face go green? You look…ill.' Tomas edged back a step as though he thought she would be *ill* on him.

'I think…' she began. Letting out a deep breath, Sheena continued. 'I think I am more tired than I thought I was. I think the journey and my worries over Wee Dubh's injuries—'

'And the thought of accompanying Robbie anywhere?' he interrupted with his own quip. She shook her head at him even though his efforts to lighten her spirits pleased her. She seemed to be finding allies in spite of Robbie's obvious dislike of her.

'Nay, not that. I am unused to such attention and so many expectations,' she admitted in a voice too low for anyone else to hear. 'I have so much to learn.' Lifting her head and glancing around the grounds, she shrugged. 'More than even I expected.'

The weight of it all pressed down on her in that moment and she wanted nothing so much as a reprieve from…everyone.

She met Tomas's gaze. 'If you do not mind, I would like to walk a bit,' she said. Before he could offer to join her, she added, 'Alone.'

'Do you have a destination in mind or do you need one?'

Thankfully, it appeared he was not going to argue with her or try to accompany her. Good. Someone had been with her every moment since her arrival, and for the days of the journey and for weeks before that in preparation. Sheena needed to find a place to hide for a bit.

At home she'd discovered a lovely room, tucked away in a little-used spot in her father's keep—a closet truly— but she'd retreated to it when everything overwhelmed her. Another secret spot of hers was located outside the walls of Broch Dubh, where she sought privacy when she needed it. But here she had no such place.

'I just wish to walk through the village,' she lied.

'As you wish,' Tomas said, tilting his head. 'Should I tell my mother, or mayhap Robbie, where you have gone?' He studied her face, waiting for her response. 'Or mayhap a maid?'

'Nay, I will be fine.'

Other than a raised brow, Tomas made no other objection and, with a nod to her, he walked away. Sheena wondered if he would allow her the privacy she craved or if he would alert someone—Robbie—of her excursion. Well, she would waste any time alone if she dawdled here, so she walked away from the stables and towards the gate.

In a few minutes' time, she found herself at the end of the path where the healer's house…and garden lay. Not wishing to trespass, she listened at the house's door for a moment before walking around its perimeter and entering.

As soon as she closed the gate behind her a sense of relief filled her. Bits of time alone, in secluded quiet places, seemed the only way to calm the terrible fears that lived within her. Fears always ready to push out and control her—her body, her very breath and her ability to think or speak. Gazing around this fertile area, Sheena saw the perfect place for her.

In the far corner, dappled sunlight filled a small alcove. Surrounded on three sides by a wooden fence, it would give her a place away from prying eyes. Making her way to it, Sheena backed into the spot and leaned against the fence and, for a moment, she felt almost invisible to the world around her. The plants that overgrew their appointed plots hid her from the view of any casual visitor. She slid down the fence and sat, cross-legged and unladylike, safe from anyone and the whole world for now.

With the warmth of the unusual bright and sunny day heating the garden and ground, it took little time for her to surrender to the exhaustion and tension within her. A wave of drowsiness drew her down into slumber and Sheena decided not to fight it. A moment or short while of sleep without care or fear would do her good.

She had never meant for hours to pass or for Robbie to be the one who woke her.

The lad approached Robbie in the hall just as his conversation with his mother ended. If only the lad had sought him out before that, Robbie could have avoided having to hear his mother's very strong disapproval of his actions. At the least, the message from Anna Mackenzie gave him a reason to leave his mother's chamber quickly.

He saw no sign of Sheena, nor Glynnis for that matter, as he strode through the hall and yard. He glanced at the stables, expecting her to be on her way to it or back, and did not see her either. Passing through the gates, he turned down the path that led to the commander's home. He would have knocked but Anna opened it before he could. Expecting her to invite him within, Robbie was surprised when she pulled the door closed and urged him down the steps.

'I did not realise it at first,' she said, leading him around the large stone house to the gate of the gardens. 'And I thought she would rouse sooner than this.'

'She?' A sinking feeling hit his gut even as he asked. He had no doubt who the 'she' was. None at all. Years of living with her family and witnessing her antics had told him that it was Sheena before Anna could speak her name. 'What has Sheena done this time?'

Anna blinked several times and he could see her bristle at both his tone and choice of words. Those who did not know Sheena would discover her lack of restraint and inability to control herself or act like the lady she was supposed to be very soon. Anna's brow furrowed and her eyes narrowed at him now.

'What a strange thing for a man to say of his betrothed.' Anna stepped inside the garden and took several steps towards one corner before she stopped. 'Actually, I thought her ill at first.'

'Ill?' A wave of guilt and unease flowed over him.

'Aye, ill. But I saw that she is indeed well and deeply asleep.' Robbie looked over the woman's head for any sign of Sheena and saw none.

'She sleeps where, Anna? I see her not.' Searching around the organised and well-kept garden, he could not see anyone else. 'Why would she sleep here?'

'Look in the corner. Behind the branches,' Anna said, pointing into a small area where the sunlight did not reach now. 'It would have been warm and sunny in the alcove for a time. The perfect place…' The woman stopped and stepped aside.

'The perfect place for what?'

'Well…' she began before meeting his gaze. He saw the challenge in hers. A glint of anger—or was it sadness?—as she watched him. 'Many things, I think. But why do you think she would seek out such a place as that?'

Memories threatened. Images of people searching for the Laird's missing daughter. Shouting her name. Hours of worry before she would turn up as if nothing was amiss. Where had she been those times?

'I know that supper will be called in the hall shortly and thought it best that a man should see to his newly arrived betrothed.'

Puzzled by the strange tones of displeasure and disappointment in her voice, Robbie turned away from the healer and stared into the alcove at Sheena. Searching her face for signs of distress or discomfort, he could see none. Her expression gave no sign of what had driven her here or why she slept hidden away. The last time he'd seen her, Sheena was walking out of the hall on his brother's arm to see her beloved horse. From Anna's words, it would seem that she'd been here since. Crouching down, he moved some of the branches aside and watched as she stirred a bit.

'I will leave you to her,' Anna said.

'Will you be in the hall?'

'Nay, Davidh and I will eat here.'

'And Iain?'

'His duties bring him to the hall.'

Robbie stood and faced Anna. 'My thanks for summoning me. I will see her safely back.'

He waited for Anna to enter her house before turning back to watch Sheena. She sighed, letting out a soft breath, before mumbling something. A name mayhap? Kneeling at the opening of the alcove, Robbie leaned in closer to try to hear what she said while slumbering.

Though she spoke not again, he studied her as she slept. This was not the girl he saw in his memories of Lairig Dubh, all lanky with a mutinous gaze. In sleep, without the constant anger in her bearing and words, her beauty lay exposed and it stunned him that he had not noticed it before. Sheena, his betrothed and, in spite of his feelings, his soon-to-be wife, had grown into a lovely young woman.

If their past was any predictor of their future, their existing animosity would build a wall more effective at separating them than the one that encircled Achnacarry's keep. And though this calm, quiet sleeping version of her belied his suspicions, he understood that even calling a truce would not bring about a lasting solution.

He let out a sigh and raised his eyes to her face, only to find her staring back at him with a confused, bleary-eyed gaze.

'Remember me?' he asked as he stood and held out his hand to her. 'Your betrothed, in case you have forgotten.'

Chapter Six

Sheena struggled against the confusion and turned her head, looking for something familiar as he watched. He remembered that feeling of waking up in a place you'd forgotten or did not know. It had taken him months to adjust after returning to Cameron lands after years of living in Lairig Dubh. It had happened again when he'd moved to Tor and back again to Achnacarry. He just did not adapt to change in his surroundings well. And it looked as if Sheena suffered from that now. So why had he immediately spoken so rudely to her? He tried once more, gentling his voice.

'You fell asleep in Anna's garden. Come, you must be chilled and uncomfortable.' He leaned over, reaching closer to offer her help in rising. The suspicion that entered her green eyes bothered him in a way he could not explain. Did she fear him? Did she think he would fool her in some way? Or had his earlier disdain shown on his face? 'Here, give me your hand.'

He remembered that same expression, but he could not bring to mind the specifics of time and place right now. She hesitated before accepting his help and he tried to ignore that as he eased her to stand. A soft groan escaped as she stood and soon another.

'How did you ever find such a place?' he asked as he guided her to the bench a few steps away.

'Have I missed supper?'

'Are you hungry?' His question surprised her, from the frown that formed on her brow. 'How long have you been here?' When he heard the sharpness in his own tone of voice, he gentled it again, from an accusation to a question. 'Are you well, Sheena?'

She released his hand and stood on her own, stretching herself to her full height and rolling her shoulders and rocking her head back and forth. Though she'd been a short lass, her head now reached above his own shoulders. After a moment, she met his gaze with clear eyes.

'I did not realise how tired I was when I first sat in the sunlit corner.'

A final shiver trembled through her body, causing a shake of her head that loosened more tendrils of hair from the plait, and the sight of it brought heat rushing through his body as fragments of the vision of her before the fire flooded his memory. If only he could remember the whole of what he'd seen in his drunken stupor. Her stomach erupted in grumbling, breaking his reverie.

'And aye, I am hungry, but more than that, I do not want to insult your mother or her hospitality by being late once more to her table,' she said. Her hands shook as she smoothed out her gown, trying to ease out the wrinkles gained by her recent position. 'Am I, are we, late?'

If he'd not been looking at her face, he might have missed the expression of insecurity that flitted over it. Strange that, for she'd never showed any hint of uncertainty in all the years he'd lived at Lairig Dubh. As she drew in and released a deep breath, she replaced anything he thought he'd seen with the familiar visage of the headstrong, the mutinous daughter of The Beast.

When the urge to jab at her swelled, he tapped it down. His feelings about their marriage were as clear as hers. Worse than that, as his mother had pointed out in words he did not ever remember hearing her utter, it was his duty to accept her as much as it was Sheena's to accept him. And every word he spoke against the match, or against her behaviour or person, would simply make matters worse.

'We are not yet. Come. We will arrive together and give them all something to whisper over.'

This time, when he held out his hand, she took it and walked in silence at his side. Robbie led her out of the garden and along the path that led to the gates. Though he spoke a few times as they passed through the village, pointing out places and greeting people, Sheena only responded when words or questions were directed at her. And she gave only the sparsest of replies. He noticed when she dropped her hand from his arm to her side but made no attempt to reclaim it.

Instead, they walked the rest of the way through the gates, across the yard and into the keep. Soon they stood at the doorway to the hall and he stopped. Though she denied it, Robbie wondered if she were indeed ill. Or simply exhausted and too proud to admit to it.

'If you prefer, you could eat in your chambers. If you are not feeling well? I know my mother would not mind if that was the cause.'

That suspicious glint flashed once more in her eyes, a wariness of him he decided he did not like. It was not as though he would jump out and scare her as he had when they were but lad and lassie. Or pull her braid and run away.

Or push her from the water's edge into the stream when he tired of her following him.

He waited on her, feeling an echo of guilt shiver through him at those very memories. Aye, he'd not behaved well towards her when they were younger. And though he'd paid the price for it, had she?

'Nay,' she said with a shake of her head. Lifting her face, she nodded towards those gathered. 'I am well and hungry.' When she would have walked off, he touched her hand.

'I would not wish you ill, Sheena. The journey and the upset over your horse's injuries are reason enough to have a care these next days.'

'Pardon?'

'I know what it's like to wake up and not know where you are or what you should be doing,' he admitted quietly. 'It takes some time to become accustomed to a new place, a new…home.'

Sheena glanced away and when she looked back at him he noticed the gleam of tears gathering in her eyes. Before she could blink them away. Which she did. 'I am well and I am hungry, Robbie,' she repeated.

'Onward then,' he said, offering his arm once more to her.

They reached the table at the front where his parents, brother and others gathered but had not been seated yet. He released her and she moved quickly away from him to Glynnis's side. It seemed the two were on their way to becoming friends. But Glynnis was such a patient, kind and helpful woman, he expected no less than that she would help Sheena however she could. Glynnis had been raised and prepared to marry well and take over the running of a noble's estates, so her advice would be valuable to Sheena, who had avoided learning at her own mother's side at all costs.

Filled with a disquiet he could not explain, Robbie watched the two with their heads leaned in close and whispering. Other than a few missteps, Sheena was different in many ways now, and he was not just thinking on the obvious and not displeasing changes to her body. Though it would be simpler for him to continue with her as he always had, even he understood she'd been respectful to his parents.

Kind even to the servants and his cousins and his brother was now her biggest supporter. Though he could blame that on Tomas's desire to ride that brute of a horse she'd brought, no one, no one else who'd spoken to her or encountered her so far had expressed anything but good opinions of her.

Except him.

Aloud, when others could hear.

His stomach tightened as the truth and seriousness of his mother's words and warnings struck him.

It was Sheena who'd been the problem before, but here and now—it was him. He'd carried the deep resentment from so many years before and held her up to it with every word she spoke, every move she made.

'You look ill, brother,' Tomas said as he smacked Robbie on the back. 'Have you got into Father's spirits again so soon?' His brother backed away a pace, took hold of his shoulders and pretended to be examining him. 'Aye, the expression says it all.'

'You are daft,' Robbie said, pushing free of his brother's grasp. He glanced over and noticed the rest of his family were taking their seats. 'Come, we are called to table now.'

As was his father's custom, he joined his wife and closest kin at table if duties did not take his attention while he was here at Achnacarry. He did the same while at Tor Castle. The Cameron sat with his advisors and the other elders at one end of the long table. Robbie's mother sat at his side and Robbie and Tomas and the others spread out from her place. When Robbie approached, his mother's nod directed him to the seat between her and Sheena. Glynnis and Tomas and even Iain joined them.

At first the meal was passed in companionable silence, as the servants served the plain but filling food his parents preferred. Intrigued now by the Sheena who sat at his side, Robbie spoke little but listened to everything that she said. And he listened to them—mundane yet helpful bits of advice from Glynnis and nothing but horse questions from Tomas—and to Sheena's replies. Once or twice her gaze moved to him as though she waited for him to speak.

'You are pensive, my son.' His mother spoke in a low voice only he could hear.

'Am I?' He put his knife down and shifted to face her more directly. 'What are your plans for Sheena?' He'd never actually planned to ask that of his mother, but the words were out now.

'From what her mother has said in her letters to me, the lass has had little training in running a household like this one. So I will help her learn.' He heard a wistful tone in her words.

'Ah, the daughter you never had.' His mother blushed. 'One you can mould and shape. Sorcha is not here enough for you to do that, is she?'

Sorcha MacMillan was married to his half-brother Alan and travelled with him on The Mackintosh's business. Her visits here were infrequent and left little time for his mother to wield her influence over her daughter-by-marriage. Especially when Elizabeth MacSorley would prefer to dote on the two grandchildren Sorcha had given her so far during any visit to Achnacarry.

His mother's face lit with pleasure at the mention of Sorcha. She shook her head. 'I would if I could, but I cannot, so I do not,' she whispered her favourite saying. 'I know you and Sheena are not reconciled to this marriage and I would like to see you both happy, Robbie. If I can help her settle into her place here, I think she will be.' She reached out under the table and patted his hand. 'Considering that your father has no plans but to continue his rule, and is comfortable knowing you will follow him, you both have time.'

He glanced over at Sheena, who showed signs of fatigue and discomfort even now. Shaking his head, he met his mother's intelligent gaze.

'She is not looking forward to it, Mother. And she is yet exhausted in body and spirit after her journey here. Give her some time before you make demands of her.'

He noticed his mother's silence and looked at her face. It was clear she was fighting the urge to splutter at his words. Had he rendered her speechless? Glynnis caught his gaze and nodded at Sheena. The lass was falling asleep while she sat at table. One by one, those around her began to notice and look to him, waiting on him to do something.

'I will escort her to her chambers now. May I tell her you have no expectations of her for the next few days?'

His mother's shocked gaze swiftly softened and she

nodded at him. 'Her own maid will return to her on the morrow. That should give her some comfort.'

'Until that damned horse is healed, I fear she will not be at ease.'

'I never thought you would have to fight for the affections of your betrothed with her horse!' She covered her surprised laugh behind a wipe of her lips with her napkin before nodding her permission.

Robbie stood, bowed his head to his father and turned to help Sheena. He leaned down close to her and whispered his words, so as not to startle her too much.

'It seems my task this day is to wake you from your slumbers, Sheena.'

When she woke gently and leaned back against his body, Robbie had the most surprising reaction. Her feminine scent and the soft sigh that escaped as she opened her eyes sent waves of heat through him. Her head tilted back until she almost rested against his shoulder, leaving her neck exposed to him. The desire to taste her skin in that spot shocked him. His mouth watered at the thought of kissing her.

She startled awake, pushing up from her chair and back against him, forcing them both off-balance. It took but a moment for Robbie to wrap his arms around Sheena and right them. Only when she glanced up and over her shoulder at him did he realise where his hands lay.

Beneath his right hand was the soft curve of her hip and belly. But it was his left hand that was more provocatively placed, for it rested across her shoulder and over her breast. Her body tensed in his grasp and her indrawn breath spoke of surprise and yet her gaze did not move from his.

He was certain he felt the watchful eyes of everyone at table on them. Robbie eased his most intimate hold and inched back, allowing Sheena room enough to stand without his support. Which she did, as she turned away from him. Concern that she would be embarrassed by what had happened pushed the unexpected words out of his mouth.

'May I escort you to your chambers?' His raised forearm waited for her hand. Had he imagined the soft gasps that echoed around them? One hadn't come from Sheena for he was watching her and, after only the briefest of pauses, she placed her hand on his.

The tension around them, as though all those seated at the high table held their breath, grew stronger as he walked her down the steps and out of the hall. A few paces into the corridor that led to the stairway to the family's chambers, Sheena slowed and took her arm away, facing him.

'I can find my way now, Robbie,' she said. 'You can return to the hall.' Crossing her arms over her chest only served to remind his body he'd touched the softness of her flesh just moments before.

'I told my mother I would see you safely to your chamber. I…she was worried about your fatigue.' The words sounded weak even to his own ears. 'So, lead on or walk with me. That choice is yours.'

She bristled at being given no true choice at all but, within the time of a breath, she nodded and turned back to the stairs. When they reached the first landing, she looked left and right. Part of him revelled in the fact that she was lost but unwilling to admit it. He'd seen that stubbornness before and knew she would never relent.

When she stepped back and motioned for him to lead,

Robbie wanted to laugh at the frank frustration in her gaze. And he might have, but something was different now. Something within him had shifted and he found the urge to torment her had waned. But she followed him wordlessly. Up two more flights of stairs and down another corridor to her bedchamber. They reached it and he stepped aside to give her access to the door.

'My mother will not expect your attendance or have duties for you for a few days,' he said. 'I think the journey and, well, all of this—' the motion of his hand was meant to encompass all that was new to her '—and I asked her to give you time to…' Her gaze narrowed. 'Time to reconcile yourself to all that has happened and what is yet to come.'

'You did?' A curl of her hair came loose and he struggled against the need to tuck it back inside the braid that could never seem to tame her wild locks. 'That is kind of you.'

'It is.' Robbie stepped back as she lifted the latch and stepped within.

'Are *you* ill?' Sheena reached out as though to test his cheek for fever. Her fingers stopped a scant few inches before touching him and she drew back.

'Nay.'

Should he tell her the truth he'd realised when he'd found her in that alcove, asleep? When he'd seen the confusion in her eyes upon waking, not knowing what time it was. Would she laugh at such an admission or think him jesting once more?

'Rest well, Sheena. We can speak on the morrow.'

She watched him with a troubled expression, the area between her brows tightening in a frown.

'Speak?' Her voice cracked a bit on the word.

He took a step away from her door. 'We are betrothed. We will have to speak of matters between us at some point.' He did not like this vulnerable side of her. Robbie understood how to deal with the mutinous, stubborn part of the Beast's daughter. This softer version was dangerous in a way he could not explain and did not wish to examine too closely. And yet…

'On the morrow, Robbie.' Sheena nodded and pushed the door closed.

He waited, listening to her moving about within the chamber. The promise of speaking to her should fill him with hesitation. He should be trying to avoid her at all costs. Yet, he understood now that behaviour such as that was worse than what he expected of her. So on the morrow he would begin again.

They would begin again.

Surely that was the right thing to do.

Chapter Seven

The bright, brilliant blue skies filled with clouds that raced across above her head surprised those living in Achnacarry. Three days in a row without a storm blowing in off either of the lochs that lay nearby was simply unthinkable, she'd been assured. The maid Isabel said so as Sheena had passed her by in the corridor outside her chamber this morn. As did Geordie and one of his helpers in the stables. The good thing about bad weather, as she knew, Geordie explained with a wink and a nod, was that it didn't last long here in the Highlands. In his long life, he'd always thought a day in which all the seasons had not made an appearance was not over yet.

With another warning not to be deceived by the brightness of the day and to keep an eye to the sky for sudden storms, he left her alone with Wee Dubh once they'd cleaned and tended to the wound.

Still, she could not banish those last strange hours of yester evening, waking from an unexpected drowse to find Robbie standing over her, and then his escort to her bedchamber, where he'd acted so strangely it had kept her tossing in her warm bed for hours. He'd taunted her from the first moment he'd seen her here, even insulting her for all to hear in front of his mother. Yet his manner in waking her, both times, could be described as… kind. She sighed and rubbed the horse's back, brushing in long strokes that brought some kind of ease to her as much as it did to Wee Dubh.

'He is a strange one, Wee,' she whispered. The horse nodded, in agreement she was certain, and his short huff of breath blown in her direction told her so. 'He does not want this marriage any more than I, and yet he does not refuse.' Now, the horse stamped his hoof and scraped along the straw in the stall. He was the one male she could always depend on. Sheena walked around to his other side to groom him.

'His mother is nice. His cousins, even his brother, as well.' She leaned her head against Wee's neck, feeling his strength and warmth against her cheek as she rubbed it on his. 'But he is just as I remember—horrid, rude and insulting.' Encircling her horse's neck with her arms, she whispered to her confidant. 'Then, without warning, he was kind. I just cannot explain that.' The words revealing her worst fear to the only one she could trust with such knowledge came out.

'How will he react when he finds out I cannot read?' She rubbed once more. 'What will he do when he finds out the rest and kens his wife is not fit to be the wife of a chieftain?'

Sheena did not know how long she stood in silence hugging the huge horse, but she continued for as long as he would allow her to do so. No matter that everyone warned her about how strong Wee was. Or how she should have a care around him for he could be dangerous. None of that mattered to her, for when she needed comfort Wee was hers. The sadness soon drained away and she felt lighter.

Mayhap the extra hours of rest she'd finally claimed this morn had helped after all? Once her thoughts had calmed enough for sleep to take her, she'd not opened her eyes until well into mid-morn. The sounds outside her door had told her that the day was a busy one for those serving the Camerons in their keep, and yet she'd slept on soundly past the clamour of activity.

With no sign of Glynnis and, as Robbie had promised, no call from Lady Elizabeth, Sheena had truly been at leisure for the first time in such a long while that it felt disturbing and wonderful at the same time. A tray left outside her door allowed her to break her fast and dress without summoning anyone.

And all because Robbie had spoken on her behalf.

Though the usual daily chores had been going on around her, Sheena noticed a change in the activity of the stables. Stepping back from Wee with a final pat farewell, she shook her gown to remove any errant hay and turned to the gate of the stall. Not expecting his arrival, she was surprised to see Robbie watching her. Nothing in his expression gave her a clue as to his reason for being here...or the reason for the unusual kindnesses he'd shown.

'Good morrow, Sheena,' he said, nodding to her. 'How does he fare this day?' She glanced over her shoulder at Wee, who now nudged her forward.

'Better than we expected. He's healing well.'

'And riding?' Robbie asked.

He stepped up on the gate and held out his hand. A bright red apple that drew Wee's immediate attention sat in his palm. The laddie moved her aside now to get to the treat. Males could be so fickle.

'Not for at least a week. The tears were just along the muscle and we cannot take the chance of worsening it.' The loud munching and slurping of the fruit's juice next to her ear made her smile. When no other offering was held out and nudging her shoulder did not get the result he wanted, Wee moved away. Aye, fickle males.

'I think he misses the running as much as you miss the riding,' Robbie said.

Sheena smiled and nodded. 'I believe he does.' She walked to the gate and Robbie opened it for her. 'There will be plenty of time to do that once he heals.'

'You could be riding now.' Her narrow gaze found no sign of teasing in his eyes. She waited for whatever he would say next. 'Geordie!'

The stablemaster came in through the side door, leading two horses behind him. Both were beauties, dark in colour and lively in step.

Robbie frowned even as he held out his hand to her. 'This is not—' he began.

'Nay, my laird. I wouldna insult the lady with the one you requested. I couldna guess which one might fall asleep on the road first—Lady Sheena or Old Megs.' Geordie laughed aloud. His words and manner of being light-hearted and respectful at the same time warmed her heart.

Sheena walked to the horse he'd chosen and took hold of the reins. 'Well, good day to you, my pretty one.' She stepped closer and Wee Dubh let out a loud whinny and stamped his hoofs to get her attention. 'You have made my wee laddie jealous, I think.' She laughed and rubbed the horse's nose. 'If this is not Old Megs, what do you call her?' When she looked at Robbie, he shrugged.

'Mo Chridhe, my lady.' Geordie gave the name.

'My heart?' she asked.

'She's quite the popular lassie in the stables.' Geordie winked once more and she laughed. He had such a way of saying things.

'Do you wish to ride?' Robbie asked. ''Tis a fair enough day.'

Sheena met Geordie's smiling gaze before Robbie's waiting one. She nodded. 'Aye.' Why deny it? Why not ride with him? It was better than remaining inside and feeling the tension grow tighter within her. It was a way to see more of the Cameron lands. 'I would love to, Robbie.'

'Only two seasons have shown themselves so far this day, my lady. Have a care now!' Geordie tightened a strap on her saddle and patted the horse's flank. His warnings made her laugh for she had lived only in the Highlands and understood the way the weather could change from one moment to the next.

In a short time they mounted and were riding through the gates towards the village. When they reached it, a few of the villagers, those who Glynnis had introduced to her, waved this time. At a place where the road divided, going north or west, Robbie nodded to the west. For now, it was too rough and twisting to give the horse her head and she was unwilling to risk any harm being done to a horse, even if it wasn't her own.

They reached the edge of the River Arkaig as it flowed eastward to Loch Lochy and crossed it by means of a small wooden bridge so dilapidated that it gave her little confidence that they would make it to the other side. Every creak made her cringe, but Mo Cridhe took it without any hesitation at all.

'Lively and sure-footed,' Robbie said as he waited for her to draw up closer. 'She is familiar with this path, even though the main road goes further towards Loch Lochy. 'I wanted to show you a place that only Camerons know of here.'

They rode on side by side for a short while, in silence as Sheena took in the beauty of the land around them. The loamy smell of the lush and thick growth on the ground was familiar to her, as was the scent of the tall pine trees that surrounded them. Well, at least something was in common with her home.

She noticed the sound before she could identify what it was. It grew louder and louder until Robbie had to shout his words for her to hear.

'I brought you in from this direction because it is more impressive to see it from here for the first time,' he shouted. When he smiled at her she nearly lost her seat.

Something unfurled in the pit of her stomach as she watched a genuine smile light his face. For the first time since her arrival, other than that drunken, dreamy expression the first night, this smile made his blue eyes soften from their icy shade to something closer to the sky overhead now. Without the frown that he usually wore, it was clear that Robbie had grown into a quite handsome man from the lad she'd known.

Though others wore their hair much longer—some loose and some tied back—his dark brown locks fell nigh to his shoulders and curls made it appear tousled and eminently touchable. But it was his eyes that changed the most when he smiled like this.

At that realisation, memories flooded her thoughts of earlier times she'd forgotten about for so long.

Robbie running through the keep, chasing her brother…and winking at her.

Robbie laughing as he rode past, following her father out into the yard.

Robbie…smiling…at her and her heart melting from the warmth of that smile.

'Take a look,' he called out.

His voice pulled her from the strange, forgotten memories and she looked up at the road ahead of them. Her breath rushed from her body in a huff at the sight before her.

Just off the road sat a waterfall, one that ended in a large pool at the bottom. From this angle, it appeared to be one long cascade, beginning beyond some cliff high above their heads. As they moved closer, the truth was revealed.

Sheena had seen waterfalls before, even ones larger and higher. What made this different was that it was divided into two sections. The brownish flow of the longer segment fell from the top of the cliff, crashing and collecting into a pool halfway down. The water gathered and swirled before rushing to the left and falling even faster and harder down to the bottom. The wooden bridge they approached crossed over the stream of water that escaped the lower pool.

'It goes out to the river from here,' Robbie shouted. He raised his arm and pointed out the path of the stream after it passed under the bridge.

Spray from the churning waters misted around them as they walked their horses across the bridge. Sheena studied the falls and the pool as they rode over its edge.

The sound of crashing water surrounded them so speech was impossible without shouting. Robbie nodded and motioned for her to follow him and soon, not far from the bridge and with the falls still close, he led her to a small clearing in the forest trees. Though still very loud, the noise had lessened enough that they did not have to shout.

'What think you of the sight?' he asked after they'd climbed down from their mounts and he'd taken hold of her reins.

'I have never seen the like,' she admitted. He walked the horses a few paces farther and flung the reins over a branch to let them graze. As she looked around, she remembered something Glynnis had told her. 'Is Anna's garden around here?'

He nodded and tilted his head towards the top of the falls. 'There.'

Sheena's gaze followed the falls backwards, from the pool nearest them and up to the top of the cliff from where the rushing torrents first appeared. Nothing she could see gave any sign of being a place to grow plants. Other than the place where the first pool gathered before crashing down, the falls simply went up and up. Just when she would have questioned him, he held out his hand to her.

'Come. I will show it to you.'

Expecting that the path that led to whatever place lay at the top must go through the forest and the hills, Sheena was surprised when he led her to a thick copse near the base of the falls. He reached out towards a large bush but stopped.

'Only a few Camerons are privy to this, so I ask you to keep it secret.' He waited for her nod of agreement.

'Most who live hereabout know of the road that leads off from the loch several miles to the north, but not this way up.'

'This is a path?' Other than the thick bushes, she saw no clearing or other way up the hillside.

'Have a care, for it is steep.' He stuck his arm into the thicket and lifted part of it out of their way.

Now she could see it.

A small tunnel had been cut through the thick undergrowth and appeared to run along the falls, up the steep side of the hill to the top. Sheena paid heed to his warning as she climbed over the gnarled roots that made up the first step of sorts at her feet. A series of indentations, some bordered with rocks or pieces of wood, allowed her, them, to climb up and up until they broke through a covering of thick branches and walked into a clearing.

The place was like something out of a story of old—a small, snug cottage sat in the middle of the clearing, and in between the croft and the stream that led to the falls was a well-tended patchwork of plots which must be Anna's garden. Robbie still led the way until they reached the cottage.

'Does someone live here?' she whispered into the stillness. The quiet of this place, above the nearby noisy falls, surprised her.

'Anna did live here for a short time after her arrival from the north. But now she uses the cottage as a still-room to prepare the herbs and plants she grows.' He stepped back and motioned her forward. 'Occasionally someone will stay here when the harvesting is under-way in the autumn.'

Robbie lifted the latch and tugged the door open. His height forced him to lower his head to enter and she followed. A plain but large table was at one side of the cottage with a smaller pallet on the other. A stone hearth sat between the two with a few stools and a chair scattered about. As she watched, he sought and found a bucket in the corner.

'I'll get some fresh water from the stream and then we...' He paused and stared at her as though deciding whether or not to finish his words.

'And then we can...?' she prodded.

'And then we can talk about our betrothal and forth-coming marriage.'

Her stomach tightened as he turned his back and walked out. Better now than later, she whispered over and over, trying to make herself believe it. What had been a pleasant surprise and experience so far, had now turned into something dreaded.

From his inexplicable behaviour last evening at sup-per—nay, from the time he had found her in Anna's gar-den—and during their ride, Robbie had been almost... caring. Well, that might be too strong a word for it. But he had been kind.

Sheena walked to the open door and watched him fill the bucket at the rushing stream. Before he turned back, she studied him closely. Other than his tall, muscular, very masculine form and the obvious strength in him as he held the heavy bucket out into the strong current to fill it, she noticed nothing untoward or different about him. As he stood, she hurried to the cupboard to find cups—and to avoid being seen watching him.

His steps behind her told her he'd returned. It was time.

Time to make him realise she could not marry him.

Time to gain his help in forcing their parents to see the truth of their betrothal.

Time to confess her truth?

Shame filled her at the thought of exposing her darkest secrets to him, but if that was the only way she could avoid this disaster before it happened, she must.

Sheena turned to face him, all the while praying she could make him understand.

Chapter Eight

Something was wrong.

As soon as he entered and his sight adjusted to the darkness within the cottage, he saw the pallor of her face. She held onto two battered cups as though they were her only hope. Her mouth was drawn into a tight thin line, constricting the usual fullness of her lips and cheeks. Robbie put the bucket on the table and crossed to her in two strides.

'What is it, Sheena? What is wrong?' He tugged the cups free and dipped one in the bucket. Holding it to her mouth, he waited for her to take it. 'Here. Drink.' He watched her even as he retrieved the chair and placed it behind her. 'Sit.'

Robbie crouched before her as she sipped the cool water and hoped it would improve her condition. What had caused the change in her, he knew not. She'd seemed well as they rode and even the climb up the steep hillside had not tired her. She'd been fine until he'd left the cottage with the bucket.

'...then we can talk about our betrothal and forthcoming marriage.'

His words came back to him and revealed the cause for her distress. Her gaze flitted to his and away when he met it. She held onto the cup and took small sips as he waited. Moving back so as to not crowd her, he grabbed one of the stools for himself and placed it next to the table. He sat and waited.

Soon the water was gone and he asked his question. 'Does the thought of our marriage upset you so much that it brings on such upset?'

He'd thought he had approached her well this morn. He'd planned an outing that he knew she would enjoy. Horses. Riding. He knew that the sight of the falls from below would impress her and saw how she was intrigued when he'd led her to the hidden path upwards. Her curiosity was one of her strongest traits and had led her into trouble, or discovery, throughout her life. From her nervousness and hesitation now, Robbie suspected that they'd slid back to the hostilities of her first two days here.

'Do you wish my honesty, or should I dissemble and give the expected answer?' she asked.

Robbie could not help himself—his first reaction to her disgruntled expression and tone of voice was to laugh. Aloud and loudly.

'I think you just answered me, Sheena.'

She glanced away, seeming to study the way the roof sat on the walls around them. She huffed out a breath and faced him. 'And you, Robbie. Do *you* want to marry *me*?'

When their eyes met, he shook his head. Another little huff and nod from her before she looked away at the damned corner were her only reactions.

'So why did you agree to it?' she asked, shifting in the chair as she placed the empty cup on the table.

Damn it, but he should be angry about her lack of enthusiasm to marry him. He should be insulted. And yet a deep sense of relief filled him as he understood that, after years of being opposed to each other, at least they agreed on something.

'Loyalty and duty to my clan and to my father.' It was the reason behind almost every one of his actions. 'I will be faithful to my promises and to the duties I carry out as tanist.' The left corner of her mouth lifted, whether beginning to smile or sneer, he could not tell. 'And you?'

'The decision was made for me and, as is expected for the daughter of a powerful man, 'twas made without consulting me. I was a child when the betrothal was signed and no more in charge of myself or my future when I was told to travel here a few weeks ago.'

She stood and filled a cup from the bucket, holding it out to him. He accepted it and she filled hers once more before walking outside. Robbie followed her around the side of the cottage to the garden. She approached the first of the well-tended plots that lay in an orderly pattern and were covered with an assortment of plants, flowers, herbs and bushes. Anna used everything grown here to treat those in her care.

Sheena stood, facing the sun with eyes closed and chin raised. The winds, though gentle breezes now, lifted loosened strands of her hair to catch the flickering rays of the sun. Glints of gold and auburn made it look as if her tresses were aflame. A few moments passed in silence and she opened her eyes and met his.

'I cannot marry you, Robbie.' The stark admission hung in the space between them.

Cannot? Cannot? Robbie searched her expression for

something more to explain her meaning. A shrug of her shoulders and a shake of her head was all she gave him.

'You cannot? Or will not?' he asked.

Crossing his arms over his chest, he faced her and waited for her words. Was she being wilful, as he'd known her to be in the past, or was something else going on here? One breath expelled, followed by another and another, as she paused before giving him an answer.

'Cannot.' Regret tinged her words and it surprised him.

'Is there another you prefer? Another you…love?' he asked, unable to keep the words behind his teeth.

A quick shake of her head answered his question.

'If neither of us want this, we must find a way out of it,' she said. 'Will you help me, Robbie? Help me find an escape from this well-woven betrothal?'

Of all the things he expected her to say, that was never something his wildest imaginings would have considered. Though he was not against finding a way out of their betrothal. Truth be told, he did not wish to find them married either. He lifted the forgotten cup to his mouth and drank the water down while trying to find the words he needed.

'Give me a reason why you cannot marry me, Sheena. I do not understand your objection.' His gaze narrowed. 'Mayhap there is another whom you wish to marry in spite of your denial?' A sudden and inexplicable pang of jealousy rushed through him at the thought that she had some other man in mind rather than him.

'Nay!' she cried out. Shaking her head, she continued. 'Nay, I told you. I want no one else.'

He nodded, trying to accept her words even while puzzled about his reaction to the thought of her affections lying elsewhere. That would make this strange request more fathomable than her words so far.

'Robbie, did you ever have a moment, even one single moment, when you smiled as you thought of marrying me? When your father told you of the plan, did you think you were blessed at such an arrangement? Even for the blink of an eye? Or the length of a breath? Did you ever want to marry me?'

Robbie did not wish to be mean, but she seemed to want the truth. Yet she was younger than him by nigh on six years and clearly had a woman's softer disposition. Admitting the truth—that he'd never wanted even for a moment to marry her—would insult and injure her in a way he did not wish to do. Before he could speak, she did.

'As I thought. And I understand how much you hate me after…after…' She paused and motioned with her hand as she tried to describe the incident that had ended in his humiliation. 'And I cannot say that I blame you.' She let out another sigh and shook her head. 'I have always known I would not marry for love, but I do not wish to marry a man who cannot stand the thought of being my husband.'

'As you cannot stand the thought of being my wife?' he asked, his sharp tone evident to even him as he looked away from her. Her hand on his arm surprised him. 'I cannot be your wife, Robbie. I am not…able.'

He could tell from the pain that entered her gaze that the words, the admission of such a truth, cost her.

Robbie frowned at her. 'But you will not tell me why that is? Why are you not able?'

Now he took a step closer to her, forcing her to look up at him. He saw nothing about her that would be a de-

formity serious enough to call off a betrothal. She had
her wits about her, for a dim-witted woman would never
say such things to the man involved. An angry woman.
An obstinate one, mayhap. The realisation struck him
hard.

'You do not trust me.'

The truth was right before him in the way her emerald-green eyes widened at his words. If a man, a warrior
or villager or any Cameron, had insulted his honour like
that, he would have challenged him without hesitation.
In some deeper way he could not understand or explain,
her mistrust struck him at his heart. His anger flared.

'You do not trust me and I do not want you,' he cried,
releasing the harsh truth that lay between them. ''Tis the
usual way of most marriages between people and families of our position.'

Sheena stiffened at his deliberately hurtful words and
threw the cup she'd been clutching at him. Not waiting
to see if it hit her target—and it had—she turned and
ran back around the cottage. Whatever good intentions
he'd had at the beginning of this day mattered little now
for, once more, he had lost control with her and allowed
his temper to rule. Robbie gave himself a moment to yell
out his remaining anger before following her.

She was gone.

He ran to the opening of the path and could see no
sign of her below, on the steep steps cut into the hillside.
Damn, but she was fast. His feet lost contact with the
slippery steps, sliding over a few of them in his haste to
catch up with Sheena.

When he finally reached the bottom he saw the horse
she'd ridden go around the bend in the road, heading

back towards the bridge. Mo Cridhe moved so quickly he could not tell if she carried Sheena or not.

He would pay a high price for his inability to control himself. As always. This time though, so much more was at stake. He cursed himself as he climbed on his horse and made his way back to Achnacarry.

She'd asked for his help to work out the situation they were in together, one neither of them wanted. And his reaction had been to shout at her. If nothing else, he'd convinced her how correct she was about their future. His betrothed had asked for his help and he'd failed her.

Worse, he'd hurt her.

Strong, resilient, stubborn even, Sheena MacLerie did not deserve his disrespect. She did not deserve his disdain. Most of all, Sheena did not deserve to be forced into a marriage that would see her under the control of a man who did not want her. A man who wanted anyone but her. A man…

Him. Even she did not deserve to be forced to marry him.

When she was certain he'd left, Sheena waited a while longer, tucked behind the trunk of a fallen tree, before leaving the seclusion of her hiding place. As she'd hoped, Robbie had been fooled by the sight of Mo Cridhe galloping down the road towards the bridge. The sound of the falls, loud though it was, soothed her somehow. Once she thought him gone, she gathered the length of her gown and climbed over the decaying branches. Her unravelling braid allowed the breeze to catch hold of her hair and pull more of it loose. As she walked, she gathered it together and tied it more securely.

Now, calmed from the spike of anger that had forced

the cup from her hand at him, she did not mind having freed her horse. Walking miles around Lairig Dubh was something she enjoyed. Sheena paused for a few moments before the falls for one more look and followed the road around the bend, over the rickety bridge and back towards the village.

The first rumble of thunder roared above her in the pitch-black clouds she'd not noticed were gathering. Just as she reached the first cottage along the road, lightning split the sky and a fat raindrop struck her cheek. With Geordie's words now echoing in her thoughts, she searched ahead for some shelter from the coming storm. Picking up the length of her gown so she could run more easily, Sheena had only taken a few strides when a door opened ahead.

'Come in, my lady! Here, now!' a woman called out to her as she pulled her door open wider so Sheena could enter. The moment that Sheena stepped within, the threatening rain came down in torrents.

'My thanks, mistress,' Sheena said as she shook out her gown and pushed her hair from her face. 'You have saved me!'

'Oh, pish! A little rain willna hurt ye, my lady.' The woman laughed as she held out a length of cloth to Sheena. 'But here now, dry yerself off so ye dinna melt.'

It took a moment or two for Sheena to realise that the woman was jesting with her. With her. A stranger who'd just arrived here in Achnacarry. Sheena accepted the cloth and nodded.

'Geordie warned me the weather was not done with us, but I did not pay heed to his warning.'

'Ye will live and learn, will ye no'?' The woman rushed around, pulling a stool closer to the hearth and dusting it off, scooping something bubbling and hot from a pot over the fire and into a cup and smiling all the while. 'Here, now, we canna let ye catch a chill, can we? Sit—' she pointed '—and this will warm ye up.'

Sheena found herself bundled up in a length of warm wool and sipping on a cup of some mulled cider as the woman moved and spoke without pause. In a way, though not in appearance or age, she reminded Sheena of the cook at Broch Dubh. Capable, bold, opinionated and experienced, Glenda ruled the kitchens with equal measures of absolute control and good humour and patience. This woman had that same attitude and manner about her.

'What are you called, mistress?' she asked.

'Yer pardon, my lady. I am Tavie Mackintosh.' Sheena noticed the loom now, off in the corner of the cottage. 'Aye, I am a weaver.'

'And are you married?' The way that Tavie's face lit at her question, Sheena could guess not only the answer but also the state of their marriage.

'Aye, my lady. My husband is Kincaid Cameron and he serves the Laird.'

'And…?' Sheena could tell Tavie wanted to tell her more.

'A son who is nigh on ten-and-five and a daughter who has nearly ten years.'

Sheena sipped the delicious cider and listened as the rain and thunder continued unabated outside. Tavie began humming some sprightly tune under her breath and she seated herself before her loom. Sheena stood and walked over to watch the woman.

Within a short time, Tavie's hands moved quickly and smoothly across the surface of the cloth she was weaving. No hesitation or pause slowed her movements as the woman moved the wooden shuttle through the warp threads that were weighted down by stones. Darker hues similar to the surrounding hills and forests coloured the spun wool.

'How long have you done this?' she asked. Sheena had seen weavers work before, for such cloth was always in demand in their keep and village too.

'Since I was a wee lass. My mam taught me and I am teaching Keita.' Tavie nodded to a smaller loom sitting nearby. The woman narrowed her gaze at Sheena. 'Would ye want to try it yerself, my lady? If ye havna before.'

'I do not want to waste your time, Tavie.'

Aye, Sheena did want to try it. But knowing that she had not inherited her mother's skill with needlework and embroidery, no matter the time or effort spent in trying to master it, made her hesitate now. Her stitches were uneven and misplaced in spite of her best attempts. *'Woefully bad,'* her mother had said with a sad smile.

'Come now, lady,' Tavie said, walking to the other loom. 'Seat yerself on this stool, and ye can give it a try. If Keita can do it, ye can.'

'But this is her work—'

'Ye canna harm it,' she assured her. 'We can pull yer threads out if need be.'

Soon the crashing thunder and slashing rains faded away while Sheena followed Tavie's instructions and guided the shuttle back and forth along the tight lines made by Tavie's daughter. Though her lines, the weft threads she laid down, were not as even or smooth as Keita's, Sheena was bursting with pride and pleasure at seeing them accumulate before her eyes.

With all of her concentration on the movement of her hands and the leading thread, she never noticed the storm move on or the door open. Only when Tavie coughed several times did she raise her eyes and see Robbie watching her over the loom.

'Oh.'

Surprised, Sheena dropped the shuttle, which unravelled as it rolled along the floor at her feet. Bending to grab it, her hand touched it the same moment that Robbie's did. When she would have pulled away, he covered her fingers with his and lifted the wooden tool from the floor.

'You are well?' he asked, his gaze searching her face.

'I am.' He released her hand and she wound the thread around the shuttle and stowed it within the warp strands as Tavie had shown her. At the woman's nod, Sheena smiled. 'The storm—'

'The storm,' he began. 'I made it back to the stable, to find Mo Chridh safely in her stall without you. I worried you might have fallen off and been caught in the worst of it.' His intense gaze made something tighten in her belly.

'I would have if not for Mistress Mackintosh's help.' Sheena nodded at her rescuer. 'She offered me shelter.'

'And it looks as if you two have been busy.' He walked closer to the loom and she held her breath.

'Only the top rows are mine. Keita is more proficient than I am.' Her hands began to sweat, awaiting his reaction—to her running from him, to her hitting him with her cup…and to her handiwork now before him.

'The lady is a quick learner,' Tavie said, coming over to the half-made work. 'See how tight those last bits are? Aye, a quick learner.'

'Aye, Tavie,' Robbie answered. ''Twould seem she

is very skilled at weaving.' He lifted his hand and ran his fingers over her work and, for a moment, she swore she could feel his touch on her skin. 'Is this something you practised at home, Sheena? I do not remember you spending time at the loom.'

'This is the first time I've tried,' she said. 'I never had the patience... I never really learned before.'

'Well, Mistress Mackintosh has uncovered a new skill of yours.'

Neither of them understood that their praise, whether true or simply being kind, meant so much to her. The tears that filled her eyes surprised her and she blinked them away before they would be seen. She'd expected the next encounter with Robbie to be filled with anger and confrontation and never this.

Never this.

If he sensed her weakness, he gave no sign. Instead, he held out his hand to her and waited for her to take it. When she looked up at him, the bruise on his chin made her wince.

'I am...' Sheena lifted her hand towards the swollen area along the edge of his jaw.

'Nay,' he said, taking her hand in his and entwining their fingers. 'I should not have spurred you to anger.'

A cough reminded them that another was watching and listening to everything. Sheena turned to Tavie.

'My thanks for the shelter, Mistress Mackintosh, and for your help in showing me how to weave. I hope Keita does not mind I added to her work.'

'Och, nay, my lady! Dinna fash over it. If ye come back, I will show ye how to change out the colours to get the pattern straight.'

Even if she was simply being polite to the woman

who would marry her chieftain's son, Sheena accepted the kindness as she allowed Robbie to lead her outside. The darkness of the storm was gone and the puffy white clouds had reclaimed the sky. Camerons of all ages were already tending to their tasks, scurrying around the paths of the village.

Robbie climbed up on his horse and leaned down, hand extended to her. It would be better than trudging through the mud that now filled the road to the keep. She took his hand and, with her foot on his, mounted behind him. He tugged the reins to keep the horse from dancing as she threw her leg over and settled her gown around her.

He rode at a steady pace back through the gates and to the keep, not pausing at the stables as she thought he might. Instead, he rode up to the steps of the keep and stopped. When a servant came running to help them, Robbie waved him off and jumped from the horse without unseating her. Rather than offering his hand, he reached up and took hold of her waist, plucking her from the horse as though she weighed nothing.

He held her close, his arms strong enough to hold her up and ease her down to her feet. If he seemed to slow her descent those last few inches before she touched the ground, that might explain how she was more aware of the muscles of his legs as she nigh on slid down his body.

Unsettled and uncertain of what to say, once again she noticed the purplish bruise blooming on his jaw and met his gaze as he released her.

'I am sorry for losing my temper and throwing that cup at you, Robbie.' Her fingers wanted to test the edges of it, but first he needed an unguent to relieve the swelling. 'Should I seek out a medicament to reduce the bruising?'

'Nay, 'tis not bad enough for all that,' he said.

'I want you to ken that I enjoyed our ride and seeking out…' she paused and lowered her voice '…that place above the falls.'

'Sheena,' he whispered, 'I will help you.'

'Help me? Oh! Find a way to end the betrothal?'

'Hush now. I want this to be kept between us. No others should know.' He yet held her waist in his hands and a shiver echoed through her body as his fingers brushed up against the sides of her breasts. ''Tis a delicate matter that could undermine existing treaties and others yet in negotiation.'

'I understand.'

'Give me a day or two to find and read our betrothal contract and afterwards we can speak about it.'

The possibility of success filled her, and she smiled at him. He would help her. He would help them extricate themselves from their unhappy future. So relieved of worry for the first time in months, she threw her arms around his neck and kissed him. His mouth was hard when hers touched it, but it softened after a moment and he allowed the intimate contact.

His arms mimicked hers, gathering her closer still. Now all the strong parts of him were pressed against her softer ones. When the truth struck her about which part of him was now tucked between their bodies, she released him and jumped back.

His eyes were different when she met them, somehow softer as he stared at her with an unidentifiable mix of reactions in his expression.

Surprise and suspicion were part of it.

Desire too.

His gaze dropped to her mouth and she held her breath, waiting for another touch of his lips on hers. Instead, he released her slowly and Sheena tried to balance as he did. Once she was settled on the ground, he grabbed up the horse's reins and turned from her.

'I will see you at supper.' His words, tossed over his shoulder as he led the horse away, were gruff and she wondered at that.

Sheena did not allow the strange turn in his manner to lessen the excitement, the relief, growing within her. Without him, she had no chance to end the betrothal.

Wondering over the reason for his change of heart did not occur to her until the middle of the night. And it was too late to ask him.

Chapter Nine

As it turned out, it took Robbie more than three days to find and read their betrothal documents. That was not the strangest part of their now shared endeavour. Nay, the perplexing part was how much she enjoyed those three days in his company and even the other hours spent with his kith and kin. Without their hostilities, meals became pleasant, with lively conversations and a chance to learn more about his family and Sheena discovered she looked forward to the gatherings.

Though Glynnis never lost her graciousness or patience in dealing with Sheena, the lady showed herself to be intelligent and able to contribute sensibly with a touch of mirth on most topics discussed at table or otherwise. She had a way of explaining methods or manners without making Sheena feel as uninformed or inexperienced as she was. Whether overseeing the bread-making in the kitchen or fetching the books or other materials that Lady Elizabeth requested, Glynnis responded as a true, well-behaved lady should.

As Sheena would never be able to.

And she was perceptive too. For it took only a day

more in each other's company for her to discover that Sheena could not read. That she took care not to expose that deficiency in front of others gained her Sheena's respect and gratitude. After offering to teach her, Glynnis did not mention it again but she somehow deflected anything that would make it obvious to anyone else.

The one thing she could not work out while watching Glynnis were her true feelings about Robbie or his cousin Iain.

Sheena thought she'd witnessed something between Glynnis and Iain at his mother's house, and yet Glynnis never demonstrated a preference or attraction to him while in anyone's presence. She spoke to both Iain and Robbie—and Tomas for that matter—evenly, both jesting and discussing all sorts of concerns with them together and separately. At meals, in the yard, in the hall or the corridors of the keep, whenever or wherever they encountered the men, Glynnis was, well, gracious.

Yet something glinted in Iain's gaze as he watched Glynnis when he did not think himself observed, something she'd noticed as she studied each of them, that spoke of a deeper regard. Almost a hunger shone in his eyes. Their behaviour, towards each other or when nigh to the other, was above reproach. Sheena might have noticed because she was not familiar with any of them. Or it might have been that she'd learned to pay heed to the smallest details.

When Glynnis was speaking to Robbie, true affection filled her voice and in the way she smiled at him. Glynnis was expected to make a prominent match and if the Camerons had known that Robbie's position would be elevated sooner, Glynnis would have been the one.

Their easy manner around each other told her the match would have been a happy one.

Oh, Glynnis did not love Robbie, nor Robbie her, but the basis of a good marriage existed between them—unlike the basic dislike she shared with him.

The only one so far who'd not confused her was Tomas.

He was the opposite of his older brother. Where Robbie was serious, sometimes to the point of sullen, at least where she was concerned, Tomas was unassuming and pleasant. He'd told her with a wink that it was the prerogative of the younger brother to spend his time untethered and without any expectations. Whenever she was wanting of company or she was heading to the stables to check on her horse, Tomas appeared at her side.

The one who continued to perplex her was Robbie.

Once he'd agreed to help her, not a single rude word or act was aimed at her. It was as though all the pressure had been lifted from him and they were more at ease than they'd been. When he was not training or seeing to his own duties, they broke their fast together and he accompanied her on errands for his mother.

She tried not to examine the changes too closely for, when she had, she'd realised that he'd lost his hostility towards her once he'd agreed to find a way to rid himself of her.

Being unwanted was nothing new to her. She knew the story of how her father had chosen her mother's life over her own. How the night she was born, her mother lay near dying and her father gave the midwife orders to save his wife and not the bairn if the choice needed to be made.

For years, it was whispered in hushed tones for it defied the teachings of the Church. But her father already flouted the rules and was known as the Beast of the Highlands for his ruthlessness. It had not surprised her when she'd finally understood what the words meant. Though the story was couched as a romantic act by a man wildly in love with his wife, to Sheena it spoke of how little regard he held for the daughter born of that night.

It was easier to understand her father's disregard for her once she knew what had happened. His slights, when viewed through that perspective, were even something she could understand.

Now, just the thought that Robbie felt the same tore at her heart in a way she could *not* understand. She did not want to marry him either, but somehow he was more insulted over her refusal to explain her reasons than her refusal to marry him.

As she left Tavie's cottage for the third time in these three days, Robbie was waiting. The smile on his face pushed away all the dark thoughts and doubts. He stood leaning against the wall of the cottage, one leg crossed over the other ankle and his arms across his chest. The breeze, hopefully a sign of a continuing fair day, ruffled through his hair, making him seem younger…and happier.

'Have you finished your lesson?' He straightened and walked closer.

'Aye. Tavie is very patient but she has her own work to complete.' She watched as he smiled again and the expectant look in his gaze made her ask, 'What brings you here?'

'I am the bearer of good news for you,' Robbie said. 'Come.' He held out his hand and took hers. 'Hurry now.'

His grasp on her was a strong one and she hurried at his side as he sped up. When they ran through the gate and he turned towards the stables, her heart raced. Could it be?

She was winded when they arrived at the stable, but she kept up with his longer strides and fast pace. It was worth it when she beheld Wee Dubh out of his stall and stamping his hooves as she neared. He nearly pulled free of Geordie at her approach and Robbie laughed at the sight.

'He is happy to see you too, Sheena.'

'Aye, my lord, he's been most anxious for the lady's return.' Geordie laughed and rubbed his hand over Wee's nose. 'I think an easy ride would ease his feistiness. If ye care to?'

Her hands trembled as she reached out for the reins.

'Breathe.' Robbie stood behind her and reached out to steady her hands. His heated breath tickled her neck as he leaned closer. 'Here, let me help you.'

He moved around her and linked his fingers for her to step in. When she placed her foot in his hold, he heaved her up onto Wee's back. If the absence of a saddle surprised him, he did not say.

''Twill be hard to keep him reined in, my lady. But, even if the laddie doesna ken it, 'tis not the time for a full run.'

She positioned her legs so that her feet did not come near the healing wounds and wrapped the reins around her fingers and wrists as she liked. As she permitted him to throw his head up and neigh, Sheena laughed aloud while Robbie mounted his own horse.

'This way,' Robbie said.

Sheena followed him out, talking to Wee as they

went, urging him to have a care and not push his limits on this first ride. She did not feel the tears or realise she cried until Robbie slowed to her side and spoke.

'Is something wrong?' He nodded to her and she felt the tears rolling down her cheeks. Sheena wiped them with the back of her hand and shook her head.

'Nay. I am happier than I have been since I arrived here.'

He stared at her for a long moment before urging his horse forward and taking the lead once more. She smiled as she followed him through the gates and out of the village. This time they rode to the east when they reached the split in the path. Within a short while, the sight of a large loch opened up before them. Not the road she'd arrived in Achnacarry on, this one lay along the edge of the loch as it spread out to the north and south. It was level and straight and Robbie pulled to the edge of it, allowing her to come next to him.

'Have a care or Geordie will have my bollocks. And I neither wish to face his anger nor endanger my privy bits.'

Shocked at first by his words, it took her no time at all to accept his invitation to let Wee have a bit of a run. It took little urging for him to start moving more swiftly and she found herself struggling to keep him from galloping down the road. She leaned over his neck, drawing up her knees and calling out to him as he covered the ground beneath them. The wind tore at her hair, but it mattered little.

Wee Dubh was recovering. He would run again. Her restless, impatient actions that had endangered him had luckily not ended in his permanent injury. The relief that surged through her lifted so much weight off her spirit.

When she noticed him blowing hard, she increased her pull on the reins, slowing him from a trot to a fast walk. Robbie caught up with them and she could not keep the smile from her face.

'Ahead, a small clearing leads to the loch.'

He nodded to the left and she guided Wee towards it. The ground levelled off there and ended at the edge of the water. She slid off Wee and walked him the rest of the way, letting him cool down from his exertions. Reaching the shore, she urged him to drink while she watched Robbie.

'Geordie said nothing of this when I saw him this morn.' She rubbed Wee's nose. 'I cannot believe his improvement and dared not hope he would be recovered enough to ride.'

'You have won Geordie's respect. He did not want you disappointed if he promised something and the *laddie* was not ready.' He walked his horse up to the water and watched as both drank.

'I am just pleased he is improving. The thought of having to…' She could not say the words to describe what could have happened if Wee's wounds had gone bad. She'd raised him since he was birthed. To be the one who'd caused his end would have broken her heart.

'Was he born at Lairig Dubh?' Her eyes widened at his question. 'I ken you went to live with Lilidh a while back.'

'Aye. After she married Rob Matheson.'

'I remember him, though we did not foster together for long.'

That man was the bastard son of one of Connor MacLerie's closest friends from the west. Connor had taken him on not so much to make allies but to honour a friend's wishes. Matheson, like Robbie, was never expected to rule over his clan so they'd both enjoyed learning from Connor. Well, until both of them ran afoul of the man…and his daughters.

'Wee was foaled at home but trained at Keppoch Keep. No one expected him to be as large or strong as he is.' She smiled and glanced at the horse. 'But for me.'

'And Lilidh had no objections?' Sheena's elder sister had been gravely injured in a fall from a horse and her fear of the creatures ruled her life.

'As long as I did not ask her to come near him, Lilidh allowed it.'

Robbie untied the skin of ale from his horse's saddle and tugged the cork out with his teeth. Taking a mouthful first, he held it out to Sheena.

'Were you with her long?' he asked. He sat on a nearby rock and shifted to allow her to sit if she wished. For now, she paced.

'She married nigh to two years ago and she invited me to accompany her back to Keppoch when she left— when they left—Lairig Dubh. I came here directly from her home when the message came to do so.'

He heard it in her voice. Regret? Sadness? At leaving her sister or coming here, he could not tell, but he heard something else in her voice.

'For a short while, Lilidh, Aidan and I were all at Keppoch Keep.'

'What brought that on?' Robbie took another mouthful. 'How did your mother allow such a thing?' He laughed, for he'd ignored the more obvious conclusion. 'What part did your father play in having all three of his children fleeing Lairig Dubh at the same time?'

Sheena sat next to him, not touching him at all, and shrugged.

'Father tends to be overbearing even at his best. Things between him and Lilidh—and him and Aidan—were not the best.'

'And you? How were things for you?'

'I was on my own most of the time.'

'No different than when I was living with your family.' She'd been a solitary child, except when trying to run with him and her brother.

'And you, Robbie? When did you return here to Achnacarry? The last time I was informed, you were still at Tor. In the south.'

'When my father took his place as chieftain. Nigh on six years ago. I have been in charge of Tor's defences until called home some weeks ago.'

'So, I keep you from your duties?' She stood and stepped towards the water.

'As has been made clear by both of my parents and several other interested parties, you are my duty.'

He noticed the wince as she faced him. She waited on the details he was supposed to seek out about their betrothal contract.

'Have you found the documents?' she asked.

Her face stiffened, as did her body, as she asked. Waiting for the worst of it. He recognised the expression as one he'd worn on his own face a number of times in his life. When Connor MacLerie had summoned him that day long ago. When called home to discover his father had been cast out. And again when his uncle was chieftain and wanted to announce another wedding that would solidify his power. More recently when the call came to return to Achnacarry and her name was mentioned.

'I have.' Her hands twisted in her skirts as she waited. 'I cannot remove them from my father's chamber.'

'Is there any hope? Of breaking it.' Her hands now clasped before her, she looked both desperate and hopeful at the same moment.

'I need to study it more.' He was being honest. 'We can look at it together. Mayhap we could ask Glynnis for help.'

'Glynnis? Why would we involve her in this?' Sheena began pacing once more, this time in a smaller circle and more rapidly. 'This is a rather intimate issue, Robbie. I do not wish her involved.'

Other than the times she'd been brusque in speaking to him, Robbie had never heard a mean word from Sheena. Not as a child and not since her arrival. But a warning of some kind lay in the tone of her voice.

Jealousy? Was she somehow jealous of Glynnis? Interesting and yet puzzling.

'I thought of asking her because her ability to read Latin is far superior to mine,' he explained.

Sheena turned and walked to the water's edge now. Crouching down, she dipped her hand in the water and let her fingers trail through it. She stared out across the surface of the loch, which was so still it reflected a perfect image of the sky above them.

He stood and walked to her side and waited for her to acknowledge him.

'We do not have to ask for her help, Sheena,' he finally said after a long silence. 'My father and mother are travelling to Tor in the morning, so the steward's chamber where the documents are kept will be empty.'

'They are leaving?' Sheena stood and faced them.

'Aye, for two days. They must see to matters at Tor.' She'd never seen his other home, the place where his family had been exiled by his uncle while he ruled. 'We could join them there so you could see the castle and area.' He glanced over at Wee Dubh. 'Now that Wee is well enough to ride.'

'Mayhap we can decide after we—after you—finish examining the contracts?'

'After *we* examine them.' He held out his hand to her and guided her to stand. 'If you trust that, between us, we have enough skill with Latin, we will leave Glynnis out of the matter.' She nodded, though the expression of doubt in her eyes seemed to contradict that. 'Let us plan to linger after breaking our fast in the morn. We will read the papers and try to find a way to end this arrangement.'

They collected the horses from the place where they stood grazing on a patch of grass and he helped her mount once more. Against his will, he admired too her skill with the huge horse.

The lack of a saddle had not slowed her a bit and, as he'd watched from behind her on the road, she'd leaned down low over Wee's neck and spoken to the horse. Steady on his back, she rode smoothly along the path, and Sheena never wobbled or lost hold of the reins. With her legs drawn up, she controlled the massive beast beneath her. As they turned northward to return to Achnacarry, she spoke.

'I promised someone my help in the morn. Can we meet at midday?' He waited for her to say more about this other person and yet she did not.

Now it was his turn to feel something resembling jealousy. Why, he knew not, but a wave of it raced through him at her words. Everyone in the clan knew she was his. Well, until they broke off the betrothal, if that was even possible. Still, who was she planning to see in the morn?

Unable to voice these strange concerns, he nodded his agreement.

Soon they were back at the stables and Geordie stood waiting, hands on hips, watching Sheena and Wee Dubh like a proud father. The older man waited for their approach before taking the reins from Sheena and helping her down. As Robbie watched them, heads together, talking about her horse, a strange thought occurred to him.

If he did truly want to marry her and if he were a jealous man, a damned horse could be his biggest competition.

Chapter Ten

In the morning, very few places were filled at the table.

His parents had left at dawn for Tor. The commander of their warriors, Anna's husband Davidh, accompanied them, as did Iain and their steward Struan, who would meet with the man who oversaw Tor Castle and their southern lands. Though he'd expected Sheena, he was met by Tomas and Glynnis. Glancing around the hall and back to Tomas, Robbie realised her probable location when he saw his brother's smile.

'The horse?'

'The horse,' Tomas confirmed. 'The lady tucked some bread and cheese in a cloth and headed towards the stables with barely a pause for wishing us a good day.'

'Glynnis, she did not ask you to go with her?'

'Nay, Robbie.' Glynnis smiled as she shook her head. 'She spends each morning at the stables, seeing to the condition of her horse and taking instruction from Geordie.' Glynnis's smile was warm and filled with affection for the woman who had indeed taken her place in his future. 'She is kind enough not to ask me to attend her.'

'If you would…' he began. He glanced from Tomas to Glynnis. 'And only because I trust you both would I even ask this of you…' Wariness entered both of their gazes. 'Tell me your thoughts on my betrothed.'

'Lady Sheena loves her horse,' Tomas said. He laughed and Robbie's hand fisted, wanting so much to use it on his brother's smirking face.

'The lady is kind,' Glynnis said, 'and lovely.'

'And she loves her horse,' Tomas added once more.

'She loves to walk outside regardless, it seems, of the conditions,' Glynnis said.

'And what of her skills, Glynnis? Has she demonstrated any to my mother's satisfaction yet?' Robbie asked.

Glynnis's dark brown eyes filled with a pitying look before she answered him. 'The lady has just arrived here, Robbie, and is not yet settled into her place.'

The answer to his question was nay.

'Embroidery? Overseeing her own maid or the servants?'

'Well, she is a young woman,' Glynnis explained while that pity in her eyes deepened.

'Glynnis, my betrothed is but a year younger than you are.' Glynnis's gaze moved from his to Tomas's and back again.

'But Robbie, you must remember that I was destined to be the wife of a—'

She stopped before she said another word that would expose her change in status—or his. Glynnis MacLachlan, daughter of The MacLachlan, an ally and standard-bearer for the Camerons, had been raised to marry a chieftain's son. Trained from the moment she could walk in all the skills and arts needed to be the appropriate wife of a powerful man.

Overseeing a household? Aye. Skilled in the womanly arts? Aye, she was that as well. Skilled in numbers and letters, able to cipher and write and read? Aye to that too. She would be the perfect wife for someone of Robbie's status.

Years ago, when his father had not laid claim to the chieftain's seat, Robbie and Glynnis's possible betrothal was not a consideration because of his arrangement with The MacLerie. Even if that had not existed, Glynnis's father had not been willing to discuss a match that would not culminate with his daughter as the wife of a chieftain. By the time that everything changed and Robbie became heir, tanist to the Camerons, any possible arrangement was superseded by the alliance between his father and The MacLerie. Though Glynnis would make him the perfect wife, she would marry someone else.

He shook his head and looked away as Glynnis shrugged, her delicate shoulders lifting and relaxing in a gesture of both hopelessness and acceptance of the missed possibilities between them.

She closed her eyes, levelled her shoulders and let out a sigh. 'She is intelligent, Robbie,' she said. 'She will learn what she needs to before 'tis time for you to sit in your father's chair.'

The words, spoken in the tone she used, should have allayed his concerns. However it was in her gaze that he saw something else. Glynnis was not telling him the truth. Or, at the least, she was holding something back.

Before he could question her further, Tomas interrupted. 'Well, we ken she knows how to raise horses.'

Tomas's words broke the rising tension. Robbie

thought his brother was being the same light-hearted lad he always was. But a glance in his direction told Robbie his brother had no mirth in him this time. Nay, his brother did not laugh or offer the words in jest.

Leaning back against his chair, Robbie drank the rest of his ale and thought on Glynnis's words, both what they said and what they did not.

'Robbie?'

'Glynnis, I thank you for sharing your thoughts with me.'

'But Robbie, she truly is a kind person. And she will learn what she must.' Glynnis's lower lip trembled a bit, worry clear on her features now.

'Aye,' he said as he placed the empty cup next to his empty bowl. 'She will do what she must.' He stood, now intent on finding his betrothed, and nodded at his brother. 'Glynnis, I ken you will be at her side, helping her in any way you can.'

Without another word he left, knowing Sheena would be in the stable. Walking to Wee's stall, he found it empty of her. It took a bit to find Geordie, who was outside teaching one of his apprentices the finer points of shoeing a horse. The man could do the task himself blindfolded and in the dark with one hand, but teaching the skill to another was a different matter.

The lad was having some difficulty in holding the huge horse's hoof steady as he worked. Rather than taking over, Geordie stood to the side, offering suggestions and humorous comments as his helper did the work.

Well, if Sheena was not here, where could she be?

Robbie walked into the village and sought out Tavie to see if Sheena had come to help her in some way. The woman was not even in her cottage when he knocked, nor was her daughter. So he moved on, heading to the centre of the village. The well and the baker's oven were two gathering places for the women as they went about their day. Had Sheena accompanied Tavie somewhere?

The well was a busy place in the morn and this was no different as villagers collected water for their daily meals and chores. He searched through the clusters surrounding the well for Sheena and did not catch sight of her. The aroma of fresh hot bread caught his attention and Robbie followed it from the well. After passing a few buildings and crofts, he reached the place where villagers would bring their loaves to bake.

'Good day to ye, my lord,' Finley called out from behind the tall stone oven. Peeking around the corner of it, the baker carried more uncooked loaves to the opening and tossed them in with his flat wooden paddle. 'Here now, Jeannie, my love, give the Young Laird a fresh one!' That the man was only a year older than Robbie made him laugh.

Every time he encountered the husband and wife, he marvelled at their differences. He short and she tall. He young and she much, much older. Even their colouring was as opposite as they could be with his almost white blond hair and hers black as pitch. Finley was Jeannie's second husband and, from the way they behaved, it was a very happy marriage. He bit into the steaming roll and moaned at the flavour.

'My thanks, Jeannie,' he said, nodding. Though the cooks and bakers who prepared food for those living in or visiting the keep were excellent at their craft, nothing compared to Finley's fresh bread.

'Are ye looking for someone, my lord?' Finley asked as he wiped his flour-dusted hands off on his long apron.

He winked as he spoke and nodded at Jeannie too. 'A certain young lady was recently here, and I gave her a sample as well.' Finley took hold of Jeannie's face and pulled her down for a quick kiss. Jeannie blushed and giggled like a lass, well, half her age would.

'I might be, Finley,' he answered. Apparently, some of those living here had not heard of his resistance to marrying The MacLerie's daughter and believed there was more between them than actually existed.

'She went off with Tavie and some others to the washing place,' the baker said. 'Jeannie?'

'Aye, my lord,' Jeannie added. 'The one closest to where the river meets the loch.'

It took but a short time for him to reach the place that Jeannie spoke of. He'd been here many times and seen the villagers and servants washing on the large flat stones along the edge. A strong enough current exchanged the water in the shallow pool that gathered there and kept a good flow of clear waters in the washing area. Something made him stop on the path before he was seen approaching.

Stepping back into the shadows of the trees along the road, he made his way closer to the lively group sitting or kneeling by the rocks. Searching through the women, he found Sheena kneeling in the midst of them, looking neither like a lady nor the betrothed of the tanist. Rather, she looked like a village lass working with her neighbours.

Her hair was braided and held back from her face by the same kind of kerchief worn by all but the youngest of the lasses. The sleeves of a plain gown were rolled up to her elbows and her hands were lost in the foaming bubbles and cloth she was rolling on the flat rock at her knees. But what drew his attention was the joy in her demeanour and the smile on her face.

He saw Tavie and a few others he recognised as he watched. They chatted as they worked and Sheena stopped a number of times, asking for guidance or advice from one or another of the women. Even when she did something incorrectly, she did not hesitate to ask or to join in the laughter that resulted from some of her errors.

Something unfurled within him as he observed her in the middle of them. Her expression was empty of worry or cares. She did not shirk from the hard work of washing clothing in the river. It was clear from her garments—those of a servant rather than the lady she was— that she thought little of her appearance or her clothing.

He stood under the cover of the trees as they worked. Some of the women began humming as they washed and the others joined them, matching their pace and actions until they moved the same way. Only once did Sheena stop and that was to speak to a woman who sat nursing a bairn away from the edge. A few times they exchanged words as she continued to twist and rub the cloth.

Why was she doing this? Why had she come here this morn instead of staying in the keep or even spending time with her damn horse? Robbie watched for a short time before returning to the keep. For the next few hours he carried out the tasks he needed to, but his thoughts went back, over and over, to the scene of Sheena in the middle of the women, washing clothes by the river.

Would she tell him the reason for her absence? Would she reveal the reason they could not speak about the important matter of their betrothal and how to avoid it when they met later?

Would she ever trust him with the reasons behind her

refusal to marry him? He just did not think it was related to what had happened to them all those years ago. Though they'd managed to keep their dislike for each other alive, it did not seem enough to stop a marriage.

The real reason must lie in the truth that Glynnis knew. Something about Sheena that neither of them would share with him. He must find a way to gain her trust. For if they were going to break a betrothal and come out of it without a war between their families, they must work together. If he did not know what stood between them, that could not happen.

At midday he waited in the hall for her to arrive.

Sheena somehow managed to get back to her chambers without being seen in the keep. With the Laird and the Lady and their closest advisors away, the hall and the corridors were not as busy, and most of the servants had carried out the cleaning of the chambers in the tower that held the family's rooms. Her own maid was probably in the storage rooms or another place, finding her way around the keep with the help of Isobel. And, looking as she did in a working gown and her hair covered much like a maid at this moment, that was a good turn of events.

Hastening to her chamber, she tugged the kerchief off and freed her hair from her braid. Because of the way her gown fastened, she could loosen it without help and she did so as quickly as she could. Robbie must be wondering where she was, and she needed to change into a proper gown and find him. With haste.

After a few rushed brushstrokes to tame her hair, Sheena gathered it into a loose braid and tossed it over her shoulder. The muddied gown came off and, since her shift was dry enough, she sought and pulled on the gown she could most easily manage alone. Her shoes were the last to be tugged on before she went off to find Robbie.

Sheena ran down the steps, glad that no one saw that behaviour either. Her mother's reprimands echoed in her thoughts as she rushed along the corridor towards the chamber that sat off the great hall, opposite the kitchen's entrance.

And there he stood.

Slowing and trying to catch her breath, Sheena tried to read his expression as she approached. He appeared to be doing the same.

'Sheena,' he said, nodding in greeting. 'Come in. My father's chamber.' He stepped back and allowed her to enter before he did.

Gair, her father's steward, maintained the same kind of chamber at Broch Dubh. Trunks and shelves filled with crates and cartons were everywhere. A large table sat in the centre of the room and many parchments and books and drawn maps lay scattered across its surface. No matter how it might resemble Gair's, Sheena knew that Struan most likely remembered every piece of parchment, every treaty or contract, every document in his care and where it was at any given moment.

Robbie skirted the table and went to a strongbox on one of the shelves under the only window in the chamber. Lifting the box, he carried it to where she stood and placed it before her. The thump as it landed spoke of its weight. Robbie turned it so that the lock faced them as he stood next to her and removed the opened lock from the hinged metal on the front.

'Not locked?'

'Nay, not while it is in here. No one comes into this chamber except those permitted by my father.'

'As you are?' Sheena looked up at him.

'Aye.' Robbie opened the box and let the lid drop back. 'As tanist, I spend a significant amount of time here, reviewing treaties, maps, any document of importance to the clan and our interests. My father involves me in many of the decisions he makes now.'

She heard the pride in his voice as he spoke of his place here. As any man in his position should be. One day he would be making the decisions. One day his word would be law among the Camerons. One day his sons would follow him.

The tightness in her chest spread through her body at the thought of that future. Of what her part should be. She fought off the clawing feeling that closed her throat.

'Sheena?' Robbie touched her hand, gaining her attention. 'What is wrong?' He squeezed her fingers and when her vision cleared she saw that he'd moved closer and was staring.

They were searching to find a way out.

They were looking to end the betrothal.

She reminded herself several more times of their purpose—their joint purpose—as she pushed the breath-stealing terror back. Words would not come.

'Sheena? Lass? Can you hear me?'

He took her by her shoulders and turned her, resting her against the table. She nodded and shook off both the fainting spell and Robbie's hold.

'I am. I am well. I am just hungry.'

'You did not break your fast this morn?' Luckily her stomach growled loudly, supporting her lie, and Robbie glanced down at her body and back at her face.

'I…' What could she say? He would never approve
of how she'd spent her morning in the hours since she'd
left the keep. The betrothed of the tanist did not wash
clothes at the river's edge like a common servant.

Without another word, he turned and walked out the
door. His call to a servant, ordering bread and cheese
and ale, surprised her once again. When he returned,
Robbie grabbed hold of a chair and brought it to where
she stood. Sheena nodded and sat in the seat he offered.

'While we are waiting, should we begin with these?'
he asked.

He lifted the lid of the box and began removing its
collection of scrolls and the many sheets of parchment
within. Soon, a pile formed before her. She chose one
of the documents and brought it nearer to her. Closing
her eyes, she offered a quick prayer that something had
changed since her last attempt. She opened her eyes and
looked at the writing.

Sheena searched for something familiar in the script
on the page before her. The swirly figures of letters
seemed to push themselves together and be indistin-
guishable from one another. Squinting made no difference. Staring helped not. She tried to concentrate on
each little group of swirls and dips drawn in ink, but
they moved and twisted and became one long strip of
meaningless images to her.

'Can you read Latin?' Robbie asked over his shoulder.
'I fear I have never conquered the Roman language. At
least not as well as my tutor wished me to do.'

'I struggle with it as well,' she said. For a moment
her infirmity was safe from discovery. That scrap of joy
evaporated as he held out a scroll to her.

'Here. Examine this. Your father has some strange

ideas and demanded the contract be written in our own tongue.'

Well, it could be worse. It could be in the English form. At least Sheena could identify several words in the Gàidhlig and might be able to stumble her way through this. If the words were not written too twisting or very muddled, she mayhap could recognise them from the few she remembered.

It was as bad as she'd thought it might be.

The scribe or clerk who'd written the contract had used his most formal handwriting to solemnise the occasion of the betrothal. Sheena had no chance of reading any of it, but for their names at the top. She tried and tried and tried for a third time to find a word or even a letter that made sense to her and simply could not.

'I have read it and can find nothing I think would invalidate the betrothal.'

Robbie's words were stark and clear. Yet, without the ability to read it, she could offer nothing to reject his claim or prove it. Frustration unlike any she'd felt before filled her in that moment. Her failure to read had been brushed aside by the clerk her father had put in charge of teaching her. When her difficulties had become apparent and her parents would not follow his recommendations to punish her until she overcame them, their demands had faded as she had, out of their sight and out of their concern.

The whole matter had simply reinforced to Sheena her lack of importance. She had not wished to be forced to spend hours standing in the rain until she could identify the letters or words her tutor insisted. Or to have her hands slapped with a cane until she could pick out the words he'd demanded she read. Nay, none of those practices had done anything but torment her body when she'd already lamented her failures.

She handed the betrothal contract back to him now.

'What did you find?'

Chapter Eleven

'Kenning that Duncan MacLerie or his man negotiated it for my father, I doubted we would find anything we could use to end this easily.'

Sheena did not have to read a word to understand the strength of the binding made with Duncan's involvement—many MacLerie adversaries had bemoaned his abilities for long after a treaty or agreement had been signed. She relied only on Duncan's reputation as the MacLeries' peacemaker for decades for her comment.

When he opened his mouth to reply, the arrival of a servant bearing a tray stopped whatever he was about to say. Robbie stepped back and motioned for the maidservant to place what she carried on one end of the wide table and watched as she did so and took her leave.

'My thanks, Margaret,' Sheena said as she glanced over at the young lass and nodded.

'My lady.' With a smile in return, the pleasant girl offered a curtsy and left, closing the door behind her. It had taken her several encounters in the hall and above stairs to finally tell Margaret from her twin Marsaili, but now Sheena could.

With another loud grumble from her belly, Sheena reached over for a piece of cheese while she waited on Robbie's opinion about the betrothal. Only when the silence extended did she look up to find him staring at her with a mix of both confusion and disbelief in his deep blue eyes.

'I beg your pardon, Robbie. Would you like some of the cheese or bread?' His stare continued and Sheena worried that she had somehow misstepped yet again. He shook his head and waved off her offer to share the sustenance on the tray.

'How did you do that?'

Now it was her turn to be confused. What had she done this time?

'What did I do?' she asked. 'Ah, I ken it a lamentable habit to thank the servants when they carry out their duties. My mother explained that 'tis not a thing done often, or at all in some keeps. But I—'

'Nay. Not that.'

'Pray tell…what did I do?' Sheena waited for a recitation of a list of her sins, her failings and her missteps as that usually followed a question such as the one he'd asked.

'How could you tell Margaret from Marsaili?'

'Oh, that.'

He nodded as he crossed his arms over his chest. His expression gave her no sign of his true reason for asking, so she told him.

'Margaret braids her hair, while Marsaili leaves hers loose. Margaret is shy and will not meet your gaze, but her sister will and will not be cowed by man nor woman. Marsaili's eyes, though brown, are a different shade from Margaret's. Lighter.' She pointed out the obvious differences between the sisters. 'Oh, and Margaret has chipped her bottom tooth.' Sheena pointed to the one the maid had broken.

His narrowed gaze told her he was considering her words. He shook his head and reached out for one of the cups. Handing it to her, he took the other and drank deeply.

'I never noticed those details.' He tipped the cup and finished the drink. 'They have served me for years and I did not see those mannerisms and features that you realised in less than a sennight.'

Sheena had no idea of how her ability to tell the twins apart—and, more so, the way she'd done it—bothered him. Nay, that was not the truth of it. He was not bothered so much as stunned by the details she'd absorbed by observing the maidservants for such a short time.

And had he ever called them by name? When he wanted more ale and his cup was empty? He raised it and a servant filled it. Aye, her ability bothered him in a way he could not work out or describe. And as before and once more, it led him back to his own shortcomings and his preconceived notions about the woman before him.

He'd thought her aimless. He'd thought she avoided her duties, and, aye, she did that at times. He'd thought her ignorant of how a keep and its people were managed. He'd thought…

He'd thought many things about her, and a chill crept down his spine now as he came to realise that he might be wrong about other matters involving Sheena Mac-Lerie.

For now, though, the betrothal and its breaking must

take their attention and efforts and it might be best to turn back to that.

'So, you agree there seems no way to break this?' He watched her reaction as she glanced at the document. 'Other than one of us declaring ourselves to be deficient in some way.'

Her face lost its colour once more, as it had earlier. He did not remember her being the nervous kind and yet she had this strange reaction at times to him and his words. More than nervousness, it was that and fear close to terror mixed in that he witnessed in her eyes. After a long moment, she was able to shake herself free of whatever gripped her.

'Deficient?' she asked. Brushing a few strands of hair away from her face, she frowned. 'Deficient how?'

Robbie laughed softly at her question. Well, she was still the innocent he'd thought her to be.

'Truly, the only deficiency that would stop this, according to the contract, would be your known inability to…' He paused, taking a moment to choose his words. If innocent, he did not wish to be vulgar. 'If it is known, by you or your family, that you cannot give me heirs, I do not have to honour the agreement.'

The colour that had waned in her cheeks rushed back in the moment she understood what he—what the agreement—meant. She stammered a few words before giving up the attempt and just looked away from him.

'Drink this,' he said. Holding her cup up, he waited for her to take it. Once she'd had a few sips, he sat next to her. 'Other than lands and titles and wealth, that is the only duty for the wife of the heir. These betrothals take little else into consideration. Since Duncan was sent to negotiate for your mother's hand in marriage for your father, I suspect the wording may be very similar to ours.'

'He did.' Placing the cup before her, she shrugged. 'Though his stepdaughter and his man Farlen have taken over many of his duties, Duncan sees to the most serious or important matters. My father trusts him.' Her blush calming, she met his gaze now. 'So, can we truly do nothing?'

He wanted to be insulted by the way she wished to rid herself of him and yet he wanted the same thing. Something in the hopefulness of her eyes made him want to help.

'There has to be a way to end it. We just need to find it.'

'Without bloodshed and mayhem?' she asked.

'I cannot tell if you would prefer that way or a smoother way that does not end in the loss of lives.'

'In all truth, I do not find it such a terrible thing, but I ken of your need to protect your clan and to carry out your duties. Death and chaos would not be your way.'

Her insight surprised him, as did the humour in her tone. Only Sheena MacLerie, daughter of the ever-bloodthirsty Beast of the Highlands, would suggest that spilling some would not be a bad thing.

'So, we should continue to seek a way out of this. Without blood or destruction,' he added.

Robbie began replacing the scrolls and other important documents back into the strongbox. He could examine them again, but he doubted he'd missed anything. Though he dare not ask his father about this matter, it was possible one other person here, well, at Tor, could answer this question. Or at least tell him if any chance existed of finding an end to their betrothal.

He would wait for his parents' return and offer to take Sheena to visit. With Glynnis and his brother accompanying them, it could be an enjoyable few days and might give him an opportunity to discover more about the reason why Sheena paled at some of the things he said. Why she believed she could not marry him.

And why it bothered him when he did not want to marry her.

'Do you have matters to attend to now?' he asked. Sheena sat in silence, watching as he finished and closed the box.

'Nay.' A brief reply, yet he could see the suspicion in her gaze. In that moment, he wanted it gone. He wanted her trust.

'Have you looked in on Wee?'

'Aye. This morn.' Before she'd joined the women in washing the clothes in the river.

'Is he well enough for a ride?'

'With you or me as his rider?' she asked. Mirth twinkled in those eyes now.

'I but wait on your word for that, Sheena.' He admitted that freely.

'For now, though, I think a lighter load would be best for his continued healing.'

He smiled at her jest and held out his hand to her. When she took it, he helped her from her seat.

'Lighter load or not,' he said, still holding onto her hand, 'you must promise that I am first to ride him when he has healed.'

His words surprised her for she blinked several times and shook her head. That small movement caused the length of her hair, pulled away from her heart-shaped face and tied loosely behind her head, to swirl around her hips.

'You wish to ride him?' She tugged his hand and he stopped drawing her towards the door.

'Aye! He is a magnificent horse. A man would have to be daft not to feel the urge to mount such a creature and let him have his head.'

'Well, you may. I think that Geordie may have to ride him to assess his healing. But you can be next.'

Robbie laughed, lifting her hand to his mouth and kissing her palm. 'As long as you do not allow my brother near him, I mind not.'

'Tomas said the same thing to me the last time I saw him.'

'Damn the man!' He frowned and shook his head. 'Has he no respect?'

She laughed and he could not help but stare at the change in her as she did. Her eyes glittered like the precious jewels in his mother's ring—emerald-green—that shone brightly when they caught the light of the flames in the hearth. Her laugh was light and filled with a joy he usually only heard when she talked to or about the horse under discussion.

'You cannot allow him, Sheena. I lay first claim as his elder and your betrothed.' Although he was yet caught up in teasing her, he noticed the moment that the light fled from her gaze.

Heir.

He'd reminded her of his position once more and, as her hand slipped from his, he cursed himself.

'Wee Dubh is yours, Sheena. Certainly you may grant permission to whomever you choose.'

Her fingers entwined and her hands shifted as she

let them fall in front of her. She did that when she was nervous. Robbie wanted to reclaim that fleeting moment of joy once more. To see her eyes and her face brighten.

'Come. Let us seek out Geordie for his advice on this matter.' He reached out and touched her clenched hands, surprised when she loosened them and took his. 'And I will make it clear to Tomas that you will choose me first.'

'Do you two battle like this all the time?' she asked as he turned once more towards the door.

'Since we could both walk,' he said. 'My mother swears 'twas earlier than that, but I cannot see how.'

She tugged once more and he faced her.

''Tis clear to anyone with eyes that you care about him. That you would do what you must to protect him. Come now, admit that you love him and would see him well.'

'We are brothers,' he said softly. Glancing past her for a moment as a few memories of their good times and bad passed through his thoughts, Robbie smiled. 'And, since we are, I cannot and will not ever admit that to him, even if it is God's honest truth.'

He laughed and a gentle smile curved the corners of her bow-shaped mouth. The urge to kiss her filled him and, when she did not resist as he stepped closer to her, he leaned down and satisfied his desire.

Her mouth softened under his and he pressed against her lips. He expected her to pull away when he slid the tip of his tongue along the tight seam of her lips. When she opened to him, he swept in to taste her.

Sweet when he expected the tartness of her personality.

Surprise when he thought to find resistance.

Curiosity when he believed he would find shock.

A soft gasp escaped before she opened a bit and allowed him to move deeper within. When the tip of her own tongue touched his, Robbie's body became as hard as the steel in the sword he wielded.

Now he was the one to be shocked. At a kiss.

It was only a kiss and yet…

He lifted his mouth from hers and found himself inordinately proud and pleased that her breathing was as irregular as his. He took in the dreamy expression in her eyes and the way her mouth remained a bit open as if she'd lost herself in the kiss and forgotten to close it.

Robbie brought her hand to his mouth, their fingers entwined now, and kissed the inside of her wrist. She gasped at the intimate touch of his tongue but did not move it away. Meeting her gaze, he asked the question he should not.

The question that had plagued him since she'd spoken her objection for the first time and even more so since her request for his help.

'Are you certain you cannot marry me, Sheena?'

The way her eyes glistened with gathering tears, surely a sign of regret, should have made him feel better about her silent refusal. He could not explain why he'd even thought to ask the question when their business in his father's chamber was about severing the ties that bound them. When she glanced off towards the door, her discomfort was something he could feel.

It had been that damned kiss.

A simple touch of their mouths and he'd lost his reason. Not their first kiss, for she'd kissed him in front of the keep the other day, but this was so much more satisfying.

Now he craved more of her on his tongue.

Shaking his head over his lack of control, and over his strange reaction to her kiss, Robbie shrugged.

'Come. Let us visit Wee Dubh and see what Geordie says about other riders.'

Chapter Twelve

Glancing over at Robbie, Sheena felt that mixture of confusion and grief and regret once more. They rode south along the river that led away from Loch Lochy towards the clan's ancestral castle for her first visit. Riding near the front of their small travel party, she was glad others were present.

They passed the small *clachan* called Gairlochy on their journey. The few people living in the gathering of crofts called out greetings to them, recognising Robbie and Iain both. When they crossed the river their ride became a pleasant, easy one and Sheena enjoyed watching the trees and scenery along their path change as they neared or drew away from the river itself.

But none of that altered the situation between her and Robbie. Four days had passed since his strange plea and she'd grown more confused with each one.

For a moment, a brief, heart-stopping moment, she'd been tempted to say aye. To withdraw her objections, to ignore her weaknesses and the terrifying fear that lived within her and to accept his offer. And that was all it took—the time that passed with an inhalation of a breath—to realise she was tempted to foolishness.

And to pain and failure.

No matter the strange, beguiling swirl of feelings that had filled her at his words and at his kiss, she could not survive being the wife of a chieftain of a great clan such as his. Between her inability to read or to write other than to scratch out a few critical words and the sheer and paralysing panic that filled her at times and caused her to fall into a faint, she was unfit to be his wife.

Now, more than before, the thought of his shame at her shortcomings tore through her like a sword wielded in battle would its target.

If he'd persisted in acting towards her as he had upon her arrival—taunting her, criticising and being hostile—she could have continued to seek a way out of their betrothal without guilt. But his recent light-hearted teasing and considerate manners made her feel worse.

She wanted to feel anger instead of the regret that gnawed at her resolve. She liked the way fury emboldened her and made her feel less hollow. Now, though, he spoke to her as though interested in what she said. He was considerate and offered to take her into the surrounding areas so she could learn his lands. Worse, he allowed her as much time each day as she wished to spend without him.

Mornings she'd spent in the village, learning to weave and sew, helping out with the washing or wherever she could. She loved being out of the keep, away from judgement and the strain of becoming the perfect wife of the man who would rule the clan when it was his time.

Lady Elizabeth tried to be helpful, but her words sounded the same as Jocelyn MacCallum's—Sheena's mother—had every time she'd corrected or examined every single task Sheena performed. And in spite of Lady Elizabeth's vast patience and her soft tone of voice, to be judged and found wanting by the lady day after day wore on Sheena.

So she did as little as she must within the lady's solar or her chambers before seeking out those who lived in the village. They welcomed her. They accepted her efforts and thanked her for them. They invited her back, even as they gently reminded her of her place and position.

And not once had Robbie questioned her about her activities or how she spent her time away from him. After that day when they'd searched through their betrothal contract looking for a way out, and after she'd rejected him, he'd acted as if neither had happened.

Even this morning, his suggestion of riding to Tor and speaking with the good brother who served as The Cameron's scribe was another in a long list of kind acts he did for her. They'd met each day at the stables, after sharing a midday meal with his cousins, and usually rode short distances into the Disputed Area along Loch Arkaig, or along this very road that followed Loch Lochy to Tor and the south.

The skies had cleared and the sun shone brightly, turning a pleasant day into one warmer than was usual in the Highlands. The breeze along the loch's edge eased the unexpected and growing heat as they made their way. Glynnis rode directly behind her now on a mild-mannered mare. Tomas had remained back at Achnacarry, but Iain had accompanied them.

With a quick look over her shoulder at those two, Sheena had a feeling that something was happening between them. From Anna's words and more from her expression during Sheena's first visit to the healer, she suspected such a relationship would not be welcomed or approved.

Glynnis had, at one time, been the one under consideration for marriage to Robbie and, rather than jealousy, Sheena thought she would make the perfect Lady Cameron for him. She was gracious, even her laughter was soft and gentle, while Sheena's sometimes sounded like a choking cough. Glynnis understood the duties expected of the wife of the chieftain and her needlework was perfect. Everything about her was...perfect.

'Can I help you with your cloak, Sheena? The day is warmer than I expected,' Robbie asked as he drew up nearer to her. Because of the combination of Wee Dubh's height and her own lack of it, they faced each other at the same level.

'Aye.'

He smiled, a genuine one, as he waited for her to untie her cloak and lifted it from her shoulders. Though not her heaviest one, Sheena was anxious to relieve herself of the weight and warmth of it and feel the lovely cool air. From the laughter from the others, they'd heard the not so discreet sigh she'd let out as Robbie lifted it from her shoulders.

'My thanks.' She gathered the length of it and laid it across her lap.

'You should be able to see Tor Castle at the top of the next rise. It sits on a promontory out into the River Lochy.'

He pointed ahead and as soon as they reached the crest of the hill she could indeed see his ancestral home. Older than Achnacarry, it had been built with one purpose in mind—laying claim to the lands around it with a stone keep able to resist attacks.

They travelled on and soon approached the entrance to the small village next to the keep. Not comparable in size to Achnacarry, it consisted of several crofts, a few small, well-tended fields and some working buildings.

'But, if you will, I would like to show you something first.'

Sheena did not hesitate to accept his intriguing invitation and Robbie called out orders to the guards ahead and behind. 'Tell Parlan I will—*we* will—arrive shortly. I am certain that my mother gave instructions on which chambers to prepare for my betrothed. I wish to show Sheena something first,' he said. Strange that, for she did not wince when he spoke of her place in his life.

The guards nodded and Sheena could not help but notice the sly smiles from Glynnis and Iain. Where was he taking her? What did the others know that she did not?

With a farewell nod, she followed Robbie's lead off the road, along a path through the thick brush and trees. Careful not to allow Wee to injure his nearly healed wound, Sheena allowed the horse to move at his own pace. Robbie stayed close and did not seem in a rush. When she thought he might be taking her to a postern gate, they headed off in a direction away from the keep.

'Are we going back to the road?'

'Nay, this path curves back around and will lead to the postern gate in the keep's wall.'

'By the river?'

'Aye, but what I want you to see is here, in the forest.'

'This area reminds me of Lairig Dubh,' she said, glancing around the low hills.

Though she'd travelled little outside the lands ruled

by her father, she knew that the trees that grew around her home—the pines, birches, oaks, rowans, hollies, willows and alders—surrounded her now. Many contented hours had been spent with their healer out in the forest, gathering seedlings and leaves and other growing things for her potions, ointments and medicaments. Iain's mother, Anna Mackenzie, had invited her company to do the same and Sheena suspected she would find the very same plants and roots were her target as well.

''Tis similar, aye,' Robbie said. 'Until you leave the Highlands, much of the lands look familiar. The lowlands have not the high hills and deep glens we have here. And the isles to the west and in the north seem to be a combination of both.'

Sheena sighed. For many reasons, she'd rarely left the safety and small world of Lairig Dubh. An unfortunate episode involving her disabling panic on a trip to a cousin's wedding in Edinburgh had resulted in her remaining behind when travelling near or far was a choice.

'I will admit it, Robbie. I am suffering from the weakness of envy as you describe places you have visited and the sights you have seen.'

He stopped and dismounted, holding out his hand as she lifted her leg over Wee Dubh and slid off the horse's back. He'd moved closer and reached up to help her, guiding her to stand before him. He'd helped her before, a number of times, but this time was different. Though he laid his hands only on her waist, the nearness of his body to hers created a heat unlike she'd ever felt.

Nay, she lied to herself. She'd felt this before. Heat had filled her when he'd kissed her days ago. When his tongue had outlined her lips, he'd plunged it within to taste her.

Even now, her breasts felt swollen as her body slid along his, rubbing over his muscular chest before her feet touched the ground beneath her. Sheena clutched at his plaid for balance, for her head seemed to spin and her body ached for something. Lifting her head and gazing at him, she realised she ached…

For him.

For another of those breath-stealing kisses.

For even more than that.

How very strange! She'd thought on their long-standing hatred and planned how to end their connection for so long that she'd ignored any possibility that she might feel differently at some point.

Like this moment.

She tilted her head back ever so slightly and noticed the way his eyes darkened and his nose flared in reaction. That was the only warning she got of his intention. Her hands grabbed hold of his shoulders as he leaned down and kissed her mouth.

It took only a moment to be glad she'd held onto him. Knowing what to expect this time, she relaxed her lips and let him dip his tongue in her mouth. The feel of it, rough and insistent against hers, sent shivers from where he touched down through her core. Uncertain if he moved closer or she did, their bodies touched from chest to thighs and every bit in between. His body was hard, every part of him, and instead of fearing it, Sheena wanted now to rub against him and feel the strength of him.

Robbie slanted his face, somehow bringing his mouth even closer to hers and allowing him to dip deeper into her. His hands slid up along her shoulders and caressed her neck. Her body trembled at the intimacy of his touch.

He spread his fingers and entangled them in her hair, holding her head still as he continued the kiss.

Softer for a moment before pressing firmly against her lips. Sweeping his tongue in and feeling it slide over hers. His fingers tangling in her hair and the touch of them as they tickled her scalp. His hips against hers and his hardened flesh caught between them.

Even as the kiss went on and on, repeated over and over until she was dizzy with the pleasure of it, the pleasure of him, Sheena understood that this somehow changed everything between them. Even though, in some ways, it changed nothing.

It changed nothing.

Sheena eased away, first lifting her mouth from his and releasing her hold on him so she could move back. As soon as he realised what she was doing, he let her go without trying to keep hold of her.

'Is that what you wished to show me?' she asked in a voice that trembled much, much more than she wished it to. It made her sound weak when she did not want to.

He let out a soft laugh before answering her. The smile that accompanied the laugh softened the lines on his brow and made the edges of his strong lips curl up ever so slightly. Both changes made her accept a truth she'd long fought—Robbie Cameron had grown from a good-looking lad into a very handsome man. The memory of her body against his reminded her that he was very much a man.

'Nay, Sheena. I did not have that in mind when I brought you down this path. But mayhap I did hope such a thing would happen again between us.'

'You did?'

'Aye.' He took her hand in his and tugged her closer

once more until she had to lift her head to meet his gaze. 'And I think you enjoyed it too.' Robbie leaned down and touched her lips with a soft and quick kiss that seemed over before it began. 'Did you, Sheena? Or am I the only one of us feeling this unexpected attraction?' He kissed her, this time lingering against her lips for a moment longer than the last one. 'This rising desire.'

This time, as she expected another quick touch, his kiss became something else. Something persuasive and then possessive. Robbie touched only her mouth, but it ignited the banked heat and sent it coursing through her entire body. Before she could reach for him or touch him in any way other than the meeting of their mouths, he lifted his head and stepped back.

He watched her, clearly waiting for her to speak, and yet she could find no words to say. He was not the first to kiss her. Several lads in her father's keep and village indeed had. None had caused the reaction Robbie's kiss had. When she remained silent, hoping he did not understand that his kisses had scattered her wits, he held out his hand to her.

'Come. What I want you to see is down this trail.'

They walked a narrowing path deeper into the wooded area, leading the horses, until they reached what seemed to be a small clearing ahead of them. The rushing water of a nearby stream and the breeze moving overhead through the trees were the only sounds that broke the silence around them. Robbie wrapped the reins of his horse around a thick branch and Sheena did the same, whispering instructions to Wee to remain there.

'The rest of the way is too narrow for them.'

The anticipation in his voice made her smile. She knew not what was beyond them but she suspected something surprising and fun. When he held back a thick layer of branches for her to pass by, she walked a few paces on and turned to face him. As he approached, she examined the clearing around them and could not tell what was so special that he wanted her to see.

Now Robbie passed her and went to the edge of the clearing, where the sound of the water flowing was loudest, and waved her over. She saw an opening nestled in and nearly hidden by some thick bushes.

'In case you have need of it.'

Chapter Thirteen

Robbie watched for the moment she realised what lay hidden behind the growth of bushes.

'A cave?' she asked, bending down to glance within.

'Nay. Not a cave. My cave.'

Though any number of the women he knew would have backed away at the word *cave*, Robbie had guessed that it would draw Sheena like a bee to flowers. And it did.

'May I go within *your* cave?'

'Aye, just have a care for your head as you go.' Her excited exclamations as she moved into the dark shelter made him smile.

Seeing her tucked away and sleeping in that tight little alcove in Anna's garden had later brought memories to mind of Sheena as a lass in her father's household when Robbie fostered with them. Some of those remembrances were as yet unclear, but he did see an image in his thoughts of finding her in a similar hidey-hole in the forest outside Lairig Dubh.

Several times while he'd lived there.

He leaned down and looked inside where Sheena had

gone. The enclosed area in the cave was not large enough for more than two or possibly three people gathered close together, overlapping and barely moving. Easing into the entrance and lowering his head, which he'd already injured too many times by not doing that, he pressed along the far wall while trying to allow the sun's light to pass farther.

'The accommodations are sparse,' he explained as he crawled the last bit to reach where she sat. 'But it is mine and I do not care.'

Sheena shifted over to allow him to sit nearer to her. 'How did you find this?' Did he imagine the wistful tone in her voice? One that sounded as though she coveted this place of his.

''Twas on a visit home from Lairig Dubh. I… I sought a measure of privacy from my parents and brother.'

'The visit after…?'

'Just so.' He shifted on the cold hard-packed floor as his body seemed to remember the lashing he'd received from her father. Waiting for his shame to be exposed and for his father to punish him for his poor behaviour, Robbie had fled the keep before he could be summoned to speak to his father. If they could not find him…

'I came down from the keep, along this part of the river and stream, when the sunlight hit it at a certain angle that revealed the cleft there.' He leaned forward and pointed to the opening. 'It had been covered under thick brush and weeds and it took me hours to clean out the debris.'

'Hours that kept you from your father's sight.'

Her calm words exposed his truth—and her own. How had he never realised before? Did she even know she'd trusted him with such an intimate detail of herself?

'Aye. Even Tomas kens not about this place.' He smiled at her. 'And I pray you not tell him.'

Her hand on his surprised him. It was mayhap the first time she'd touched him.

'I do pray for your pardon, Robbie. I did not mean for you to be punished that day.'

'Sheena—'

'Nay. Let me say this.' She moved up onto her knees, bringing her closer to him. He nodded. 'I wanted so much to be at your side all those years ago. Running free and playing with you and Aidan and the other boys. Not to be under the endless scrutiny of my mother. I wanted you to know how much…' She glanced towards the light at the opening of the cave before continuing. 'I liked you so much. I just wanted to spend time with you.'

Whatever he'd thought she might say was eclipsed by the words she actually spoke. And by the honesty of her admission. She'd liked him? All those years ago? How could that be? How could he not have known such a thing?

'But I caused you such humiliation because of my actions. When I think of the pain you suffered…' she whispered as tears shone in her eyes. 'I hope you can forgive me for my childish sin against you.'

'You were but a child, Sheena. I was older and should have followed your father's instructions.' He shifted on the floor. He'd been considerably smaller when he'd spent time in this cave. 'And I do not forgive you, for it was not your trespass. 'twas mine.'

She began to object, due, he was certain, to the fact that she did think she was to blame. Was that what kept her from trusting him? Made her believe they could not marry?

'For whatever part you played in my shameful behaviour, I forgive you.'

The smile that lifted the corners of her mouth was one of genuine delight. She'd thought he'd held her responsible all these years! He'd learned too much in the short while they had been alone and needed to think on it all without the temptation she was becoming to him, being so near.

'I think we should be on our way.'

Robbie stood as much as he could in the cramped space and moved towards the entrance. Turning back, he held his hand out to Sheena to assist her. Without a heartbeat of hesitation, she took it and followed him out. Once out in the open air, Robbie took in a deep breath of the fresh breeze coming off the stream and watched as Sheena stepped out of the darkness behind her.

The sunlight glimmered on the strands of her hair loosened by climbing in and out of his hiding place. Well, and mayhap from his hands as he ran them into her russet curls while he'd kissed her. He'd almost lost his concentration when his fingers caressed her face and head and felt the soft hair curling around his fingers. He wanted to pull it free of the ties that bound it and spread it across her shoulders. He already knew the length of it would reach to her hips.

If he reached out to her now, this new and unexpected hunger would overwhelm his control and he would do that and more. So, whether because she saw something in his gaze that forewarned her or her curiosity could not be contained, she remained a pace away from him when she spoke.

'Is this your only hiding place?' Not trusting himself

to speak, he shook his head. 'Do you have one like this at Achnacarry?'

Robbie pulled himself under control and offered her his hand. Walking back towards the horses, he told her the rest of it.

'This was my home. I spent my early years here before coming to Lairig Dubh and, after my return, here with my parents and Tomas. We moved to Achnacarry only when my uncle died.'

He paused, uncertain about how to explain the upheaval that had seen his uncle, the chieftain, challenged and dead. Though rumours flew across the Highlands, not everyone knew the whole scandalous truth. Had The MacLerie explained it to her when they'd revealed the change in his circumstances and hers? When he'd gone from being the nephew of the powerful Cameron chieftain to being the heir of the next one?

'And by then you were too old?'

'Not too old, lass. Too busy. My father was the new chieftain and I was the new...' He shrugged. 'Heir.'

'Duties?' He nodded. The horses neighed at their return. 'Honour?' Another nod. What else could he say?

After the humiliating exposure of his parents' secret a few years ago before the Cameron clan and their allies, Robbie understood that all that kept them strong was duty. Honouring the fealty they owed the clan and the chieftain. Disregarding personal choices for what would be best for the clan. And, watching his mother suffer through the revelation about her son's parentage— and her own shame at their enemies' hands—he'd vowed never to allow anything but reason and measured responses be his way.

'Aye.' When they drew near the horses, he released

the reins and held Sheena's out to her. ''Tis safer that way. Not to pursue the softer things that might destroy us in the end.'

He moved to her side to assist her, but she'd already climbed on the big horse's back without his help. Mounting and turning back towards the path they'd followed here, Robbie pointed off in the distance.

'We will join up with the main road to Tor farther down the path.' She followed his hand as it pointed south. 'And I will show you the shortcut to the cave from the postern gate.'

'Why?' she asked, drawing up next to him.

'I ken you, Sheena. You will want to explore and I want you to be safe.' He'd shocked her with his honesty. ''Tis my duty as your betrothed to make certain of it.'

After his recent attentions, his insistence that his words and actions were about simple duty should have hurt her. And yet they offered some reassurance she could not identify. Marriages between noblemen and noblewomen did not depend on love. If fortune smiled on them, they might find mutual affection and respect, but a proper union never required soft feelings.

She'd lived her whole life with parents whose deep and abiding love was known far and wide, in spite of her father's reputation as a wife-killer and her mother's forced agreement. And their love had been the source of sighs and whispers for as long as Sheena could remember. If anyone knew the price of such a love as theirs, it was her.

So even if he never loved her, he could never hate her or shame her for her shortcomings and weaknesses. If the last days had shown her anything, it was that Robbie would carry out his duty to marry her. In spite of searching for a way out of their agreement, he would, in the end, marry her.

And, no matter that he was being kinder to her and that he stole her ability to think when he kissed or touched her, she would not survive a life as the wife of a clan as large and powerful as the Camerons.

'You ken me well, Robbie.' She patted Wee Dubh's neck as they reached the road. 'I would have sought out the cave and been gone for hours searching for it.' The worst of it was that he was correct.

'I kenned that,' he said as a smug expression covered his face. 'Come, let me show you Tor.'

For a moment she thought he meant to take her back to the main road so they could enter the yard though the main gate. Robbie guided his horse in the opposite direction and soon it led them down to the river's edge. Here, the river's course ran from the north, around the outcropping of rock where the castle sat and south once more.

'There,' he said, pointing to the place where a smaller stream joined the larger river. 'If you follow that upstream, past the curve, you will get to the cave.'

'Can horses make it from here?' Sheena lifted herself up and tried to see if a path could be seen.

'Aye, but only if the river is low. A full flow, after a storm up on the loch or north of here, makes it dangerous. So have a care before you follow the shoreline.'

Did he know her so well that he understood she would seek out the comfort of that secluded place? His blue gaze narrowed as he waited on her acknowledgement. Sheena nodded, giving him what he wanted.

They rode on until the river turned sharply and Tor was above them. Not as impressive an entrance as the main gate, the postern gateway was halfway up the hill's steep rise and would therefore prevent a huge force from attacking it even from the river. They had to urge the horses forward and Sheena worried about Wee reinjuring or tearing his wounds, even though Geordie had pronounced him sound for this journey. She slid off the horse and led him forward with the reins.

'Is he limping?' Robbie was at her side in less time than it took to call out to him.

'Nay, but the path is a strenuous one and I fear for him.'

They walked the rest of the way up to the guards, who stood a bit straighter as they realised who approached them.

'Lundy, Innes, how goes it here?' Robbie asked.

'Well, sir,' the first one said.

'Lundy, is your brother still beating you with the quarterstaff?'

The first one, who must be Lundy, shrugged and offered a sheepish nod. 'Aye, Robbie.'

'And you, Innes? How goes it with your training?' Sheena waited for the second young man to reply. Instead, he looked off in the distance, forcing a laugh from Lundy and from Robbie.

'This is Sheena MacLerie,' Robbie said as he motioned her forward. 'My betrothed. Have a care for her.' The men studied her for a moment, neither one seemed disrespectful in their regard, and nodded at Robbie, accepting his order. 'Keep her safe.'

Once they'd nodded, Robbie spoke to them for a short time, exchanging details of some plans for training before he led her into the dark tunnel of the postern gate. It was narrow—only one person or one horse could pass through it at one time. The stone ceiling was higher than she'd expected but once she saw the openings above Sheena understood that guards could rain down rocks or arrows or burning liquid to stop any invaders.

They reached the other side and were greeted by two more guards. Robbie repeated the introductions and orders for her protection before leading her to one of the smaller buildings in the yard. Before they could reach it, several men poured out of it and hurried to them.

'Hiv ye seen such a beauty?' one asked another.

'Nay, not in my life!' replied this one, an older man with a thick patch of grey hair that sprang up in the centre of his otherwise bald head. 'Not in my life, laddie.'

'Can I—' the first one began before a tall, brown-haired man interrupted and stepped between the men and her. Were they speaking of her? Sheena watched as this man held up his hands.

'Nay, lads,' he said. 'You can look at the beast, but you cannot take him.' He faced her before offering a bow. 'I am called Parlan, my lady. When the Laird or his tanist are not in command here, I take care of things.'

Her horse. They were talking about Wee Dubh. She smiled and caught Robbie's gaze and saw the laughter.

'My horse?' He nodded with a laugh.

'Thank you for your welcome, Parlan,' she said. 'Mayhap one of the...the lads could take Wee Dubh to the stables?'

Her words provoked a chaotic scene she'd not anticipated. Wee reacted by rearing his head and stamping his hoofs, but that only fed the excitement of those fighting for the chance to be the one to lead *her* beast away. Allowing only a bit of scuffling before he stepped in, Sheena watched Robbie gain control.

'Here now, lads,' he called out. 'Remember you cannot be riding him.' The small group yelled out in agreement and jostled for a better position. 'You will have to take turns with this. Here comes Jamie. He will assign the duty each time it's needed. For this first time, Jamie, may we let Lady Sheena choose who will take the wee lad to the stables?'

'Och, aye, sir,' the man who must run the stables agreed. 'If ye will do the honours, my lady?'

She did not know which gesture touched her more—Robbie clearly taking extra precautions for Wee or that he thought it important to include her. She swallowed against the growing tightness in her throat and blinked quickly so that the threatening tears did not fall. He slipped his hand in hers and leaned closer to say something only to her.

'I do not want you to be suspicious and think I am being considerate of your wishes in order to gain your permission to ride Wee Dubh.'

'That is precisely what I think.'

'Think what you must,' he jested. 'But have mercy on the lads awaiting your choice.'

Her heart raced and something unexpected and warm filled her. She did not doubt he wanted to ride Wee. She did not doubt that he was trying to ingratiate himself with those who worked in the stables. But the way he managed to do it showed her an entirely different part of him she'd not seen before. Here at Tor, he seemed more at ease, younger even than when at Achnacarry. Now that she knew about his cave and that he'd spent many years here, it made sense. He thought of this as home.

Sheena looked at each of the hopefuls before her and pointed to the one who looked most eager.

'Micheil,' Jamie said. 'Walk slowly to the lady and give Wee Dubh a chance to see you first.' The lad did as directed, and seeing the happiness bubbling within him over this small thing made her smile as well. 'My lady, would you place the reins in Micheil's hand and step back?'

All the time, Jamie spoke in that same soothing tone that Geordie used while calming riled horses. She did as he said and found herself pressed against Robbie as Micheil now followed each of Jamie's instructions. He spoke to Wee, and the way the horse's head nodded spoke of Wee's acceptance of this boy.

Robbie gathered her in his arms from behind and, for once, she remained still in his embrace, allowing herself to feel at ease. Feeling as if she mattered to someone. As if her wants and needs were being paid heed to.

'See,' he whispered against her ear. His heated breath tickled as it touched her. 'He is well-cared-for here, as at Achnacarry.'

He held her as the others ran off with Jamie to settle Wee Dubh. When Parlan turned back to them, surprise at seeing the embrace lit on his face for a short moment before he nodded at them.

'If you are ready to come inside, I am certain that Conran will have your chamber ready.'

'Conran?' Sheena stepped out of Robbie's arms with a strange sense of regret at doing so. 'Who is he?'

'He is steward here, my lady,' Parlan explained. 'I am the castellan.'

'I beg your pardon, Parlan.' She'd insulted the man who oversaw every aspect of this castle by thinking him only the steward. 'I fear I have offered insult with my words.'

'Nay, no insult, my lady,' Parlan said, stepping back and motioning for them to walk with him.

'Parlan is getting a bit big for his breeches, Sheena. Do not let him fool you with his grand title,' Robbie said, taking her hand as they walked. 'He is commander of the warriors here and oversees our southern lands.' The man he spoke of turned and nodded.

'How far do the lands extend?' she asked. Certain that someone, most likely her mother, had told her about the Camerons' claims and the lands they held, Sheena had never been able to remember such things. As they walked to the keep, Parlan answered.

By the time they reached the keep and entered into a smaller great room than the one at Achnacarry, Sheena had forgotten that Robbie held her hand, as she had forgotten almost every detail that Parlan had shared. Only when Iain's eyes widened and Glynnis let out a soft gasp as they approached the large table near the hearth in the front of the chamber did she realise that the small gesture had been seen. After a slight hesitation, she released his hand and followed the man introduced as Conran to the chamber above stairs that Lady Elizabeth had selected for her on her recent visit.

But she could not help glancing over her shoulder as she did. Robbie watched her every step as she left the hall and, for some reason she did not wish to study too closely, it felt good to have his attention.

Chapter Fourteen

Sheena stared at Conran, trying to make sense of his words. She did not dare look at the list he'd handed her a short time ago. Concentrating on the explanation of his request, she tried not to let panic rise within her.

A roar grew in her head and her gaze flitted from Conran to Glynnis across the small table where they sat, to the servants milling about carrying out their tasks. Farther away, a few guards, workmen and others needed within the keep worked. Though none seemed to be aware of her or her nervousness, she thought they all glanced her way and could see the growing unease inside her.

'Lady Elizabeth suggested you should be the one to choose since this will be your household once you are married,' Conran explained once more.

'Conran,' Glynnis said, 'if you leave the list with Lady Sheena, she can study the names and let you know her decision when she has made it.'

'Very well, my lady.' Conran offered a bow to her and a nod to Glynnis before leaving them.

'Sheena?' Glynnis spoke her name softly even as she reached out and touched Sheena's hand. 'Are you well?'

'I cannot…cannot…'

Fear. This was what she feared the most. Though not the entire length and breadth of Cameron properties and holdings, running Tor and its surrounding lands was terrifying enough.

She noticed Glynnis summoning one of the servants before coming to her side. After whispering to the maid, Glynnis guided Sheena to her feet and she allowed it, following them without knowing their destination. Each step brought on more trembling in her hands and her legs and, by the time Sheena sat down, her limbs were shaking so badly she could not move.

As her heart raced and pounded within her chest and blackness surrounded her, Sheena lost all hope of keeping her affliction a secret after all.

Robbie rushed behind the maid who'd sought him out with Glynnis's call. Something was wrong, very wrong, with Sheena. The lass stopped before the door to his mother's solar and stepped aside with worry covering her face. Robbie lifted the latch and entered.

Sheena lay on the cushioned bench in the corner, as pale as death and barely breathing. Glynnis knelt at her side, stroking her hand and whispering her name. As he moved closer, he prayed to the Almighty, because he had no idea of what else to do.

'What happened? What is wrong with her?' he asked, crossing the last few paces in a near run and touching Sheena's cheek and brow. Covered in a fine sheen of sweat that he would have thought brought on by fever, the coolness of her skin startled him. 'Is she breathing?' Again, he prayed as he leaned down and watched for the rise and fall of her chest. Instead of an even movement, her breaths came in shallow, rapid panting.

'Conran was speaking to her about organising her household here and she became agitated. She struggled to breathe so I brought her here. I did not think you would wish her exposed to everyone in this…this distress.'

'Nay!' He knelt at Sheena's side as Glynnis answered a knock on the door. 'Nay,' he whispered. 'Has she spoken at all?' He smoothed her hair off her face and took her hand in his.

'She has not spoken since I brought her here.' Glynnis returned with a bowl of water and a cloth. 'Here, wipe her brow and neck with this.' Robbie took the cloth and did that several times under Glynnis's direction.

They continued to tend to Sheena in silence until her breathing seemed to slow and grow deeper. Her cheeks regained their usual blush and Robbie let out the breath he did not know he'd been holding. She seemed to be sleeping now rather than in some kind of illness.

'Has this happened before, Glynnis? Have you seen the like of it?' Robbie tossed the wet cloth into the bowl and placed it on a table. When Glynnis did not reply, he turned to face her and saw the truth in her sad eyes.

'Nothing as bad as this, Robbie. I would have told you.'

'But something similar?'

'When faced with something unexpected.' Glynnis looked away.

'Is this the meaning behind your words of warning when I asked what you thought of her?' Glynnis had known something, for even that much was clear to him from her reticence. 'Did you ken of this?'

'Robbie, I pray you not to…' She stopped abruptly and he realised Sheena's eyes were open and staring at him.

Robbie watched as Sheena gained awareness of where she was and who was with her. When she tried to rise, she groaned and laid her head back down.

'Rest a bit more here, Sheena,' he urged. Her distress was clear in the way her lips drew into a tight line, driving all the colour from them. She looked away from him to Glynnis.

'What happened?'

'You grew overwhelmed at table and I brought you here before you fainted.'

'Are you in pain, Sheena?' Robbie asked, softening his tone.

'My head. My…'

She slid her hand down over her belly. From the growing green tinge in her neck and around her face, he understood and moved aside just as Glynnis stepped closer to help.

Robbie walked across the chamber and stared out of the window that opened over the yard, giving the women a measure of privacy to deal with this unsettling situation.

Sheena had hidden this from him. From her family as well? Did this happen often? If Glynnis knew of it, it had happened since Sheena had arrived at Achnacarry. How had he missed such a thing?

'Robbie, Sheena would like to go to her chamber.'

He turned back to find Sheena sitting up but leaning against the wall, as though she could not sit on her own. Her expression was one of undisguised misery— her eyes dull, her face pale and drawn.

'If I could just sleep—'

'Can you summon a maid to help me take her—?' Glynnis began.

'Nay.'

Both of their expressions in that moment were the same, for their eyes widened at his refusal. But they misunderstood his intention. He motioned Glynnis aside in order to lean in and lift Sheena into his arms. Her body shivered and pressed against his chest as he shifted her closer and nodded to the door. Glynnis rushed to it and opened it for him to pass.

He moved swiftly from the room to the stairway leading up to the bedchambers. He felt her strength give out and she collapsed against his chest. Glynnis reached the door before him and opened it. When she would have followed him inside, he shook his head.

'I can see to her, Robbie. I do not have need of the servants if you wish this kept out of their view.'

'I thank you for what you have done to shield her so far, Glynnis. Truly. But I will tend to her now.'

He could see that she wanted to argue with him and he also recognised the moment she relented. Well, almost relented.

'I will bring some ale and watered wine and bread. They may help to settle her stomach. I can send to Anna for a—'

'Bread and watered wine will be perfect. If Sheena has need of anything else or more, I will send to you.'

Glynnis nodded and stepped back from the door. As she pulled it closed, he could swear she was smiling.

He walked to the bed and climbed on the edge, easing Sheena down onto its surface. With little difficulty, he managed to adjust her on the pillows and remove her shoes. She did not stir at all, but this seemed more like a deep sleep than the faint she'd suffered before.

Pushing himself up to sit against the headboard, he thought back to her arrival and the time he'd discovered—well, Anna had discovered—Sheena asleep in the garden alcove. She had been sleeping so deeply he could not rouse her for some time and she'd been drowsy the rest of the evening. Did these…spells cause her to fall into exhaustion?

As he watched her sleep, he tried to remember back to his years at Lairig Dubh. Other than a fleeting memory of some good times and some bad, he remembered very few specific details about Sheena as a child. He'd been too busy learning to fight and how to lead and the manners needed of a knight and a nobleman. Connor Mac-Lerie was not an overly harsh foster father, but he held those he accepted to foster to high standards and pushed them to excel in their training and in their studies.

He'd paid little heed to Connor's eldest daughter Lilidh and even less to Sheena. At least he and her brother had until she'd forced herself into their attention. Remembering her words in the cave just a few days before, he had indeed missed the point of her bothering them and trailing them through the keep and village.

'I liked you so much. I just wanted to spend time with you.'

She'd been so young when he'd lived with her family. Could she really have cared so much about him? He smiled now as he did remember some of the words her mother had spoken to him, and to Aidan, about their deplorable manners and lack of proper behaviour towards those of the feminine gender. Lasses had just not been important to him when he was but a young lad.

Sheena had not been important to him.

She stirred next to him and he reached over to soothe her restless movements. With gentle caresses, he smoothed her hair back and watched as she settled deeper in sleep. Remaining closer to her, he pressed a kiss to her forehead and another on her brow. That she turned and followed his mouth as though seeking another touch of his lips surprised him.

He smiled at the fanciful thought until she turned towards him, yet fully slumbering, seeking him. Stunned at such an action, Robbie slid down until he was lying next to her and gathered her in his arms.

For all her opposition to him while she was awake, she seemed to trust him while asleep.

Leaning his face against her hair, Robbie knew he was lying to himself. Lately, since they'd begun sharing kisses, Sheena had not pulled away from him at all. She allowed his touch. She reached out to him. She'd accompanied him on his visits the last few days to those who lived in the small collection of cottages and buildings that made up the village.

Her behaviour, if not her words, gave him hope that she might find a way to accept their betrothal. With this exposed secret—though he had not the full understanding of it yet—more questions than answers stirred. So many questions.

The next time he opened his eyes, the chamber was completely dark—no candle or lantern or fire in the hearth threw any light at all. He lay on his side, draped over the soft lovely form that was Sheena. So close that he could feel the curve of her back, the fullness of her hips and thighs as she pressed against him. His aroused flesh had noticed before he did, for it lay tucked tightly between them, fitted nicely against the full globes of her behind.

His arm and his hand were the true problem.

When he shifted his hand, he discovered that her breast filled his palm nicely. Robbie ached to caress it and the tight tip that now teased his hand. He wanted to do that and more to her, with her. His wee Highland beastie had grown into a beautiful, bold, kind, desirable woman and she lay in his arms. But even though he was comfortable, and they had privacy, this was not the time for it.

He wanted her awake so he could watch her eyes as he touched her and tasted her. He wanted her to be part of their joining when it happened. And, most of all, he wanted her to want him. Want his touch. Want to marry him.

Robbie lifted his arm slowly so as not to disturb her rest and shifted away until he could slide off the bed. Without opening the door he could not tell how much time had passed since he'd brought her here. He lifted the latch with care and eased the door open.

Glynnis had returned for, on the floor next to the door, was a covered tray. Though shadows filled the corridor, night had not yet fallen. From the sounds and aromas drifting up from below, supper was being eaten in the hall without them. Glynnis would have seen to that and found some excuse for it too.

When he turned back towards the bed, carrying the tray into her bedchamber, Sheena was watching his every move.

'Ah, you are awake.' He walked to the table and placed the tray on it. After lighting a candle from one of the torches in the corridor, he lit several candles before closing the door. 'Glynnis brought you some...' Robbie lifted the cloth covering the wooden tray and told Sheena what was there. 'Bread. Cheese. A jug of—' he lifted the jug to his nose and sniffed '—wine. One of those sweet rolls the cook makes that you liked. And some butter for the bread.'

'Glynnis is kind,' Sheena said. She pushed the length of her gown down to cover her ankles before climbing off the bed. She wobbled and he was at her side before she could tumble.

'Here now.' He guided her to sit on the bedside. 'You had a...faint.' Stepping back, he searched her for any sign of that previous distress. 'Are you well? Now?'

She looked away and he thought she was not going to answer him. Her green eyes reflected the flickering light of the candles spread around. And staring back at him was the suspicion that had only recently fled her lovely gaze when she looked at him. He had not realised how much he hated that expression until he saw it again now. When she shrugged, he expected that she would not speak. Her words surprised him.

'I am...better, Robbie.'

'Do you hunger or thirst?' He lifted the bread out to her.

'Not yet,' she whispered. 'I need to sleep.'

'More?'

Confusion showed in the tightening of her brow and mouth. 'It can take a day or more to recover when it is this...strong an...event.'

Robbie put the bread back on the tray and pulled a stool closer to the bed and sat down. 'Is it this strong often, Sheena?'

'Robbie...' she said before shrugging again and shaking her head. 'Nay, I think not. Usually it happens in times of great challenge or uncertainty. Less often over the last few years.' She met his eyes and nodded. ''Tis grown worse since—'

'Your father informed you of our impending marriage?' The slightest of movements of her head, not a true nod, gave him his answer. 'The day in Anna's garden?'

'Aye.' She let out a sigh and he heard the exhaustion in it. 'I met so many people that day. So much was unfamiliar. You were—'

'Being difficult?'

'It happened without warning. Glynnis helped me but the feeling never left. Later, I just needed to flee. To hide away. To find silence and quiet. I sought out Anna's garden because it had been all of that when I'd visited it earlier, but I do not remember sitting in that alcove. I do not remember falling asleep there. I only kenned I was awake when I saw your face.'

'Why did you not just tell me?' he asked.

Sheena slipped off the bed, unable to remain still in spite of the growing lethargy spreading through her, as it did after one of these *spells*, as her mother called them. She needed to sleep. Her thoughts were confused, as though the thick mist that gathered around Lairig Dubh in the mornings filled her head. Instead of collapsing back on the bed, she walked to the table and poured some of the wine into a cup.

'It is a weakness, Robbie. Something is wrong with me. I cannot control it or explain it and, for a certain, I did not want someone who hated me to ken my sorry state.'

'I do not hate you, Sheena.'

'Well, my father and mother are ashamed of it, of me.

For many years they tried to ignore it, ignore me. That is why they allowed me finally to move with Lilidh. They did not have to suffer the humiliation of a daughter fraught with fainting spells and worse and could hide me deep in the Highlands where no one would see and no one would gossip.'

She drank down the wine, glad it was watered down, and put the cup on the tray, fearing that she would lift the jug and empty it to soothe her fraying control. She'd spoken of her shame to no one. No one knew the whole of it, no matter what they suspected. And now she'd told the one person she wanted the least to know such a thing.

As she returned to the bed, Robbie took hold of her hand and made her stop before him.

'I do not hate you, Sheena,' he repeated.

'Nor I you,' she whispered as she freed her hand and continued away from him without looking at his face. 'Though I did try. For many years, I tried.' She turned to see the disbelief on his face at her words. 'It was easier to accept the truth of it—that you could not stand being near me—if I convinced myself I hated you in return.'

'And did you convince yourself?' He walked over and sat next to her on the bed. Reaching over to take her hand again, he shook his head. 'I already ken the answer, for I remember the things you said and the way you made certain to avoid me.' He kissed her hand where their fingers entwined and released her. 'And I you.'

Walking around the chamber, he blew out the candles but for the one nearest the bed.

'I think you should rest now,' he said when he reached the door. With his hand on the latch, he turned back to her. 'You do not need to leave your chambers until morning, but I will not be able to keep Glynnis from coming to check on you.'

Sheena smiled at that. Glynnis was now her fiercest protector and, she prayed, friend. 'My thanks for remaining at my side,' she said.

With a nod, he opened the door and stepped into the hall, leaning back just before closing it. 'How did you ken I was here?'

'I woke several times to find you keeping me warm and safe.'

He let out a sound that was something between a sigh and a snort before nodding. 'Seek me out in the morning,' he said.

The door closed and she sank back onto the bed. What strength she had gained during the short rest was gone, used up by facing Robbie and admitting her affliction to him. She should have allowed him to think she did not know he'd slept at her side. But, in her confusion and exhaustion, she'd told him.

She remembered the touch of his mouth against her forehead. And the warmth of his body as he'd lain behind her. And the reaction of his flesh to her nearness. She remembered that and all the soft whispers and words as he'd cared for her.

Sheena dragged the bedcovers down and climbed under them, not bothering to undress. Once settled, she offered her usual prayers, but this time she added one more.

She prayed that Robbie would not realise the weapon she'd placed in his hands with her admission. She prayed that her shame would never be known or used against her or, worse, her father and mother.

If Robbie decided now to seek a dissolution of their

betrothal using her affliction as a reason, it would call her father's honour into question. Which would make the Beast of the Highlands regret her birth and survival even more than he did already.

Considering Robbie's devotion to his sworn duty to his clan, she'd put him in an impossible situation. If he exposed her truth, as he should to protect his clan, he would insult her father and draw both clans into a new war. If he kept silent, he would marry someone unfit to be the wife of the great Cameron chieftain and it would destroy him and any chance of them making even a tolerable marriage.

If he had not hated her before, he would now.

The sound of servants moving along the hallway of bedchambers told her the day had dawned and it was time to face her fate. A soft knock alerted her to Edana's arrival. The young woman served both her and Glynnis on their visit here and, if Sheena made the choices Lady Elizabeth asked of her, she might be assigned to be her maid.

'Good day, my lady,' Edana said in a soft voice. 'Are ye feeling better this morn? May Mungo enter?'

Sheena smiled, unsure of what else to say, and nodded. The maid carried a tray and, as she opened the door widely, a tall and able lad followed, bringing in a large and steaming bucket. Edana stood guard as the boy placed the water next to the hearth, which he quickly and efficiently stoked to life. Only when Mungo bowed and left did Edana put the tray down and ready a basin for her to use.

'With yer stomach upset, I wasna certain ye would want to break yer fast below or no'. So here is some porridge and some bread and cheese. Lady Glynnis said ye didna eat at all last night after all and ye might be hungry.'

'I am better this morn, Edana. I will have some porridge.' The maid looked happy and she scooped some of the hot and creamy mixture into a bowl and placed it on the table.

'If ye sit here, I can see to yer hair, my lady.' Sheena moved to the table and Edana placed a stool there. 'It looks like—' Edana stopped speaking and choked a bit. As she untied the vestiges of Sheena's long braid, she attempted to stave off another laugh and failed.

'What does it look like, Edana? Now you must tell me.'

'It looks like the cats that live in the stables got into a fight in it...my lady.'

The only thing that saved her was that Sheena had swallowed the mouthful of ale before the maid answered her. Even so, she was choking and coughing and laughing when Glynnis arrived. Edana stepped back and waited for Sheena to take a breath.

'Well, this is not what I expected to greet me this morn,' Glynnis said.

'I thank you for coming to see to me, Glynnis. As I told Edana, I am better for the rest I got.'

Sheena nodded at the maid to continue and she motioned to Glynnis to join her there.

'There is plenty of porridge if you have not eaten,' she said.

'Your stomach has settled now?'

Sheena nodded. 'Although this was worse than some occurrences, sleep is the best thing for me.'

'My lady, my aunt is known for her herbal concoctions, if ye hiv need of something to calm yer belly,' Edana offered. The skilful servant had loosened Sheena's braid and now ran a comb through the snarled lengths, smoothing out the tangles more with each stroke.

'Does she work here in the keep?'

'Aye, my lady. She works in the kitchen with my uncle Brodie.'

'Your uncle?'

'Aye, he is the cook, my lady.'

'Are you related to everyone in the keep? I mean other than being Camerons?' Sheena asked.

The comb had sorted out the tangled mess and Edana was weaving the sections of hair into a tight braid—one that would resist movement and Robbie's touch. For a moment she could feel the strength of Robbie's fingers as they'd caressed her head, sending the loosened locks of hair falling about her shoulders.

'Weel, my lady, Parlan is my cousin on my father's side, and hiv ye met Jamie yet?'

Sheena nodded.

'He is a cousin on my ma's side.'

As she helped Sheena dress and tidied the chamber, she never stopped talking and by the time the maid left Sheena knew more about the inhabitants of Tor Castle and the area around it than she'd thought possible.

As she pulled the door closed, Glynnis smiled.

'You now have little need of Conran's list,' she said. 'Edana has given you more knowledge of how this household is managed than Conran would ever willingly share. More than he may ken himself.'

Some of the dread that was building within her dissipated at the realisation that Glynnis spoke the truth and that Edana was an informative source and willing and anxious to share her thoughts.

All she needed to do was face Robbie now that he knew one of her truths.

Chapter Fifteen

'I thought you were my friend.'

Robbie wiped the sweat off his brow with the back of his hand and spit in the dirt at his feet. Lifting his sword again, he turned slowly, following Parlan's movements. He was paying the price for underestimating the older man's abilities and would not be fooled again by the warrior's feints and distractions. If his father had seen his last error, The Cameron would be doubting his son's rightness as tanist.

'That was your first mistake. Friend or not, I never promised to give you an easy time of it, Robbie.' Parlan laughed as he swung his sword and positioned himself for another attack. 'Your brother Tomas fought better than this the last time he was here.'

The sting of the insult drew shouts from the men around them. Robbie laughed it off until Parlan yelled another. 'Iain, come fight me and show your cousin how Camerons fight!'

His younger cousin laughed now, not accepting the invitation and seeing it for what it was. Iain had not been raised as a warrior. Instead he had lived with his mother in the lands of the MacKenzies to the north until a few years ago. He'd begun training with his stepfather once they'd moved here, and showed great promise.

It was a matter of common knowledge that Iain had as much claim to the clan chieftain's high seat as either Robbie or Tomas. Mayhap more of one since Iain's father was the son of the only male heir of the Old Laird, Euan Cameron. But Iain had never shown an interest in being considered for the role of tanist, in preparation for leading the clan.

Iain's talents lay in woodworking and carpentry rather than swords and shields. Though Robbie did not doubt his cousin's ability to lead if he had a mind to, he did doubt his desire to seek that position of power. Glancing over at him for a moment, he nodded. Iain laughed and returned his nod.

'So, 'tis but you and I now, Parlan,' Robbie taunted. 'And I am coming for you now.'

With no other warning, Robbie raised his sword and charged the man. Parlan stood still and watched his approach. Only four paces divided them and Robbie crossed them quickly, not allowing Parlan the opportunity to discern his method of attack. Soon the fighting was so fierce, Robbie had no time to think about much other than protecting his head and tender parts. The sounds of the yelling and jeering of the crowd disappeared as he concentrated on trying to pull Parlan off his balance when the man struck each blow. By parrying just outside his reach, Robbie forced him to overextend once and twice and thrice. It was that successful third time that finally allowed him to rush in and push Parlan back and to the ground, sword at his throat. Breathing hard now, he stood over one of the best warriors he'd faced. Robbie moved his sword and held out his hand.

Dropping his sword to the ground at his side, Parlan nodded and took Robbie's offer of help. Climbing to his feet, the castellan brushed off the dirt and bowed to Robbie.

'My lord, you are improving,' he said. Robbie smacked his back at the mocking compliment. 'Clearly, though, Davidh allows you to meander through your training with him.'

'I wish that were so, Parlan. Iain will attest to Davidh's full attention to both of us.' Robbie picked up his discarded shirt and was using it to wipe off the dust of the yard when Parlan nodded past him.

'Good day, my lady,' Parlan called. The others yet circled around the fighting men turned and nodded or bowed.

Robbie turned as well, not knowing what to expect when he saw her. He let out his breath when he noticed that she did not appear ill or pale. He offered a quick prayer of thanks as he handed his sword off to his cousin and walked to her.

'You look well,' he said. 'You must have got the rest you needed.' The wariness was there once more in the way she watched him.

'Aye. You also look…well.'

Her eyes moved over him, taking in, he was certain, the dirt and sweat of the fight and the recently acquired bumps and bruises. A man did not train with Parlan, or Davidh, and come away unmarked. He tied his shirt around his waist after he'd mopped away the worst of it.

'How much did you see?'

She shook her head and shrugged. 'I've only just

walked up. So only the last triumphant moments of your battle.'

'Ye did not see his disgrace a little while ago, my lady?' Parlan walked over and stood next to Robbie. 'If ye wish to, I can do it once more.'

'Your cousin spoke of your wit, Parlan. I am glad to see it,' she said with a smile at his nemesis.

'Who spoke of such a thing?' Robbie asked, shoving Parlan aside.

'Edana, my maid.' Sheena nodded.

'You are well?' he asked. With a nod he sent Parlan away and watched her face for any hesitation.

'Aye.'

'Walk with me?' He held out his hand to her and waited. He felt as if they'd moved past the distance of their initial encounters last night. When hers slipped into his, Robbie smiled. 'There is another place I would like you to see.'

They walked together through the yard and out through the main gate. Though they'd been together over the last few days, their duties had seen them in the keep more than out of it. Or so he'd thought.

In the time it took them to reach the river's edge, no fewer than ten villagers had stopped to greet her—not him. To give their best wishes to Sheena. To ask her questions. Or to suggest a place to stop or something to do. When he finally guided her to a secluded pool that formed where the river's current slowed, he felt ignored and invisible. As though he had not lived here many years and had even seen to its protection for the last six.

Only one person, one of the men from the stable, even had a word to say to him and it was only to ask if he'd ridden Wee Dubh yet. It had taken Sheena no time at all to gather all those around her into being her supporters. He was about to wave the stragglers away and pull her through the last line of bushes to the water when he realised he could use this time to clean up before she finished speaking to the final few women.

He walked to the edge of the pool and tossed his shirt into the water and stripped out of his breeches and boots. His sigh of relief echoed over the river's surface as he made his way into the waist-deep water of the pool. The sun had been shining on it for hours so it was not as icy cold as he knew it could be. The swirling water relieved the heat of his sweaty skin and cooled him down quickly. Grabbing his shirt before it floated downstream, he swirled it in the water a few times before wringing it out and tossing it over the branch that reached out above his head.

Robbie knelt down and dunked his head under, shaking it before standing and sluicing the excess water with his hands. Not wasting time, he rubbed his chest and face with the water and stood, heading back to the shore and his clothes.

He needed to talk to Sheena about her illness or condition or whatever it was. He understood that it was the perfect reason to end their betrothal. Perfect except it would expose Sheena and her family to shame and her father to dishonour if he knew of it and had signed the betrothal in spite of it.

And if there was one thing he'd learned after living in the man's home and with his family, it was that Connor MacLerie knew everything that happened in or around or affecting Lairig Dubh and the Clan MacLerie. More, if Connor did not know it, his wife Jocelyn did. Nothing escaped them. Nothing.

'Damn him to hell!' he said through clenched jaws. His fists pounded the surface as he stepped closer to the water's edge. Wiping the splashed water from his eyes, he found Sheena staring back at him.

'You must be thinking of my father,' she said.

Her eyes met his, but he could see she fought the urge to lower them. Hell, his flesh rose at just the thought of her staring at him, cold water be damned too. Her gaze fell as he knew it must and when she neither looked nor turned away, he continued walking out of the water.

And he would have simply pulled on his breeches and wet shirt and boots if she had not let that tempting mouth of hers drop open as he moved closer. But it was the sound she made that made his control fly away.

A hungry gasp followed by her tongue sliding over those lips he knew would be soft beneath his. When he reached her and took hold of her shoulders, she did not pull away. Nay, the bold wench stared directly at his cock and licked her lips again. Robbie's knees nearly buckled at the thought of her tongue on him, but he managed to guide them down to kneel with their bodies touching.

He would have kissed her. He planned to kiss her... he did. But she did the most surprising thing—she leaned up and kissed him. Her hands slid up to cup his face and she pressed her mouth to his. Robbie held his breath, waiting for her to take the next step. The tentative and testing touch of her tongue on his lips nearly unmanned him. He opened for her and was rewarded with her tongue seeking and touching his.

It was the sweetest thing he'd ever felt. And the hottest and most provocative, for his body wanted what she offered. He wanted her. She tangled her hands in his wet hair and pulled him closer, even though he was wont to move not at all. He wrapped his arms around her, sliding his palms down her back and caressing her buttocks, lifting and pressing her against him. He heard her moans in his mouth and smiled against hers.

'Sheena, lass, you are sweeter than I imagined,' he whispered when she allowed them a breath.

She panted in steamy little puffs against his mouth before he kissed his way over her chin and down her neck. He slid one of his hands between their bodies and covered her breast. He flicked his thumb across the tip, enjoying the way it tightened under his caress and the way she pressed against him.

Robbie moved her hands onto his chest and guided her body and his to the loamy, grass-covered ground there. Lying on their sides, he took her hand and led it down and down until she touched him. His hiss and her gasp blended into the most arousing sound he'd ever heard. She kissed him again, furiously and fiercely, at the same time she gently stroked the length of him.

The urge to turn her on her back and fill her as hard and as deep as he could almost overwhelmed him at the pleasure of her hand on his flesh, but he knew she was an innocent and rutting by a river was not how he would take her body for the first time. But he could offer her a taste of the vast passion that could be theirs.

With an arm over her shoulder and the other free to slide along her side, he gathered the length of her gown in his hand and he waited until he exposed her skin to his touch before guiding her leg up onto his hip. She opened her eyes and stared at him.

'I want to touch you as you do me,' he whispered. Her body eased against him and his hand moved between her legs. She tightened her grasp on his manhood when his fingers touched the curls there. 'Easy now, lass. Easy.'

He held her close as he slipped between the heated folds of flesh between her legs. She gasped once and again when the tip of his finger pressed deeper and found that place within her where another part of his body urgently wanted to be. Did she realise she stroked him as he did her? Did she know she was driving him to madness with her innocent and aroused sounds and tremors? Just as he rubbed between the folds and found the spot he wanted to caress, he took her mouth and swallowed her gasps and moans.

The tiny yet hardened bud of flesh would be too sensitive to touch, so he circled around it, sliding past it and gliding out and towards it. Sheena's body arched into his hand with each stroke. Finally, he touched it and she moaned against his mouth. Her hand released his flesh and covered his hand, urging him on.

'More, lass?' He laughed against her mouth. 'Like this?'

He stroked slowly and gently, using one finger and adding another within her flesh to draw her body's weeping and spread it over the bud. She whispered something—some words he could not understand but that were clearly in approval. Allowing her body and the sounds she made to guide him, he shifted his hand so that now three fingers filled her woman's core while his thumb found and caressed the bud of flesh. Her hips thrusted against his hand, pushing him in deeper and urging him on.

'Faster now, lass? Deeper like this?'

The moan that escaped her told him what he needed to know—her body was ready. His was as well but this would be for her. He kept his fingers deep and stroked faster and harder until her hips arched off the ground and her whole body trembled. When she cried her release out, he kissed her, thrusting his tongue in her mouth as he wanted to thrust his body within her tight core. He pressed his thumb there until her body stopped arching against his hand. Slowly, he eased his fingers out and his hand free of her heat as she collapsed against his side.

It took some time for their breathing to calm and their hearts to slow and he just held her close until they could speak. He would have spoken when someone else's voice echoed through the trees.

'I just hope she's not ill again, Iain. We must find her!' Glynnis's panicking voice was the only warning they got.

Sheena's eyes opened and she began to struggle to rise. When she got to her feet and looked down at her now soaked, muddy gown that was also marked with handprints, Robbie knew she did not wish to be found so. Looking at the trees and the river, he also knew there was only one thing to do. He gained his feet, wrapped his arms around her and whispered a warning to her…

Before he threw both of them into the river.

Glynnis squawked louder than the geese that ran free in the yard and village as she and Iain broke free from the trees and saw them in the river there. As he and Sheena gained some footing there in the deeper part of the pool, he whispered apologies that only she could hear.

''Tis not the way I wanted this to end, lass.' He held her by her hips and kept her in front of him lest Glynnis get a better view of his nakedness. 'But I thought it better not to be caught as we were.'

She shivered and he wondered if it was the memory of what had happened between them or the cool water rushing around them now. When she pressed back against him, he had his answer and he could not help the smile that broke out.

Iain noticed it and, worse, he saw Robbie's clothes in a heap near where he and Glynnis stood. With a knowing smirk, his cousin moved away from them and drew Glynnis's gaze as well. He owed Iain for his subtle help. Now if he could only do more. As if he'd heard Robbie's unspoken plea, Iain called out.

'Can I help you out, Sheena?' Iain asked. 'If Robbie has his way, he will remain there for hours.'

'Come, Sheena,' Glynnis said. 'I do not wish you to get ill, not after…not after last night.'

Iain and Glynnis came to the edge and Sheena moved towards them, accepting their help in wrangling her long, wet gown out of the water. With a wink over Sheena's head, Iain guided both women back to the path and away from the river. Robbie waited a short while, letting the cool water calm the heat in his blood, before climbing out.

He still needed to talk to Sheena and settle things between them.

And they would. He was certain of it.

Chapter Sixteen

Her body ached. Not from the cold of the river's water. Nay, her body ached with the heat of his touch. It ached for more of it. More of him.

Sheena sighed at the memory of his hardness in her grasp. Long and thick, she'd barely been able to encircle its width, but she'd tried, and he'd moaned as she'd caressed that flesh that had one purpose.

Another sigh escaped as she thought of the way he'd stroked her in her most intimate place. A place no one had ever touched. Her hips arched and her body shuddered. Sheena could almost feel the way his finger, his *fingers*, had pushed inside her and touched a sensitive spot she did not even know existed within her own body. Her breasts swelled at the very thought of his touch.

When that next sigh echoed across her chamber, Glynnis cleared her throat and Sheena remembered she was not alone.

'You have had a change of heart, Sheena?' the lady asked.

'Change of heart?'

'Since your arrival, I have sensed that neither of you

wish to marry. Well, not marry each other. But this…' she paused and nodded towards Sheena '…these sighs speak of a change.'

'I had never thought past my old hatred of him, Glynnis. He surprised me with his affection and his…appeal.'

Glynnis walked over and took the comb from Edana, nodding for her maid to leave. Once they were alone, Glynnis pulled a stool behind her and took up the maid's work.

'I kenned not of this past hatred,' Glynnis said.

'Every Cameron must ken of it. The humiliation I caused to their chieftain's son,' Sheena said. 'But you were not living here then, were you?'

'Nay, not until just over a year ago, but Sheena—' Glynnis lowered her hand and moved to face her. 'I have never heard such a thing from anyone here. Not even Robbie.' She shook her head. 'And Robbie said many things on learning that your arrival was imminent. And suggested others until the chieftain put an end to it.'

'He did?' Remembering that he'd insulted her to her face and in her presence during those first days, she nodded. 'Well, it was because I caused him great shame in my father's house. Before all the MacLerie elders and counsellors.'

'I would say from the glances exchanged by the two of you each time you passed in the yard or keep in these last few hours, all past grievances have been put aside.'

Heat filled her cheeks at Glynnis's words. Robbie's gaze had been filled with hunger of a different sort when it met hers across the entryway into the keep earlier. And when they'd passed by each other on the stairs as she'd returned from changing. Indeed, he had reached out to touch her hand before realising that Glynnis followed closely behind. Her body had been filled with an awareness of the meaning and an awareness of his touch ever since. Each time she saw him, she could feel his fingers again.

Within her.

She shifted suddenly, startling Glynnis.

The perfect lady narrowed her gaze at Sheena and nodded knowingly. 'I think if we'd arrived a moment or two sooner at the river's edge—'

Sheena put her hand over Glynnis's mouth to stop her. 'It changes nothing, Glynnis. I cannot be the wife of the next Cameron chieftain.'

'Do you wish me to braid it for you now that it is dry? Or do you plan to take supper here in your chambers and so leave it loose?' Glynnis waited on her reply but her words did not fool Sheena. Glynnis was waiting for some revelation or admission.

'I cannot marry the heir to The Cameron,' she repeated. Turning her body on her stool, she took Glynnis's hands in hers. 'I will bring shame and failure to Robbie and his family, as I have to my own, should my affliction be known.' Sheena stood and moved away from her. ''Tis worse even than that. How can I be trusted to carry out my duties if I cannot ken when those spells will come upon me?'

'So now that Robbie kens, he will break the betrothal?' Glynnis asked. 'What would happen if he does that?'

Sheena rubbed her forehead at the sudden tightness there. She did not want to think about the consequences yet. She wanted to bask in the warmth of the feelings that Robbie had caused within her. It might be shallow and dangerous, but once again he'd made her feel wanted. Important. Alive and excited.

Having been humiliated and unwanted by her father and mother had created an emptiness she could not seem to fill. She knew how little she mattered to them and now knowing that she would shame them again when Robbie exposed his discovery about her inappropriateness to be his wife tore her apart in a different way.

'I have been a fool,' she whispered. 'I asked him to help me find a way to break it—I just did not intend to give him the reason he could do it on his own.'

'Sheena, I do not think that Robbie would expose you to shame.'

'If it were only my shame, it would matter not. But to protect me, it forces Robbie to ignore his duty, his loyalty, to his father and his clan.'

She sat on the bed. She could not say it all, mention all of the ways this would come back and hurt her. Because, in the end, if he used this to break their betrothal it would be worse for their clans and their people. And that failing to act on his part would destroy him.

Glynnis said no more, able to sense her upset at the direction in which their discussion was moving. She kindly did not mention the other failure in Sheena's character at this time. Glynnis had been the only one to notice it—so far. The woman who would make Robbie a perfect wife stood and, after placing the comb on the table there, made her way to the door.

'Speak to him candidly, Sheena. I suspect that together you can find a way to work this out.'

Just as Glynnis lifted the latch, a knock came at the door. Sheena waited as she opened it and found Edana there. Glynnis nodded back at Sheena before allowing the maid in and leaving.

'My lady, your presence is requested below,' Edana said. A soft smile told Sheena that the maid was caught up in some manoeuvre or another. Robbie was the only one here to summon her.

A part of her warmed at the thought of him. For now, she concentrated on that warmth and would leave the rest until it happened.

'Here, now, let me fix yer hair, my lady,' Edana said, guiding Sheena to sit. 'A braid will do ye nicely.'

Edana would not share any details, but within a very short time Sheena followed her down the stairs to find the great hall empty.

'This way, my lady. Come along this way,' Edana urged.

They went not to the main door, but back along the kitchens to another. Greeting each of the servants working there quickly, for Edana did not slow her stride, they reached the door that opened to the yard from the back of the keep. The heavy, metal-wrapped wooden door creaked loudly as Edana pushed on it, forcing it to give way slowly. When it swung open, Robbie stood there.

With Wee Dubh and his horse, ready to ride.

'The weather will not hold for much longer. I thought not to waste these hours before supper.' He held up the reins.

If they were not surrounded by others, they might be able to speak plainly and sort out what to do. She nodded. Within moments, they rode through the gate and headed south, past the place where the stream joined the river and farther beyond. After staying close to the river for several miles, they finally left it and headed east. When they reached the rise of a hill there, Robbie stopped and dismounted.

Higher than most of the area around them, this hill gave her an awe-inspiring view back to Tor, another castle farther south and to a huge mountain to the east. The winds whipped around them here, with few trees to protect them. But Sheena found the brisk winds soothing and she closed her eyes and turned into them. Without a cloak, it grew cold and yet she did not wish to leave. Soon she felt Robbie at her back, standing close enough to strengthen her stance and to share his body's warmth. When he wrapped his arms around her, holding her close, she felt safe.

Safe in the arms of the one man who could destroy her.

'That is one of the highest mountains you will find anywhere in all of Scotland,' he said against her ear. He pointed into the distance at the mountain she'd noticed when they stopped. 'And there, if you look past that castle, that is Loch Linnhe.'

'That is not a Cameron holding?' she asked, shading her eyes with her hand as she stared south.

'Nay, the Comyns hold Inverlochy and the lands around it.'

'And you are not at war with them?'

'Och, nay,' he said, shaking his head against her shoulder. 'We are in good stead with them for now. Though if my father had not finally claimed his place as chieftain, they might have made an attempt or two at Tor and our lands here.'

'So the Camerons save all their feuding and fighting for the Mackintoshes?'

'Until Brodie Mackintosh won back the high seat and forced my uncle Euan to help him solidify his claim.'

'Euan?'

'Aye, Iain's grandfather.'

She wished she could have read the charts and lists of his clan and their connections. The words swirled together and the sketches of their likenesses did not help her follow the various lines of succession. All she could remember was that all the males seemed to pass down a very large nose through the generations of Camerons.

'And now your father tries to solidify his hold and power by allying with my father.'

''Tis the way of things.'

She let the silence surround them for several moments before turning in his embrace. The winds took hold of her braid and tugged at it. Robbie reached out and grabbed the end of it, wrapping it several times around his fist until he held her head steady in his grasp.

'You gave me a weapon to wield against you,' he said, staring at her face as he spoke, as though he searched there for some truth. 'And against your father.'

Sheena held her breath, looking in his eyes for some clue to any plans to use his newfound knowledge of her weakness. She clenched her jaws together, trying not to cry out.

'And if I hated you it would be very easy to wield it.' He leaned closer and touched his mouth to hers so gently it made her want to weep. 'But I do not hate you, Sheena. Or wish to see you shamed or your father dishonoured.'

'You see now why I cannot marry you, Robbie. I cannot control these spells. What if it happens in the hall in front of your clan? Or worse, your enemies?' She pulled free of his hold and he allowed her to go. Crossing her arms over her chest, she shook her head. 'How can you think me able to carry out the duties of a wife to the chieftain when I ken that I cannot?'

The panic was rising again, at the thought of what faced her. What faced them if he would not believe her. A vice tightened around her chest, keeping her from taking a breath and forcing her to gasp. It was happening now. Right in front of him. And there was nothing she could...

'I have you, lass,' he whispered as he pulled her into his arms and held her. 'I have you.'

He'd seen the exact moment it had begun this time. Her face had turned ashen grey and her features had frozen in an expression of horror just before she'd started gasping. Not certain of how to stop it, or even if it could be stopped, he did the only thing he could—he held her.

He held her and waited to see if this fear would grow or ease. Could these spells be stopped or were they pre-ordained somehow to reach some level of debilitation before releasing her from their grasp?

Robbie leaned away and looked at her face to see if she'd fallen into that stupor, but her clear gaze stared back at him. He eased his hold and allowed her to stand on her own.

'What will you do now?' she asked.

The quiver in her voice tore him apart. Before, and when she'd arrived at Achnacarry, he'd thought her rude and overbearing, selfish even. He had allowed his foolish behaviour years ago to dictate his feelings and his actions for far too long regarding Sheena MacLerie.

The worst part of this was that he wanted her as his wife. He could imagine living with her and loving her as they ruled and protected the Clan Cameron after his father. She was bright and curious and kind. She responded with honest passion at his touch and he could see nights and days of pleasure between them. But Robbie could not work out a way to keep her without destroying her. Or give her up without doing the same.

'If you cannot marry me and take your place as the tanist's wife, we have no choice but to return to Achnacarry on the morrow and continue to seek a way out of the betrothal.'

'We do not wait for your priest? The one you thought might help us?'

'Nay. Parlan said that Father Donald should return from his visit to his family on Skye some time in the next fortnight. So he will be of no assistance if we want this handled sooner rather than later.' With regret, he shook his head.

A strong burst of wind pushed her off-balance and he took it as a sign to leave. He only hoped that he could ease her fears over what her life would be like as his wife.

And now understanding, or beginning to understand, this affliction of hers created a bigger problem. As heir, as a loyal son who honoured his duties to his father and his clan, he could not marry a woman who was deficient in some way. It could endanger the future heirs of the clan.

He needed to seek advice about this. He needed someone he could trust and who would be knowledgeable in matters of the heart and body.

'Come,' he said, stepping back and offering his hand. 'No good will come from allowing you to freeze to death and I do not wish to face the viper's tongue if Glynnis hears I kept you out in this wind after tossing you into the chilled river.'

'Viper's tongue? Glynnis?' Sheena laughed aloud and he was glad of it. 'She is the most perfect woman I have met in my life. Patient and kind and accomplished and skilled and...' Had she run out of terms to describe Glynnis and all her perfection? She sighed. 'Aye,' she admitted to him. 'She can be dogged when protecting someone she cares about.'

He suddenly felt a great relief that Glynnis had taken Sheena under her wing and thought it important to defend her. It was critical to have someone around Sheena who understood the dangers she faced. Already Glynnis had shown her quick-wittedness in assisting Sheena and covering up her weakness when needed.

The winds eased as they rode down the hill and back to the road along the river. Glynnis studied them closely, both when they arrived back at Tor and through supper.

The next day surprised him for it dawned warm and bright, unusual for their area, when showers should have poured down on them several times a day. As they broke their fast, Sheena asked for a bit of time before they left for Achnacarry. As he'd done before, he followed her to see where she was going.

The cook and his wife, Edana, the lads in the stable and even several villagers who provided game for the household were her targets. As in Achnacarry's village, she spoke to each one and they held onto every word she uttered. He was never close enough to hear the topic being discussed, but it was clear on every face that she'd taken some interest in them and they were glad of it.

As their travelling party gathered in the yard to begin the ride north, a messenger arrived and handed a scroll to him, rather than Parlan. He met Sheena's anxious eyes and tried to smile.

'What is it, Robbie?' she asked, approaching Wee Dubh to mount him.

'Visitors have arrived from Lairig Dubh.'

Chapter Seventeen

When Wee reacted to her rising level of anxiety on the ride north, Sheena asked Robbie to ride him. What should have been a moment to savour was instead one she could not enjoy. His stunned expression at her request gave way to an excitement in him that should have given her a measure of the same.

His horse required her full attention and control, which were frayed as each mile brought them closer to Achnacarry and facing her parents. The only thing keeping her calm enough to ride was Robbie's sheer joy. He heeded her every word about placement of his legs and feet to avoid the worst of the injured area on the horse's belly. He accepted her suggestions about how much control to exert and when. When he asked her permission to run him ahead of the group, her heart nearly burst.

This was not the same leisurely ride as the one they'd had going to Tor. Nay, it was as though everyone travelling with them sensed her growing fear and discomfort. That they reached Achnacarry in much less time than it had taken to travel in the other direction did not surprise her. And no one questioned it. Due to their later departure though, the sun was setting behind Achnacarry when they rode in, only an hour or so of daylight left. As they passed through the gates, the guards who'd travelled with them separated off to see to new duties while Glynnis and Iain followed them to the stables, where Geordie stood watching. Geordie nodded at her as he took the reins from Robbie. He'd given her the word that Wee was healed enough, at her judgement, to be ridden by others larger and stronger than herself.

As she slid off Robbie's horse and gained her feet, Tomas came running towards them. Smacking Robbie first, he greeted her.

'They arrived late last night, just before the gates closed,' he said. 'How was it to ride him, Robbie?' And before giving his brother a chance to speak, he looked at her. 'I cannot believe you let him ride.'

Trying to follow his words, his change of topic made her smile. If riding Wee Dubh brought such joy to her, it should not surprise her that Robbie and Tomas would want to as well. And for the moment it took her mind off those waiting within the keep.

'Come, lass,' Robbie said softly as he took her hand in his. 'I have not seen your father in some years. Let us face him together.'

If her grip on his hand was too tight and if she stumbled once or twice on their path to the keep, Robbie remained silent and steadfast at her side. He stopped them just before the steps up to the door and nodded for Iain and Glynnis to pause behind them.

'What worries you, Sheena? Is there something I should ken before we speak to them?' She noticed he pulled her closer and still entwined their fingers as he held her hand. A far cry from the first time they had walked up these very steps.

'I have not seen them since I moved with Lilidh. Well, they came to Keppoch Keep but were busy dealing with Aidan and his problems.'

'How did you find out that you were to come here?'

'They sent a messenger.' She shrugged.

'So how did you tell them you did not wish this betrothal?'

His eyes were intense now, and he stared at her with anger. He was angry?

'I told them before. Years ago when it was first discussed.'

'And they went on with the arrangements? In spite of your refusal?'

She nodded. 'My mother said that I was too young to ken my mind on such matters and they would make the best decision for me.'

He mumbled something under his breath and she thought she heard several vulgar words as he did.

'Did your parents ask you again?'

'Robbie, what is it you want me to say? Did I tell them again? Aye, I did. Before I went to Lilidh's I begged my mother not to force me to this marriage. You'd been named tanist and I kenned…'

'That you could not marry me.'

Whatever he was searching for in her words, he must have found, for he nodded, and they continued up the stone steps and through the open doors. Sheena glanced over her shoulder and saw the concern on Glynnis's face. Iain, as usual, only watched Glynnis.

Just before they entered the hall, Robbie released her hand and placed it on the top of his arm. Puzzling over that, Sheena did not realise they'd reached the front of the hall and stood before his parents and her…

Cousin.

Farlen MacLerie, now serving as Duncan the Peacemaker's man, stood and walked to her. Looking around, he was the only MacLerie she could see, but for several others who travelled with Farlen on Duncan's work.

'My father? My mother?' she asked as he approached. Mayhap they had not entered the hall yet. She glanced past him to the corridor leading to the stairs of the tower where they would be given a bedchamber for their visit. 'Are they above stairs?'

'Sheena, I bring greetings from the earl and your mother,' Farlen said as he nodded to Robbie. Taking her by her shoulders, he pulled her closer and kissed her on the cheek. 'And from Duncan, Marian and your cousins as well.' He released her and stepped back.

She had no words. Nothing would form on her tongue to reply to his greeting. Farlen was here and not her father nor mother.

They'd sent Farlen in their place. Not Duncan even. Farlen.

They'd not come to make the final arrangements for her wedding.

They'd sent Farlen instead.

They could not have shown their disregard any clearer than that. They'd sent Farlen to deal with her.

'It has been a long ride from Tor,' Robbie said, taking hold of her arm and guiding her around Farlen. 'Let us sit and refresh ourselves from it.' He almost dragged her to the raised table and into a chair there.

The pain slashed through her so deeply she could not even speak. She felt him put a cup in her hands and formed her grasp around it so it would not drop. She must have sipped it, for it was soon empty.

Talk went on around her. Robbie might have boasted about riding Wee Dubh. Tomas might have begged her permission to be next. Glynnis's tear-filled eyes surprised her. The Cameron and Lady Elizabeth were there, but she did not know if they spoke to her or not.

Her heart bled there before them and she could not say a word. Farlen must have called her name several times before Robbie touched her arm to gain her attention. 'Farlen asked what you thought of Tor Castle.'

She blinked several times as she sorted through the dark, jumbled thoughts and pain for some correct thing to say.

And she could not.

They'd sent someone else in their stead.

'Sheena mentioned to me that the lie of it reminded her of Lairig Dubh sitting high on its cliff,' Glynnis said.

All Sheena could do was nod.

'There is a stream and river nearby that the lady said brought the area around her home to mind,' Iain added. That he spoke surprised her, for he had little to say most of the time.

'Aye.' She forced out one word. And all she could do now was fight the overwhelming need to cry.

Nay, not cry.

Keen. She needed to wail from the pain of this public rejection of her worth to them.

Soon they turned their attention away and the voices merged into a confusing tangle she could not understand. Robbie stroked her hand, and it gave her some sort of comfort. A reason to keep from running and running and running. From his gaze she knew he worried about one of her spells taking control of her now. She wanted to reassure him, to ease the worry in his eyes, but she could not.

There was no fear building inside her now. No darkness threatening to pull her down into its grasp. The only thing she felt was pain.

Pain where her heart should be.

Pain where she'd begun to feel something else when with him. Joy and safety. And wanting. And…

'I—' she began, not knowing what she wanted to say. She stood and Robbie rose at her side, not letting go of her hand.

'Before you take your leave, Sheena…' Robbie's mother said. Nodding at them and at Farlen, she smiled. 'The final arrangements have been made for the wedding.'

She would have stumbled if not for Robbie's strong hold on her. They'd sent Farlen for this. Sheena lifted her head and looked at Lady Elizabeth. 'Very well.'

She had not changed her decision, but in this moment she could not argue.

'I would see my cousin to her chambers,' Farlen said. He walked to her and held out his hand. 'I would speak to her of her father's wishes.'

Robbie suggested to Farlen that he should wait until morning and remained at Sheena's side.

Farlen laughed and clapped Robbie on the back. 'I can see you're anxious to make her yours. Soon enough she will be, but this day her kin would like time to speak to her of family matters.'

She recognised the begrudging consent in Robbie's movement away from her. He let her hand go only at the last moment before Farlen took hold of her.

'I leave at first light, so this will be my only chance to gain her attention,' Farlen continued.

Sheena nodded at Robbie, who took a step back, clearing a path for them to leave.

She walked along with Farlen in silence, leaving only an uncomfortable quiet behind them. Sheena pointed them in the direction of her bedchamber and soon, too soon, they stood at her door. Now, she would hear the true reason for his contrived encounter. He let go of her arm and took a few steps away before facing her.

'Sheena, you must ken that word of your behaviour would reach your father. There is little the man does not find out,' Farlen said. She struggled to listen to his words. 'You must take your duties seriously, lass. Be attentive to Lady Elizabeth's counsel. Put your best efforts into learning what your duties will be.'

'I—'

'Washing laundry for the villagers? Playing at weaving when your lack of skills in working with needle and thread are kenned and lamented over by your mother?'

She stared at him. How had her father learned of her daily actions here?

'And after fighting your father over that monstrous horse, you nearly killed him with your reckless riding. Will you never accept your duty? When will you leave the wilfulness of childhood behind and do what you must?'

Shame now filled her, twining its way around and throughout her heart and soul. It took her a few moments to realise that Farlen held something out to her.

'From your father. He wants you to heed his warnings and not bring shame to him by failing to honour this betrothal, Sheena.' When she did not accept the packet, he reached for her hand and placed it there. 'Three weeks. You have three weeks to sort out your behaviour and show him you are worthy to be called The MacLerie daughter.'

She stared at the parchment in her hand and at the man who'd been sent to tell her of their displeasure. *His* shame.

'Make him proud, lass.'

She remained standing there for some time after the echo of his footsteps drifted into the night. She should seek her bed. She should...

She would think on all of this in the morning, when her thoughts were orderly and her heart had stopped bleeding.

But they'd sent someone else.

Robbie followed his parents into the steward's chamber where—only days? a week? ago—he and Sheena had searched for a way out of their betrothal. With this man Farlen's arrival, that now seemed an impossible task. He waited only for his father to close the door and for his mother to sit before he asked, 'What is the meaning of this? Farlen is to discuss the wedding? Not Duncan? Not Sheena's parents?'

He felt the hot shame and pain that had filled her the very moment she'd realised they were not here on her behalf. That they had sent someone else. Her words about not mattering to them were proven to be truth by this man's arrival.

'The earl sent a letter explaining his absence and setting up the final terms of our arrangement.'

'You did not wait on our arrival for that discussion?'

he asked. Anger filled him—for the complete disregard of both him and Sheena.

Yet this was a side of Connor MacLerie he had not seen before. Oh, he'd seen the man's ruthlessness and his way of getting what he wanted through whatever means were needed. He'd seen his firm methods of discipline and the iron hold he had over all matters MacLerie.

The one thing he'd never seen before was this clear cruelty.

'Why do I feel that there is more going on than we are party to? Like we have been drawn into some game the earl plays around us.'

His father did not flinch from the accusation made. 'The MacLerie has his reasons and we have ours for pursuing this marriage. We have from the beginning of it, years ago. It took many years, a cessation of hostilities with the Mackintoshes and a new king to bring it to fruition, but 'tis close now, Robbie.'

The entirety of Scotland was filled with powerful men manipulating others and leveraging their power through marriages, deaths or recapturing lands taken by the English, while the previous King was held hostage in London. Now King Robert Stewart was parcelling out pieces of the Highlands to his sons and other relatives to concentrate his own power over the unruly clans.

That Connor MacLerie and Robbie's own father did the same was not a surprise—it was a prudent move to secure their clans' futures. He'd just never expected Connor to trample over his own daughter to get what he wanted.

'Unless you can give me a valid reason to break this betrothal, you will marry her in three weeks.'

The silence was so profound he swore they could hear

his heart beating. His father and mother stared at him, awaiting his reply.

And he should reply.

As the tanist, who was responsible for protecting the future of his family, both in matters of leadership and providing heirs, he should expose what he knew about Sheena. Tell his parents about her spells when she lost her wits, her control and her consciousness. Tell them the other secret he'd discovered—she could not read or write. She could not follow written instructions or read the important documents that the wife of The Cameron would need to. Her ability to oversee the servants was negligible. She neither excelled, nay she was not even competent, at the womanly tasks expected of a noble-born woman. The only unknown was her ability to breed heirs.

She would make the worst wife for the future chieftain of the mighty Camerons.

While it was his duty to seek out the best wife, who would bring the most to his clan and buttress their position in the Highlands and in Scotland.

It was his duty to reveal the truths he'd discovered about her to his parents so that they did not agree to a marriage beneath them…without added benefits that could be leveraged by this knowledge.

He'd sworn to carry out his duty and all he had to do now was reveal the truth. All he had to do was shame her, first before his parents and before hers.

In that moment, when duty and loyalty—the two responsibilities he took most seriously and the guideposts for how he lived his life—lay heavily upon him, all he could see in his thoughts was her face at the news that her parents had sent someone else to oversee her marriage.

As he watched his parents waiting on his final word, he understood how his father had felt all those years ago when faced with the grievous task of honour that now faced him. His father's only choices had been to put aside the woman he loved because of her brutal disgrace or to turn from his rightful position as the next chieftain.

Robbie had always believed that his father had not been strong enough to do the right thing. That love was not reason enough to endanger his clan and to disregard his duty and his honour. How foolish he'd been to believe that claiming love or satisfying honour was a simple choice to make!

For it was not pity he felt for Sheena when he watched her almost overpowered by distress. When he saw the deep shame she carried within her that was now threatened with exposure. Nay, some time after hating her and then disliking her, and finally seeing the truth and the kind heart within her, Robbie had fallen in love with Sheena MacLerie.

He let out a breath and shrugged at his father's question. 'Other than the fact that Sheena wishes to marry me even less than I her?'

'Aye,' his father said. When his mother would have spoken, he shook his head at her. 'Elizabeth, you know we need this marriage treaty.' At her nod he repeated his concern. 'Is she deficient in some way that necessitates calling this off?'

In that moment of clarity, Robbie understood that he must lie to his father, to his chieftain, to protect the woman he loved. And so he did.

'There is no reason.'

He would tell himself later that it was part of a plan. A plan to continue to work together to find a way out of this that would keep both of their families safe and keep honour intact. He would lie to himself that there would be time to help Sheena learn what she must and to help her find a way to deal with the terrifying spells. A way to become the wife of a chieftain.

But right now the only thing he knew was that he must find a way to protect her. Save her honour and her heart. Make right the way she'd been treated or take away their power to hurt her.

And as he nodded, the confirmation of that lie to his father still lying fresh on his lips, Robbie prayed there was time enough to help her change. And that she would see reason and accept that she must become his wife.

Strange, but a cackling laugh seemed to echo through the keep as he left his parents behind. And the icy shiver that tracked down his spine made him wonder if he had somehow tempted the fates.

Now, only time would tell.

Chapter Eighteen

Within two days after Farlen left, Sheena had changed. The Sheena he knew had gone to bed that night and this new, strange one had awoken the next morning.

Not her appearance but her demeanour. Well, her appearance did change, for she began wearing more formal gowns and she covered her hair, and nothing ever seemed out of place on her. If someone pointed out some loosened locks from her braid or now elaborate hair arrangement, she took leave of his mother and went to her chambers, not reappearing until it had been *tidied*.

Her gown, her hands and her face were never dusty or dirtied because she did nothing that would make them so. She remained at his mother's side and call from the time she broke her fast in the morning until she was in her bed at night.

And Robbie hated it.

He'd tried to tempt her to escape with him to that place above the falls, but she had tasks to see to for his mother. He'd invited her to ride, even saddling the wee laddie and bringing him to the keep. She'd given him a sad little smile and asked if he would see to Wee Dubh's exercise from now on. Though she visited the village, she did not stay to chat or weave with Tavie or Jeannie or to help them, not even with the new bairn.

The worst change was the way she did not respond to him. To his kisses or caresses.

He pulled her into an alcove in the corridor leading back to the kitchens, determined to tell her about his plan, such as it was. Distracted by the curve of her lips and soft smile, he wrapped his arms around her and kissed her. She'd spent so much time in his mother's company since their return that he'd not had the chance to do that. Now, he did. Touching his tongue to her mouth, he teased her lips, waiting for her body to melt against him and to open to him.

She did neither.

Instead, she stood quietly, neither participating nor fighting him, until he realised it. And he understood that he did not want her acquiescence. He wanted the secret passion that dwelled within her. Passion he'd tasted and felt and knew it was true.

'What is wrong, Sheena?' he asked when he released her and watched as she straightened the fall of her gown and tucked non-existent hairs back under the veil she wore.

'Not a thing, Robbie. I am just on my way to get something from the kitchen for your mother and would not want her to be waiting for my return.'

He grabbed her hand before she could move away.

'The weather is fair, and I am certain my mother would give you leave to accompany me on a ride. Wee Dubh misses you,' he said. He was not above using her damn horse as leverage in this. 'As do I.'

He lifted her hand to his mouth and kissed her palm

and the inside of her wrist. The slightest of shivers gave him some hope, which she dashed on the cold stone floor with her next words.

'Mayhap once I have improved in my duties she will allow it.' She pulled her hand free, rubbing it on her skirts as though it would remove his kiss before smiling at him. 'I will see you at supper.'

As she walked away, never even glancing back at him over her shoulder, Robbie knew what bothered him. That smile. That false pleasant expression she wore on her face now. From morning until night and every hour in between.

He hated it, along with every change that had been made to the lively, curious, kind woman he loved. He just needed to speak to her and explain that it would work out between them. That he would help her. That she would be safe with him.

Each day he waited for the chance to get her alone and each day he failed. Robbie approached Glynnis and was met not by the 'perfect woman' as Sheena would describe her, but by a woman growing angrier by the day. She rebuffed his attempts to discuss Sheena and removed herself from the table as soon as she could. Even Iain appeared frustrated by this change in Glynnis.

Finally, he asked to speak with Davidh and Anna, hoping for advice from them—either as the happily wedded couple they were or the commander and the healer who were both familiar with dealing with difficult people and circumstances. He walked out to the stone house on the first path outside the gate that night after supper was done.

'Come inside,' Anna greeted him and pulled the

door wide to allow him entrance. 'Davidh is here as you asked.'

The man who Robbie had trained with for years and who was Parlan's closest friend stood as he entered and pointed to a chair by the large hearth. Before anyone spoke, Anna put a large, steaming mug of...something in his hands. She always had some concoction or another in the pot over the fire to serve to visitors. Inhaling deeply, he noticed the aroma of honey and some spices he could not name.

'She is not trying to poison you,' Davidh said. Taking the mug his wife offered him now, Davidh took a mouthful and swallowed. ''Tis only betony and honey...'

'And a touch of this and a pinch of that,' Anna added with a laugh.

Davidh took her hand in his as she sat down closest to him and pulled her to him. Robbie took a moment to look away as the couple kissed, staring at the various racks and bunches hanging overhead and the pots and plants scattered on every open surface in this large chamber.

'So, what is so important that you come in the dark of night to consult with us?' Davidh asked.

''Tis important and I would seek your advice in confidence,' he explained. 'A delicate matter I do not wish to spread through the village, or even the keep.'

'I am intrigued, Robbie. Is this a matter your father should be aware of?'

Now the difficult part came.

'I would keep this discussion between the three of us, if you would, Davidh.' He saw the looks exchanged by the commander and his wife.

'Does this matter impact the clan?' He nodded. 'Is there any danger to the Camerons?' Davidh asked very direct questions that Robbie needed to consider how to answer.

'I do not think so,' he said. He was not being completely candid with Davidh, for breaking a betrothal and halting the coming wedding could be dangerous if objections were raised.

'Ken that I will bring anything I think may endanger us to your father, Robbie.'

'Aye, he trusts The Cameron fully,' Anna added. 'He told your father my secret when I could not trust anyone with it.'

Finding out that there was another with a strong claim to the high seat would have had a different result had the one holding the seat been ruthless and without honour. But his father had welcomed Iain Mackenzie as the grandson of his older brother and brought him into the clan.

Davidh drank down the rest of the contents of his mug and stood, winking at Anna as he did so.

'I have just remembered something left undone outside,' he said. 'My wife can offer her counsel to you and you can have no fear that she will break your confidence.' Once Davidh left, they sat in silence as Robbie thought on how to broach this topic with her.

Anna made it easier for him. 'How does Sheena fare these days?' she asked. Sipping her cup, she watched him over the rim.

'I think you ken that she is what brings me here, Anna. I think you witnessed Sheena having a...spell on her first days here.' Robbie studied her now. 'The day she ended up sleeping by your garden wall.'

'She had a milder one earlier than that. While walking the village with Lady Glynnis, they met Iain on

his way here. They brought her to me when she was…
overwhelmed.' Anna nodded. 'I suspected something
more, but 'tis not something I could just go up and ask
her.' Anna smiled. 'I tried to ask Lady Glynnis and she
brushed off my concerns.'

'She has appointed herself Sheena's guardian.'

'Have you seen one of these episodes of illness?'

'Most of one. While we were at Tor. She grows overwhelmed by fear and loses control of herself. Suddenly
she cannot breathe, she loses all colour and becomes
agitated. Finally, she loses consciousness.' He remembered the look of her in the solar at Tor when he'd arrived
at Glynnis's call. 'For the first while, 'tis not sleeping.
Once it passes, she falls deeply asleep.' He ran his hands
through his hair. 'And she needs hours and hours of
sleep to recover.'

Though nothing he'd said seemed to surprise her,
Anna did not speak at first. She stared at the low flames
under the pot and remained silent.

'Is fear the only thing that brings these on?'

'It seems that when she feels threatened in some way
it happens. Too many new people. Too many things happening around her.' Robbie met her gaze. 'Do you have
something, a concoction or tisane or something, that can
help her? That could ease these symptoms?'

'I have seen this before,' Anna said. 'In my mother's
village when we lived there. It was a man who suffered
them. Though it was not fear that would bring his on, it
sounds like the same thing. He would complain that his
heart was beating out of his chest and that he could not
take in a breath, in spite of breathing as though running a
race. He would talk very quickly without slowing and he
would pace around very quickly.' Anna nodded at him.

'It sounds similar, from what Glynnis would tell me. Is there something that would help her?'

Anna rose from her chair and filled her cup once more from the pot. He shook his head at her offer of more and waited for her to sit again.

'We, my mother and I, could find nothing that kept them from happening. Oh, sometimes, if what brought them on could be interrupted, they would be less severe. But nothing we made rid the man of them.'

'So there is nothing you can do for her?' he asked.

The healer studied him for a short time and smiled.

'You love her.'

'It matters not. If you cannot help her—'

'Never say love does not matter. But more the matter is the issue of you marrying her without revealing the extent of these spells to your father.'

'She is ashamed of this weakness. I do not want her shamed more because of its revelation.' Robbie asked the question he needed an answer to. 'Will this endanger her if she does marry me?'

'Ah, so she does not wish to marry you.' Anna drew the shawl tighter around her shoulders.

''Tis more complicated than that, Anna. It would take me hours to sort through it and find the key to it. But more than the time it would take, it is worse because I do not ken all of it.'

'You just want to help her.'

'Aye.' He let out a breath. 'Aye.'

'I can only tell you to make her feel safe. If she feels safe, the spells may not be as serious.' He nodded. 'There are restorative brews I can make for her, to strengthen her afterwards.'

He stood and thanked her for her time and the betony

tisane. As he reached out to lift the latch on the door, she spoke again.

'Another thing that could help her would be to have a place where she can seek refuge. Like the alcove in my garden. If you find such a place in the keep, she may feel better that it is there for her should she need it.'

'I will seek out such a place,' he said. Finally, something tangible he could do to help her.

'My workroom on the lower floor of the keep might be such a place. There is a small nook there that is unused at present. See if you think it practical.'

When he opened the door, he found Davidh sitting on the step there. If he'd heard any of the details, he gave no sign of it.

'My thanks, Davidh.'

'Robbie, I would urge you to speak to your father about any matter involving the earl's daughter. Too much is at stake to keep such knowledge from him.'

Robbie acknowledged his counsel and took his leave, making his way back to the keep. He would examine Anna's workroom in the morning and see if it could be that safe spot that Sheena might have need of.

The next day he went to the workroom and was pleased by what he found. After clearing out the space, which was only just bigger than a closet, he found a stool, some cushions and two blankets and placed them within it. If she sought this place, there would be some comfort there and not a stone floor and cold wall against her back.

Now, all he need do was get her alone and show this to her. To make her understand that she could marry him. She could live the life they were meant to have.

It did not happen the rest of that day, but he knew it

would soon. He could not stand by uselessly as she became a shell of the woman she'd been. As she withered right before his eyes.

A few days later, the middle of the night brought a crisis and a revelation he'd never expected.

Chapter Nineteen

'Robbie… Wake up, man!'

He did just that, reaching for the dirk he kept close by his pillow.

''Tis me, Martyn,' the voice whispered.

'Martyn? What are you doing here?' Martyn worked in the stables with Geordie. Dear God! 'Tell me nothing has happened to Wee Dubh!' Sheena could weather many storms, but the loss of that horse would strike her down. Especially now.

'Nay, not the wee laddie,' Martyn explained. 'Geordie needs the lady's help.'

Robbie sat up and pushed the bedcovers aside. The scraping of metal on flint and the flash of a candle's light revealed it was the man he'd thought. Martyn stepped back as Robbie grabbed his trews and tugged them on.

'Why?' Robbie pulled his shirt over his head and looked around the floor for his boots. 'In the middle of the night?'

'The brown mare is slipping her foal and willna let Geordie near her. The lady has a way wi' the horses and he thinks she may be able to calm the puir thing down so he can help the foal.'

Dressed and ready, Robbie still could not work out his part in this. 'Did you send the lady's maid to her? Is she on her way?'

'Aye, I did that. Geordie said to do that. But the lady refused.'

Robbie stopped before he took another step. 'The lady refused Geordie's call?'

'Aye. She said that 'twasna her place to do such things.'

This had gone too far. The Sheena he knew would never hesitate to help Geordie. Hell, the Sheena he knew would have lived in the stables had the old man allowed it. He shook his head in disbelief.

'Wait below stairs. I will bring her along.'

Martyn was gone before Robbie entered the corridor. Walking to her chamber, he knocked softly before opening the door.

'Sheena,' he said. Stepping within and closing the door behind him so as not to wake anyone else, he walked to her bedside. 'Are you awake?'

'Robbie,' she said, pulling the bedcovers up to her neck, 'what are you doing here?'

'Geordie sent for you. He needs your help.'

'I cannot go.' How could there be so much pain evident in just those three words? Regret. Pain. Loss. Those and more filled her tone as well.

'Lass,' he said, sitting now on her bed. 'I ken that everything is wrong. I ken you are trying to be different. But how will you feel if the mare and foal die? Will you regret not heeding Geordie's plea for your help?'

'You do not ken what you ask of me, Robbie. You do

not ken.' Once more he could hear how pain infused her words.

'I do not ken,' he said. 'Tell me. Or come with me and we can sort this out later.'

In the shadows and light thrown around the chamber by the flames in her hearth, he could see the indecision and struggle on her face. Something else was at play here. Part of whatever was the conflict between her and her father, he guessed. But something kept her frozen when she should have been halfway to the stables by now.

Robbie saw the moment she decided to answer Geordie's call. She tossed off the bedcovers and ran to the trunk in the corner.

'Should I summon Isabel to help you?' he asked, already turned away from the attributes the firelight exposed to his sight.

'Nay, I will be out in but a moment.'

The woman who came out into the corridor was the Sheena who'd walked at ease among the villagers. This was the one he'd witnessed scrubbing laundry by the river. With her hair pulled back in the kerchief worn by most of the women while working and the plain woollen gown with an apron tied around her waist, this was the Sheena who found joy in life and in people. Seeing her as she was now told Robbie how badly things were going with her.

Because she must marry him.

Robbie took her hand and guided her down the darkened hallway and stairs to where Martyn awaited them. Soon they arrived at the stables and were led to Geordie. Before she followed Martyn to the stall where Geordie worked with the mare who was losing her foal too early, an animal's roar filled the stables.

Sheena shuddered at it but kept moving. It came once more as they arrived at the large stall being used for this mare. When it came for a third time, Robbie stared down the row of stalls, knowing which horse made such a sound.

''Tis Wee Dubh,' Geordie said as he walked over to the gate. 'He kens ye're here, my lady.'

'He sounds in pain,' Robbie said.

'He is.' Geordie's words sent a tremor through her.

She could not... She must concentrate on this task, one that she would rather avoid.

'Tell me what I must do.' She ignored her beloved horse's distress, for she could not see him or her reserve would crumble.

She stepped inside and waited on Geordie's directions. The mare's sides heaved, and her eyes were wild with pain. When the horse turned, Sheena could see one of the foal's legs dangling out of the mare and blood tracked down it, dripping onto the hay strewn over the floor. This was bad.

'If she willna calm, we could lose both of them,' Geordie explained. Sheena frowned. Both? 'The foal is dead so it willna deliver. In that position, the other legs will tear Muirne's insides. I need to get some of the sleeping potion in her so we can take the foal.'

The mare groaned and flung her head back. Her eyes rolled and she bared her teeth. Did the horse know her bairn was dead? Did she feel her own impending death?

This was the same situation her own mother had faced on the night of her birth. A bairn who would not be born. A mother's lifeblood draining away with the passing of every second. Both may die. A choice to be made. Had her mother known? She shivered as she realised it.

'My lady, talk to her if ye will. If yer voice can calm her, I can get closer.'

She turned towards the mare and began whispering words of encouragement. Words of hope. Nonsense words. Sheena even sang a lullaby until the mare responded.

'Easy now, Muirne lass,' she said, taking one step closer and another. 'Come to me and tell me your troubles.'

She continued for a short time, the silence broken only by the mare's grunts and groans of pain. The men working with Geordie and even Robbie, who watched, spoke not a word and made not a sound that would distract the horse. Sheena took one careful step and another until she was able to touch the mare's bowed head. With gentle strokes, she convinced the horse to allow her closer. Once she could wrap her arm around the mare's neck, she whispered only to her.

'I am so sorry, lass,' she repeated, only feeling the tears when they trickled down her face. 'You did well, lass. Here now, let Geordie come closer. Let him help you.'

When the mare seemed ready to fight, Sheena stroked down her nose and breathed on her slowly. Finally, Geordie offered the horse the bucket with the potion in it. The worry on his face told her she must hasten. Working together, they got enough of the potion into Muirne to slow her down. With Geordie on the other side, they guided the horse down to the floor and onto her side. Sheena sat holding her head as the potion drew her into a deep sleep.

The rest took little time at all once Geordie could proceed and Sheena openly sobbed as the wee body of the foal was removed from within its mother.

''Twas too soon, my lady. No way to save it,' Geordie explained. 'But, with yer help, Muirne is alive and can have another, God willing.'

'God willing,' she repeated.

But her mother had never had another bairn after Sheena was born and she—they—almost died. In all the years, as her kith and kin had bairn after bairn, Jocelyn MacCallum had no more. Was that another sin her father held against her?

'Sheena, I can take you back to your chamber, if you are ready?' Robbie offered. It seemed strange to hear him speak after such a tense, silent time here.

'Geordie?' she asked. At his nod, Sheena accepted Robbie's hand and help to stand. Her legs trembled through the first steps away and again when she glanced back at the body of the foal now lying in the corner.

'Would you like to see the wee laddie before we go back?'

She wiped the tears away with the end of her sleeve before shaking her head and walking away. The only way she'd been able to get through these last days and nights was by staying away from Wee Dubh. The urge to saddle and ride him out of Achnacarry and never return was too strong and she feared she did not have the strength to resist it if she saw him.

The only thing that had kept her here was accepting that she finally had a way to find worth in her parents' eyes. And the only reason she was willing to become someone she was not was that, if there was no way out of this, she would marry Robbie and he deserved a wife better than she could be.

Glancing over at him as they walked through the yard, she knew that she would do what she must because of him. She owed him that much, and even more. Because of the way he'd accepted her refusal and offered to help her. Oh, at first he'd done it because he'd wanted out too. But more recently they'd found a certain level of companionship and comfort and co-operation between them. She stumbled at the memory of his touch and the taste of him and the way he'd brought her pleasure she'd no idea existed. Aye, although the thought of marrying the next clan chieftain terrified her, marrying Robbie Cameron did not engender the same fears.

'Before you go to your chamber, I would show you something,' he said, as he took her elbow and kept her from pitching forward.

When they entered the keep, Robbie led her to the stairs that led down to the lower level. Various store-rooms and supplies, the storage place for some weapons and a few chambers left open for unexpected needs were down there. He grabbed a torch from the wall next to the entrance and held it above them.

'I do not think this is a good idea. If your mother learns of this, she will not approve.' She whispered the words, not knowing if others were nearby. At times, people slept in the hall. There were guards who also walked the corridor to protect those who lived in the keep. Any of them could report seeing Sheena skulking through the keep in the middle of the night with Robbie. She did not want to jeopardise whatever progress she'd made with Lady Elizabeth now. 'I think I should seek my chamber.'

He faced her, the light thrown by the torch illuminating him, changing his expression as it flickered. He put his other hand on her cheek, stroking down with his thumb, much in the same way she had calmed Muirne in her distress.

'I do not understand why you are doing this, but I see what it is doing to you, Sheena.' He leaned in quickly and kissed her. All she wanted to do was throw her arms around him and hold him to her. Luckily for her, he stepped back. 'I ask you to see something I think you need. I will not keep you against your will or delay you in returning to your chambers once you see it.'

How could she refuse him this? He'd protected her and cared for her when she'd needed his help. If she was truthful with herself, Sheena wanted to spend as much time with him as possible.

She sighed and nodded.

He went first and she followed and soon they stood in front of the large room that Anna used as a workroom for her herbal remedies and healing potions and ointments. Though she did most of her work in the home she shared with Davidh, this was useful when she needed to tend to those in the keep or prepare plants she, and the clan, would need over the winter.

Robbie opened the door and put the torch in the holder above it. But he did not stop there. With a wave, he took her to the corner of the room farthest from the door. There, a small closet of a sort opened into the wall.

'This is…if you have need…this is for you.'

She stared as he stumbled over his words, trying to explain. Leaning into the narrow alcove-like indentation, she noticed a stool, pillows and some blankets folded and laid there. He took her hand and kissed it.

The truth and purpose of it struck her—like his cave

and the enclosed spot in Anna's garden, this was a sanctuary for her. A place to hide. A place to recover. A place to try to regain control when the spells tried to strike her down. A safe place in a keep where she was always on display.

'You do not leave the keep often. I just did not want you to be without a place where you can seek the quiet you need. If you cannot summon me when—' he nodded at her '—find your way here for a time and I will come to you.'

She could not bear it.

She must do her duty and show her parents she could. Yet this acknowledgement and acceptance by Robbie of the woman she was, faults and weaknesses and all, made her want to give up her quest and be herself with him.

'Do not give up on me yet, lass. I will find a way out of this for you. For us. Have faith.'

Sheena glanced once more at the extreme kindness he'd done for her and wondered if he truly believed his own words. She could not, so she did the only thing she could—she ran.

Out of Anna's workroom, along the darkened corridor to the steps and up. And up again to her bedchamber. She tore off the now stained gown and apron and kerchief and tossed them in the corner. She made it to her room with scant seconds to spare before the torrent of tears began.

He understood so much and yet so little. She could not fail and yet she knew she would. She must change. She must overcome the fears of her childhood and become the woman her parents wanted her to be. But every effort to do that in the past had been an utter failure. As the sadness poured forth, Sheena understood one thing that had changed within her since Farlen's delivery of her father's message.

Fear had been burned from her and all that was left was sadness and shame. And a heart broken that not even the love she felt for Robbie could mend.

Chapter Twenty

I f he'd thought watching her last night as she'd worked to save the mare and lose the foal was hard, meeting that false smile over the table as they broke their fast made it seem the easier task.

And though that smile might fool others, it did not hide the puffiness of eyes that had cried as much as hers had on her return to her bedchamber. He'd followed her, in spite of her being unaware of his presence behind her all the way up to her room. Standing outside her door and hearing the heartrending sobbing, Robbie had been tempted to take her away from Achnacarry and keep her to himself.

Watching her tear her heart and soul apart to become someone else, he wanted to roar out his displeasure as Wee Dubh had in the stables last night. Even the horse knew something was wrong with her. Yet his mother and father seemed pleased by the changes in Sheena. As his gaze moved down the table and met Glynnis's angry brown one, Robbie was glad that he found a kindred spirit here.

The bad part of finding her angry stare was that it

seemed directed at him. Her heart-shaped face softened whenever Sheena spoke to her but took on that sullen expression once Sheena looked away.

His mother announced her plans for the day and spoke to Sheena and Glynnis about what she would need from them. Just when he was losing patience and control, his mother stood to leave. Like younger versions of the lady of the castle, they both rose gracefully and bowed to his father before beginning to follow his mother away.

Sheena paused and stepped back to the table.

'Robbie, your mother has reminded me of my increasing duties and preparations for the wedding,' she said, that false smile sitting on her face and daring him to kiss it off. 'I had planned—' She stopped.

For a moment he thought she could not force out whatever words she'd planned. She swallowed several times, took a breath and began anew.

'I was thinking on this last night.' Another pause but this time her eyes flared at him as she referred to what had happened. As far as he knew, no one had spoken of her involvement in the shocking event in the stables. 'With all of my duties and as a marriage gift to you, I would like to give Wee Dubh to you now.'

Robbie felt his brother slap him on the back and congratulate him. His father clapped his approval. His mother nodded gently and he suspected this had been her idea. Glynnis's expression grew darker and even more dangerous. He'd not even begun to accept that she'd spoken the words when she finally met his eyes.

Empty, broken green eyes stared back at him.

No regret. No anger. No fear. Nothing. As though this action had not killed her. As though giving her beloved horse away was something she did every morning after breaking her fast. This was wrong. So very wrong that he could not even speak.

'Well, come now, Sheena.' His mother took Sheena by the arm and walked with her out of the hall.

'I need to fetch something from my chambers, my lady. I will join you in the solar,' Glynnis said. The stare promising him death told him to follow her.

As she left, Robbie was still stunned. In any other circumstance, receiving the gift of a horse like that would thrill him. Wee Dubh was incomparable in size and height and heart. When he regained his full strength, which was progressing well, according to Geordie, he would be a brute once more on journeys or even in battle when trained for it.

The price of this gift was too high and he could not— would not—accept it. Not if the cost was Sheena's to bear. He did not understand the reason behind it— behind Sheena's acceptance of this transformation. Behind her acquiescence in giving up herself.

But he knew someone did.

Someone who was as furious about it as he was.

Someone who was seeking something in her chamber and expected him to meet her there.

Robbie delayed not and followed just behind Glynnis, making certain that the corridor leading to her room was empty of servants or prying eyes. His mother would be waiting on Glynnis's arrival, so he could not delay. He did not bother knocking.

The barrage began as soon as he closed the door behind him.

'How can you let this happen?' From her tone, Glynnis would be spitting fire if she could. At him. 'I thought you—' She stopped and crossed her arms over her chest.

The tapping of her foot was the only sound echoing through the distance between them.

'You thought what, Glynnis? That I can put a stop to something that I have no control over?' he spat back. 'I have asked her about this. I tried last night—'

'Last night? What happened last night?'

'Geordie needed her help with a mare. I was with her. I tried to make her see Wee Dubh. She refused.'

'So you kenned what she would do this morn?' Glynnis's usually pretty face was contorted with anger and pain. 'How can you accept such a thing when you ken—'

'I ken she, the Sheena who arrived here, who I hated…' He raked his hands through his hair, trying to sort this out. 'Nay, I never hated her. I hated what I thought of myself and my actions because of her.' He shook his head. 'Sheena would never willingly give up that horse to me or anyone. Never. But I do not ken what is behind her change in manners,' he admitted.

'Truly? You are telling me that you ken nothing of her parents' wishes? Their letter to her?' Glynnis's gaze narrowed and he felt her judging his answer.

'My parents received some word from her father, but they've not spoken of it to me. Other than that the date is set for our marriage.'

'Come with me. And be quick and quiet.'

She gave him no chance to question, for she turned and left her chamber without delay. He saw her path— to Sheena's chambers—and he went.

Glynnis peeked within first before motioning for him to enter. He remained by the door while she walked to a small closet opposite the bed and took out a wooden box. It was clear she was looking for something specific and she found it and held it out to him.

A folded parchment addressed to Sheena. And this was not written in the flowery script of a scribe or priest. Nay, he recognised the writing of Connor MacLerie, for he had seen it many, many times. Why would Connor write to Sheena when she could not read?

'Read it.'

He unfolded the parchment sheet and did so.

Dearest daughter...
...wilful...pride...obedience...ashamed...
...demand...marriage...
...duty...duty...duty...

His blood boiled with each demand he read. By the end, anger prevented him from seeing any of it. He would have crushed the parchment in his hand had Glynnis not saved it.

'And you think I had knowledge of...that? That I would stand by and watch her be destroyed?'

'You did not want to marry her, Robbie. Everyone here kens.'

'I did not. When she arrived here, I was as opposed as she was.' Robbie looked at the parchment in Glynnis's hands. 'She asked me to help her find a way out of the betrothal. Because of her...affliction she said she cannot be the wife of a chieftain.' He thought back on Glynnis's own observations and reminded her. 'There is more about her inability to learn the simplest of tasks, to accomplish all the things expected of a chieftain's wife and more that she would not reveal to me. You and Tomas both hinted at it when I asked you about her progress in settling in. But if my parents kenned the full truth, it would give them reasons to object to the contract.'

'And war would be the result?'

Robbie looked at Glynnis, who was canny and more intelligent than most thought.

'We have been looking for a way out together,' he said.

'But her affliction is just that. So—'

'Using that will expose her to shame. She has lived with this shame her whole life. That shame and fear brings on these attacks. You must have read the letter. You ken.'

God Almighty! She'd not just read it, she'd read it…

'You read it to Sheena.'

Tears filled her eyes and she nodded before dashing them away with her hand. 'Aye.'

'Because you ken she cannot read or write either.'

A stiff nod was all the reply he got. A long moment's stalemate was finally broken by a brittle laugh. 'How did you learn of that?' she asked.

'I paid heed to her. Watched her when she was not aware of it. She hides it well enough.'

'Another deficiency that could be brought to bear.'

'Another weakness about which to shame her?'

Robbie shook his head. 'I will not use those against her. Not even to get her out of this marriage.'

Glynnis's eyes and mouth grew wide at that admission. 'So you are caught between exposing her to more shame or keeping such knowledge from your father… your chieftain.'

He paused before nodding. 'And she is caught between shaming herself and her father and bringing his honour into question and marrying a chieftain's heir when their life together will force her to face everything she cannot do.'

'You violate your own oaths either way.'

''Tis worse still, for Sheena ceases to exist with each passing day of trying to prove her father wrong and to gain his approval. The Sheena I marry will not be the Sheena I I—'

He stopped before saying it. He'd not spoken of it to Sheena and he would not to another until she knew his feelings.

Glynnis searched his face, as though he would reveal some solution to this situation. And he wished to God he had one.

'Lady Glynnis? Lady Glynnis, are ye here?'

The call, a woman's voice coming down the corridor, silenced them. She motioned for him to move behind the door and to be quiet.

'Aye, coming!' she called back. Glynnis lowered her voice and handed him the parchment. 'Put this back and wait for me to lead her away before leaving,' she whispered. Grabbing some small thing off the table next to Sheena's bed, Glynnis lifted the latch and stepped out of the bedchamber.

'I was on my way to Lady Elizabeth when I remembered Lady Sheena had asked about this.'

Their voices drifted off as they walked away from Sheena's bedchamber and to the stairs. Robbie turned to place the parchment back in the box when he stopped. Staring at it, he comprehended he'd been looking at this matter in the wrong direction. Its solution did not lie with Sheena. The solution to this belonged to the one who'd begun it—Connor MacLerie.

The Beast of the Highlands.

Instead of returning the missive, he tucked it inside his shirt and replaced everything else that had been in the box on top of it. Satisfied that it looked undisturbed, he put the box where Glynnis had taken it from and left Sheena's chambers.

She would never look for it, because it meant some- one else would have to read it to her. And having heard it once aloud, he was certain she did not want to hear it again.

When word arrived that Connor MacLerie's party was journeying to Achnacarry, Robbie knew what he had to do and he thought he might have a way as well.

If it went as he planned, Sheena would be free of their betrothal and not forced to marry a man she believed she would only fail.

Sheena would be free of him after all.

And he would carry out his duties and marry another.

He went to the stables and had Wee Dubh readied. Geordie gave him a piercing look—one that told him exactly what the man thought of Robbie now owning Sheena's horse. But as soon as he whispered his mis- sion to the horse, the wee laddie accepted Robbie on his back without argument.

It took almost the entire day of riding west to finally reach the place where the messenger had said Connor would camp for the final night before riding on to Ach- nacarry.

She did not have any reason to seek out this place, but when the lady gave her leave Sheena's feet just brought her here. No sounds emanated from within when she knocked, so she opened the door to Anna's workroom and entered.

Wooden shutters covered the small windows high on

the wall and yet the weak light was enough for her to see her way and avoid bumping into any of the tables or shelves of delicate plants and unguents scattered around the room. She eased into the small closet-like part of the chamber and she would swear she could hear his words whispered in the air around her.

'I just did not want you to be without a place where you can seek the quiet you need... I will find a way out of this for you. For us.'

In these last weeks, though surrounded by people at all times, she'd felt alone. Always performing like a trained pet. Always being judged. Always being found wanting.

Worse, she had lost faith that he would do what he'd agreed to do. Not for want of intent but for want of an actual solution.

Lady Elizabeth had explained that Sheena's mother had written several times to explain her shortcomings in detail and had asked the lady to help Sheena prepare for the role she would play in life. The lady was not unkind, but clearly relished having Sheena under her tutelage. She had even offered to give Sheena time away from her duties. It was those kindnesses that helped her keep her fears at bay.

Sheena had, in contemplating matters in the middle of the night, come to understand that if she faltered or turned her efforts away from her attempt to do what her parents wished, she would indeed fail. When the fear had been replaced by a deep sadness in its stead, Sheena wondered if she would ever be without one or other emotion. Not willing to risk it, she had pitilessly pushed away anything or anyone that threatened her progress.

A sad laugh escaped her at the thought that her father would have been the one to appreciate her ruthlessness.

Sheena sat on the stool, wrapped one of the blankets around her and closed her eyes, missing Robbie with every breath she inhaled and let out.

Missing his laughter. Missing their walks. Missing riding the paths around Achnacarry. Missing his scandalous kisses and caresses by the river. And praying nightly, daily and other times in between that he would find a way out as he'd promised.

But she knew that the fear and the fits were never gone for long. And when they returned they would be worse than ever, and they would be seen. People would point. Whispers would begin. Suspicions would spread, for even the powerful MacLerie could not stop those. She'd heard them in Lairig Dubh, even while her father exerted his iron-handed control.

The Church already looked askance at the man who'd been rumoured to have killed his first wife for not giving him sons. All they needed to hear was that The Beast's offspring, his daughter, suffered from unholy fits. It would bring church officials looking too closely at the story of her birth and her father's choice.

She sighed and opened her eyes, Sheena wondered what the next weeks would bring. She was damned no matter what—she'd not managed to learn the tasks and skills that she'd never learned before. Even Glynnis's secret efforts to teach her to read had failed. So, if forced to it, she would go into a marriage guaranteed to be hell on earth for her.

Oh, Robbie would be kind for a while, until she brought shame to him. It might even take a long time, but it would happen. And she would have to watch his regard for her—and the genuine affection she thought he did feel for her now—die.

Why had her parents forced this on her?

Why had they forced Robbie to suffer once more because of her?

Chapter Twenty-One

Robbie was challenged only once while crossing Mackintosh lands. One of the guards his father had sent after him handled it and they travelled on. Whether his father suspected his intent or not, he must have witnessed him leaving Achnacarry—or someone had reported him leaving—and sent along a few warriors to protect his heir.

Instead of the fair weather that had favoured his last long rides with Sheena, the skies opened and storms dogged his every mile. The torrents of rain were so heavy that part of the only road through the hills in the Disputed Lands had washed away.

But rain, and even thrashing winds, would not stop him.

Just as he'd thought, they arrived at the large camp just before sunset. He was escorted to the biggest tent, set up in the middle of the dozens, next to the river. The whispers and pointing told him that the horse he rode had been recognised. When his escorts stopped he slid off Wee's back and rubbed his nose, praising him for not tossing his sorry arse in the mud when he could have along the way.

'Why are you riding my daughter's horse?'

Robbie did not turn immediately at Connor's voice. He waited for several moments and faced the man who had made him the warrior and dutiful son he was now.

The man behind so much of Sheena's torment.

'My lord,' he said, bowing when he met Connor's gaze.

'Why do you have her horse?'

'And a good evening to you, my lady.'

Unable to avoid being involved and as yet unseen by the earl, Jocelyn MacCallum, Countess of Douran and Lady MacLerie, walked to her husband's side and nodded at Robbie. Although the earl shifted his stance, edging slightly towards the lady, he gave no other acknowledgement of her arrival. The woman who'd helped in raising him, who'd taught him manners and grooming…and fairness and the softer side of life that her husband routinely ignored.

'Do not make me ask a third time, Robbie.'

Connor's tone changed enough that a massive man now moved from the shadows to his side. Rurik Erengislsson, half Highlander and half Norse warrior, and probably the best and most dangerous fighter in all the Highlands. And he stood at his cousin's side, awaiting orders. Another man resembling Rurik also moved into position and Robbie realised it must be the man's son. A younger warrior, almost as tall, with his father's build but his mother's colouring, Young Dougal as he was called, stood, hand on hilt, waiting.

'Wee Dubh is not Sheena's horse. She gave him to me.'

Connor's reaction to his wife's loud gasp was swift—

he lifted the flap of his tent and, while guiding Jocelyn inside, he told Robbie to follow with a jerk of his head. Rurik remained at the opening, not entering but not moving his gaze from any possible threat to his chieftain, even if that threat was from someone he knew.

Robbie held out the reins to one of his men before following them in. He paused just before lowering his head and offered up a prayer for wisdom. For anyone confronting the Beast of the Highlands certainly needed the Almighty's help. In that last moment, though, it was the image of Sheena—pale, terrified and ashamed— that gave him the strength and the courage to do what he must.

Robbie stood watching and waiting as Jocelyn ordered the servants about—bringing him a cup of something hot, taking his soaked cloak and giving him a length of cloth to use to dry off—without speaking a word. Nothing of worth would happen or be spoken of until the pleasantries in which she excelled were accomplished. Only as he observed the lady's flawless polite conduct did he see the difference between her and her daughter.

Lady MacLerie *saw* to visitors' comfort while her daughter had the ability and desire to make people comfortable. As the daughter of the most powerful noble in this part of Scotland, she should not have to exert any effort at all, let alone serve or help those below her. But Sheena enjoyed it. She liked people. She found a way to comfort anyone in need of such. It was a skill not measured the same way, but a skill or talent regardless.

As were other things about Sheena.

Her kindness and interest in the villagers and those

who were in the clan. The way she knew and understood each person's place and talents and, more importantly, their needs and wants. How Finley lived for her compliments on his bread. How allowing Tavie to teach her to weave gave the woman something to brag about at the well. How the young woman with the bairn, damn him for not remembering her name, needed help with her laundry.

And that she knew and remembered each of their names and kith and kin and what they did and what they needed.

She needed no lists to read or parchments to keep records of the people around her—the people she cared about. She kept it all in her heart.

He was thinking on their conversation about Margaret and Marsaili when the last of the servants finished and departed, leaving him alone with Connor and Jocelyn. This was so different from their last encounters, when he had not yet stepped into his place as tanist to The Cameron.

'So, what brings you here on the horse we ken my daughter would not give up unless something was seriously wrong?' Connor asked. 'Indeed, what have you done to her to force her to give up her most prized possession?'

Jocelyn hissed in a soft breath, reacting to her husband's accusation. He watched as Connor took a long mouthful from his cup before meeting his gaze.

''Tis not what I have done or not done,' he began. 'But more about what you have done and not done to Sheena.'

Robbie reached inside his leather jack and pulled out the letter. He held it out to Connor, positioned so that Jocelyn could see the writing on the front. It did not take her but a moment before she saw it, recognised it and took the parchment from him before Connor could.

Connor's brow lifted at Robbie as he watched, but did not try to stop his wife from reading the missive. Robbie had learned much about them in watching them over the years and he knew that little to nothing stood in Jocelyn's way when she decided her path.

'Connor...' Her husband's name came out of her mouth as a mix of whining, cursing and frustration. Robbie had heard it before. He could not help the wry smile that broke forth on his face at the sound of an aggrieved Lady MacLerie. 'Why would you send something like this to her? Firstly, you ken she—'

Jocelyn broke off her words quickly, so he completed it for her, and the secret was no more.

'Sheena cannot read.' He nodded. 'And she cannot write or do sums.' Robbie shrugged. 'I ken.'

'Is that what brings you here? Because you discovered this and mean to make demands?' Connor asked. 'What is it you want? To keep Sheena's...*condition* a secret?'

He should have expected this from one of the most ruthless, most powerful, most manipulative men in Scotland. But he'd counted on exactly this reaction. When he withdrew the betrothal document, Connor shook his head and looked at his wife.

'I expected more from you, Robbie,' he said. Rising from his chair, he walked over and filled his cup again. Facing him, Connor continued. 'What is the cost of your silence?'

His voice was bitter and dark, edged with the danger of a cornered, wounded predator. His glare was worse even than that. Jocelyn, well, she looked almost the same, which he'd also expected. She would defend any of her children when threatened, which Robbie's words seemed to do. But if she cared so much, how had she allowed any of this?

'Do you wish to end the betrothal, Robbie? Do you reject Sheena as your bride?' Jocelyn whispered. The hurt in her voice and her stance wounded him.

'Why did you put her through this? Kenning that she has not the skills needed nor the ability to learn them? Kenning that she would be held up and shamed if that became common knowledge?'

He had to lower his voice because his instinct was to shout at them. He cleared his throat and shook his head, tossing the document that bound them all together on the table.

'But worse, you ken about the…spells that steal her wits and her breath. That force her to hide in closets and garden alcoves.' His hands fisted at the thought of her hiding in shame. 'You kenned and you still forced her to this? Do you care so little for your own flesh and blood?' He looked from one to the other. 'Truly, I expected so much more from you than that.'

'What does The Cameron want to keep his silence? What do you want?' Connor asked. Jocelyn had lost all the colour in her face and she clasped her hands before her. Connor did not move.

'So, you wish to protect her now?'

'Now? I have—we have—always wanted to protect her.' Connor walked to his wife and looked deeply into her eyes. When she tilted her head in the slightest of nods, he continued. 'We have tried to keep it all from view. When the priest began to question her inability to write and saw the beginning of one of her…fits, I sent him back to the abbey claiming some offence. I give too much to their upkeep for the abbot to risk insulting me. When one clerk wanted to punish her until she would read the words before her, I sent him off to another keep.'

'We tried to help her, Robbie. You do not remember. But we made every allowance and every accommodation and we did not press her when it was clear she had not the skill nor the ability to perform most tasks expected,' Jocelyn explained now.

That was not how he, or Sheena, remembered things.

'She was terrified of me,' Connor admitted, a hoarseness entering his voice that Robbie did not recognise. He seemed…almost human. 'So we decided that I would keep my distance from her. We thought she would improve as she grew up.'

'And did she?' he asked. 'When you told her of the betrothal…how did she respond?'

'At first, when Sheena was much younger and still remembered the…incident with you, she said that she hated you and you her. But, as she grew, she seemed less opposed. I thought it may be because you were familiar to her,' Jocelyn explained. 'We sent word when your father decided it was time to move forward.'

'You sent word? You did not speak to her at all?' It was as bad as she'd described to him.

'We decided that it was better to keep it…'

'Secret?' he asked.

'Nay! Our kith and kin all ken. Some will travel in the next week to be present at the wedding. To celebrate our daughter's marriage and the new alliance between our clans.' She paused and looked at Connor.

'We thought if we treated it with less fanfare and attention then she would be calmer about it.'

'Did Lilidh tell you the fits had returned when word

came that she would move to Achnacarry? That the spells grew worse once more?'

'Nay,' Jocelyn whispered. She moved towards her husband and he had her in his arms at the next step. 'We thought…'

'All of that aside, what do you want in order for this—?' Connor interrupted.

'Your daughter's condition?'

'The matter of my daughter's condition to remain quiet. What does your father want?' Connor released Jocelyn and picked up the betrothal agreement and shook it at him. 'What do you want?'

What did he want?

He wanted Sheena to laugh again. To watch her like a fae creature on the back of her monstrous horse as they raced along the loch. To have her and pleasure her and to hear her sigh of completion. He wanted to make her his.

He wanted to marry her.

But…

'My father kens nothing of this. My mother may have suspicions but she has not raised them…yet.'

'You are tanist and have not told him?' Connor stared at him now as he pointed out Robbie's failure. 'What do you want? You wish to break the betrothal?'

'Not I. I want you to find a way out of this damned agreement and I want you to see that she is protected.'

'Protected? From whom?'

'Protected against being married off against her will.'

'And what about you? What do you get out of this?'

Robbie let out a breath. He was nearing the end of his patience.

'If you break this, I *have* done my duty and will be able to marry elsewhere to satisfy my father's needs.'

Jocelyn gasped and he could hear the soft sobs escape her control. 'I always thought, I hoped, that you would be a good match for her, Robbie. In spite of what happened between you, I thought you looked at her with some affection, caring even,' she said. Looking up at him, she shook her head. 'So, you have no feelings for Sheena?'

Robbie nodded at Connor and at the lady, taking his leave with a silent nod, not saying another word. Jocelyn followed him and touched his arm to make him stop. 'Tell me the truth of it, Robbie.'

Robbie stared over her head at Sheena's father. Though he was not satisfied that he understood how things stood between them or what they'd actually done in dealing with Sheena, Robbie thought they did care about her. That his demand would be met.

'No feelings for your daughter, my lady?' He smiled. 'I only wish that were the truth.'

He walked out after refusing their offer of hospitality for the night, preferring to begin his return to Achnacarry under the full moon's light.

What would happen? How would The Beast settle this? Robbie could not even begin to come up with a way, but he knew Connor MacLerie, and Connor MacLerie would get what he wanted.

Hopefully that meant Sheena would as well.

And him? He would do his duty, as he'd pledged to do.

Chapter Twenty-Two

Word of her parents' approach came as they were about to sit for supper. Lady Elizabeth called out orders to servants and kin alike to prepare for their arrival. By the time their outriders arrived in Achnacarry, the villagers had lined the road to the gate to catch a glimpse. But Sheena did not fool herself into thinking that they were there to see anything but her parents. Well, her father.

To a one, they wanted to see the man long called The Beast of the Highlands. By the time her father rode through the gate and up to the keep, Sheena's stomach was nearly in revolt. She felt someone move next to her and thought that Glynnis had approached until a hand slipped into hers.

'Courage now, Wee Beastie.'

It was not Glynnis at all, but Robbie who stood at her side. She fought the urge to wrap her arms around him for the warmth and comfort he would offer her. Especially now, when her parents would learn the truth—she was not worthy. She had failed again.

She had practised being graceful and curtsying as a lady should and thought herself ready for that small gesture. Her father stared at her as he dismounted and helped her mother to the ground. Sheena counted the steps as they climbed, waiting for them to be welcomed by the chieftain and his wife. So when her mother turned from her father's side and ran to her, pulling her into her arms and hugging her, Sheena could not breathe for the shock of it.

'I have missed you, my lassie,' she whispered to Sheena. Her mother leaned away and wiped tears from her eyes as she stepped back. When she glanced past her mother, she saw that her father watched them closely. 'I pray your pardon, Lady Elizabeth... Laird Robert. 'Tis a while since I saw my daughter.' Jocelyn MacCallum, Lady MacLerie, could be most gracious when needed.

As though that was in the ordinary way of things, Robbie's parents bowed and invited them to supper without blinking. Once inside, order was restored and they were seated at the high table in the places of honour. With Robbie at her side, though acting strangely, she somehow made it through the tense meal. Not a word was spoken about the forthcoming wedding, her behaviour or misbehaviour or about the couple to be married.

She listened carefully and noticed that both of her parents guided the conversation to topics like the recent storms, or travelling from the west, or the cost of goods from the south. Not a word about the wedding. When the last course was served and consumed, Sheena could feel the knot in her stomach tightening and worried that her nervousness would bring on a spell. Robbie's hand on her leg under the table seized her attention. He took her hand and tangled their fingers together.

'Fear not, lass,' he whispered. 'I must speak with my father and yours. I will return. Glynnis?'

Glynnis came around and took Robbie's place as he first spoke to his father and hers before the men strode off the dais without a sign of what was to come. Her cousins Rurik and Struan followed and positioned themselves near the entrance to the chamber off the hall. Those remaining at table found it very uncomfortable and conversation on lighter topics was difficult since it was clear that something was happening. Or so she thought, for once the men, or most of them, had left, her mother began asking questions—about her.

Lady Elizabeth spoke highly of her efforts and her demeanour while Glynnis praised her willingness to work and more. Her mother smiled at her, truly smiled, for the first time in so long that she could not remember the last. The roiling in her belly eased…until the shouting began.

The men who served under Rurik—his son and the guards who ate at the tables below—tensed. No one would draw or brandish weapons, but clearly her father's men were ready to fight to defend their chieftain. The Cameron's guards did the same and tension filled the hall as they waited on some signal. When the voices grew louder, no one made a sound or dared move. Struan approached Lady Elizabeth while Rurik returned and spoke to their lady before he spoke to her.

'Lady, your father wishes your attendance in a matter. If you would accompany your lady mother?' he said in a very formal way. A glance at her mother revealed nothing, for she looked at ease as she waited for Sheena.

Soon, too soon if it was her choice, the steward's chamber was crowded with her parents and Robbie and his. Although anger sat plainly on Laird Robert's face, her father's expression appeared quite at ease. But the

Beast of the Highlands was renowned for his prowess and calm under attack.

Finally, when she could no longer remain silent, she blurted out, 'What is the matter? What is going on here?' Strangely, no one reprimanded her for speaking up.

''Twould seem that all your good efforts are for naught, Lady Sheena,' The Cameron said. His voice was filled with anger and frustration, a familiar condition when people dealt with the Beast. 'I can find no good way to say this, I fear, so I will just speak the truth.'

'Duncan discovered a problem with the betrothal agreement, Sheena.' Her father spoke first. 'Irreconcilable issues. I fear the agreement is terminated between The Cameron and myself.'

Everything around her ceased—no sound, no movement, nothing existed in that moment. Her gaze caught Robbie's and he winked at her. Winked? A broken agreement and he winked. He had something to do with this? As her eyes swept across those in the chamber who had just heard this dangerous announcement, she realised they all looked to her.

She could not draw breath as she waited on the rest. A broken betrothal could be cause for war. It tore allies apart and fragmented clans.

The Cameron huffed loudly before speaking.

'Your father has agreed to pay for the insult and we will sort out another alliance between our clans, but you will not be marrying my heir after all, Sheena. I pray you will not hold me or mine responsible for this abrupt ending. We wish you only the best as you recover from this unfortunate incident.' The Cameron glared openly at her father as he held out his hand to his wife. 'We will speak more on the morrow before you depart, my lord.'

They left the chamber without another word, leaving only Robbie behind with her and her parents.

And still she could not move. Or speak. Or think.

'I would speak to my daughter,' her father said. 'Alone.' Her mother began to argue and he just shook his head. 'Nay, my love. I would speak to Sheena alone.'

Robbie stepped away from the place where he stood leaning against the wall and walked to her. Leaning over her, he kissed her. Three soft, quick kisses on her forehead, her cheek and her lips that were done before she could savour them. Something told her that they were the last kisses she would get from him.

Before he moved away, he whispered so only she could hear his words. 'You are free, my wee beastie. And you are now, and will ever be, safe.'

She turned to watch as he left. At the last moment, he smiled at her and nodded. He exchanged a knowing glance with her father and allowed her mother to precede him.

Then he was gone. Gone.

He'd kept his word. Somehow he had found a way out.

But now she'd simply caused more trouble for her father. Insult to The Cameron's honour? Gold out of Mac-Lerie's coffers to pay for not presenting the bride he'd promised. Another debt she would owe him.

'Sheena?'

His voice, so close she could feel his breath against her cheek, startled her. He'd moved closer and sat next to her without her even realising it. When she looked into his eyes, eyes she'd been told looked like her own, she saw such sadness it hurt.

'I beg your forgiveness, my lass. I have wronged you in so many ways and added to your suffering.'

Tears flowed as her heart heard his plea.

'I may be good at fighting and planning battles and defending castles and keeps, but I have been disastrous as a father. I made mistakes with your sister and your brother, but I have caused you so much fear and pain. I would take it all back if I could.'

He opened his arms to her and she fell into them, sobbing against his chest as he offered her the one thing that she truly wanted—his love. He rocked back and forth and rubbed her head as she cried, whispering words of comfort and begging her to forgive him for all of his mistakes.

'I am sorry that it took someone else to make me see my mistakes, but I hope you will give me the chance to make things right with you.' He released her enough to look at her. 'You can return to your sister's household if you'd like. I hope, though, when you can speak of the wrongs I have committed against you, that you will return to Lairig Dubh and let me set things aright.'

Every kind word he said made her cry harder. And yet he sat in silence at her side and allowed her the time she needed. Grief and pain and loss and fear poured out in good measure before she felt an end to it.

'I do love you, lass. I—your mother and I—have always loved you. Clearly, though, we had no idea of how to show you that.'

'Father,' she whispered. It felt so good to let go of so much and to feel cherished by him for the first time.

He stood and guided her up to her feet.

'We will leave for Lairig Dubh on the morrow. So seek your rest now. It will be a long ride the first day.' They moved towards the door. 'And fret not for Robbie has given Wee Dubh back to you.'

'He has? When?' And the larger questions loomed about Robbie. 'What will happen now with Robbie?'

'He is tanist and needs a wife. His father will seek out a suitable one for him and he will marry.'

Glynnis MacLachlan, Lady Paragon MacVirtue she'd thought of her before understanding the depth and breadth of the lady's character and kindnesses.

The perfect wife for The Cameron's heir.

Gracious and kind. Patient and loyal. Proficient and skilled. The perfect wife for Robbie Cameron now that he needed one.

The thought of Robbie married to her and loving her sickened Sheena. And yet Glynnis had been raised from birth for that marriage and now it would be hers.

And his.

As she walked out into the now empty hall with her father, Sheena felt no joy at the idea of not marrying Robbie. Oh, she would have failed, and spectacularly, when the time came, but the thought of not seeing him, not touching him, not loving him tore her heart apart.

She must honour the gift he'd given her. She did honour the freedom he had somehow arranged. She did.

So why did the thought of a life without him hurt so much?

The morning dawned bright and mocked her with its cheeriness. Somehow, a dark, damp and dreary day would have felt more appropriate for leaving behind a place and the people she'd thought were her home. She did not join her parents or Robbie's to break her fast, begging off to help the servants pack up her belongings for travel back to Lairig Dubh.

Her mother had come to her at dawn and they had

spoken of many things in the privacy of her chamber. They would have more time along the journey to sort out her next steps, but her mother assured her that they would not discuss marriage until she was ready to do so. It would take time to explain things to her, so Sheena did not press now.

It took several hours to organise the baggage and for her farewells. She invited Glynnis to visit her once everything had calmed down and she had her promise to do that.

Yet, in spite of those conversations, which comforted her, nothing could prepare her for the terrible parts of taking her leave of Achnacarry and its people later that morning.

The first was not seeing Robbie at all. He also stayed away from the hall and she had no way of knowing where he might be. So she left without saying farewell to him. She had so much to tell him, even though he did not seem to want it. She asked Glynnis to pass on a few messages to him and left the rest unsaid.

The second terrible part was when they rode out of the yard and through the village. A crowd had gathered and so they slowed to a halt for them to approach.

Tavie and her daughter were first to reach her and they handed her a small package wrapped in cloth. Her weaving, to take with her, Tavie said. Glenna held up her wee bairn for a touch. Finley's wife, Jeannie, handed her a basket of steaming bread for her journey. And on and on as every person she'd met in the village said their farewells to her.

Her parents just watched without saying a word, other than to greet anyone who called out or spoke to them. The crowd soon dispersed and they were on their way.

It took all her concentration to keep Wee Dubh under control and she could barely see anything along the road as they rode at a steady pace away from Achnacarry.

Away from Robbie.

Away from her heart, which she'd left with him.

She wondered if she could live without it.

Chapter Twenty-Three

Robbie returned to the keep after watching The Mac-Lerie and his family depart Achnacarry. He'd watched her, as he had so many times before, as she made her way through the village. It still baffled him that she thought herself unprepared to oversee the people of a keep and a village when it came to her so easily.

Once again, she spoke to each one as they approached. The wee packages and gifts surprised her, but he knew about them before they were given to her. The villagers—Tavie, Finley, Glenna with the bairn and others—had asked him if she would accept them since she was leaving.

The ones most surprised by it all were her parents. They sat stiff and shocked by the outpouring of love for their daughter by these people who should have been strangers, beneath her notice. People who should serve her, rather than her caring about them.

As he watched, Robbie understood one thing about her that had escaped him before—she was not being overly modest in saying she could not carry out the duties of the wife of a chieftain. She would need to change in order for her to live that life, with its challenges and demands.

Aye, he would help her in any way he could, if she'd let him. But this deficiency went too deep within her and it was unfair of him to expect her to accept she must change and commit to that change. And whether that would take a short time or a longer period before he took the high seat mattered not. As he observed her now, he realised he was as arrogant and ignorant as her father was in believing that she was the one who needed to fit their needs—to be the expected daughter of a Highland chieftain or to be the wife he needed.

Yet, as he observed her leave-taking, he knew he could not let her go. She would take the joy and the challenge and the spark from his life and he was not certain he could carry on without her.

He'd told Connor he would do his duty and marry as expected. His parents had, several times since last evening, mentioned Glynnis's name as though he would simply accept one woman in the place of another. Aye, the dutiful, loyal tanist of the Clan Cameron would. But how could he now that he understood the truth?

Laughter travelled in the wind and, try as he might to convince himself that it was from the villagers there, he suspected he had indeed enraged the fates and that was their response to his challenge. It was his turn to laugh when he thought of the scorn he'd felt for his father's choice those many years ago.

Choosing his love for a disgraced woman over his duty and oath to his clan. Love over duty.

Robbie now faced a similar choice, for he could not have the woman he loved and keep his position as tanist and later as chieftain without destroying her.

As she waved for the final time and headed out of the village with her parents, he made his decision. He would be taking a huge risk—giving up one on the hope of gaining the other—but he was willing.

He loved her and she loved him, of that he had no doubt. He would risk it for that love. To give it a chance to grow into something as powerful as the love between his parents or hers.

She was worth it. She had value. She was worthy.

He just hoped he was.

After speaking with Tavie, he headed for the keep and his father and the elders to do what he must.

It took hours more than he'd thought it would, but when he rode away from Achnacarry he was simply the eldest son of the chieftain, pledged in loyalty and in service to The Cameron, the clan and the one who would be designated tanist. He was now far enough behind the travelling party that he would not reach them until nightfall...again.

He managed to slip by the first line of guards and approached the camp from along a drover's path higher in the hills. They were still on Cameron— actually Mackintosh—lands, but lands he knew well enough to make his way. This time he came alone. As the sun set behind the western mountains, he finally saw Sheena walking amongst the tents. Pray God she had her own, for taking her from the same tent where her parents slept would be impossible. He let out a breath of relief when she sought a smaller tent nearby and entered it alone.

Stalking in silence, it took some time to make his way around the edge of the arranged tents and approach hers. He thought about what he would say. He crawled to the

back of the tent and listened for her movements within.
She must be asleep by now. He drew his dirk and sliced
down the side of the tent, loosening the bottom of the
canvas so he could roll under it. When he gained his
feet, he saw her sitting on her pallet and calmly watching him enter.

Even in the dim light of a few candles, she looked glo-
rious—in a shift that covered most of her while giving
him enticing glimpses of her fetching curves. Memories
of that drunken night when he'd visited her chamber and
watched her move in front of the flames flooded back.
Her hair, all its golden and auburn layers, tumbled over
her shoulders and his hands itched to touch it. To wrap
it around his fist and pull her to him.

'Robbie!' she whispered, not trying to cover herself.
'What are you doing?'

'I have been told that the best way to claim a bride is
the old Highland way.'

'Claim a bride in the old Highland way? Handfasting, do you mean?' she asked.

He smiled when he realised she'd not called out a
warning about his presence.

'Well, handfasting is at the end of it, but first it involves kidnapping the bride and having your way with
her until she agrees to the handfasting,' he said. 'Or just
having your way with her?'

Images of kidnapping and having her filled his
thoughts. From the way her mouth dropped open, she
was thinking on the same thing.

'And who told you this was the old Highland way?'

She reached back and gathered her hair in her hands,
quickly dividing it into sections and twisting it into a
braid. Did she have any idea that her movement brought

her lovely breasts tight against her shift? Or that he could see the darker circles of her nipples? She might not but his aroused fellow did. He knelt down before her on the pallet.

'What?' He'd forgotten her question at the sight before him. She drew up on her knees before him, exposing her naked legs to him as she tugged a gown from the sack lying next to her pallet. Going up on her knees, she pulled the gown over her head and smoothed it down with admirable haste. 'Oh, who told me that?'

'Aye,' she said as she leaned over the edge of the pallet to search for and find her stockings and shoes.

'Geordie did.'

She stopped and tilted her head in question at his response. 'Geordie in the stables told you that? Why would he say such a thing to you?' She grabbed up the woollen plaid that lay over the pallet and folded it several times until it fitted around her shoulders.

'Apparently, 'tis how he found and married his wife. Kidnapped her and had his way with her until she was with child and accepted him.' She was dressed now and watching him. He shrugged. 'He told me when I told him my original plan.'

'This was not yours?' she asked.

'Nay. I thought to come and ask your father for help again.'

'Again?' He noticed the moment she realised the truth. 'You arranged it with my father?' Her voice quietened. 'You found a way and went to him.' Tears filled her eyes and he shook his head. This was not a time for sadness.

'The truth made him agree, Sheena. The changes you were trying to make to your behaviour and to yourself were destroying you. I could not stand by and watch that happen.' He reached out and took her hand in his. 'First I needed you safe. I needed to ken you would be safe from his machinations and my own clan's plans as well.'

'You did that for me?' Those damned tears fell freely now.

'What kind of man would I be if I allowed harm to come to you? Betrothed or not, I think we are friends. And I would protect a friend, Sheena. I would protect you.' He gained his feet and guided her to stand. 'But I want to be more than your friend.' She did not release his hand. If anything, she clasped his tighter than before. That made it easier to draw her closer and kiss her.

He just needed to feel the touch of her mouth on his. He needed to hear the sigh he knew she would release. He just needed…her. Stepping back before he lost any semblance of control, he cleared his throat.

'You need to understand about my change in fortunes before I do the kidnapping part of which we spoke.' He saw the tears had stopped and a glimmer of something more hopeful filled her gaze. 'If you come with me, if I take you, you are getting Robbie Cameron, eldest son of The Cameron, a man sworn in fealty to him and the next tanist.'

'The next tanist?' She cocked her head and shook it. 'But you are tanist.'

'Nay, no longer. If I married you as tanist, it meant forcing you to a life you dreaded, demanding you fill a role you cannot. So I did as my father had done all those years ago and gave that up in the hope that you would marry just Robbie Cameron.' He laughed. 'And to think I thought him weak for his decision. That choosing to put love above his duty was the wrong thing to do.'

'Robbie, can you change your mind? Will your father take you back when you come to your senses and realise the bad deal you have made with me?'

'I will not. Already the elders were discussing their choice, though neither Tomas nor Iain will be happy to learn of their consideration.'

He pulled her into his arms and kissed her again, this time as he'd wanted to for weeks. Their mouths touched, their tongues explored and their bodies pressed together until they were both breathless.

'But you live for duty and honour, Robbie,' she whispered in a soft tone, her breathing still shallow and quick. 'You gave your oath to your father. Will you hate me for bringing you to this?'

'My love,' he whispered, touching her mouth with his, 'I am still sworn to my clan. I will serve however my father wishes, but I would rather do it with you at my side.'

She kissed him then and Robbie remained unmoving and allowed her to seek what she wanted of him. The softness of her mouth on his sent ripples of desire through his body.

Lifting her head, she searched his face, staring into his eyes. 'And my spells and other weaknesses do not frighten you off? I cannot say how they will be in the future. I cannot read, Robbie. I cannot write or do numbers. And I cannot—'

'Yet you are able to read people and situations with an extraordinary talent. And you remember what is important here,' he said, touching her chest where her heart beat. 'We can work out ways to do what must be done, Sheena. Together.'

Tears shone in her eyes once more, but he knew they were not sorrowful but happy ones. She accepted him with another searing kiss. If they did not stop this, he would never get her out of the camp.

'I will only do the kidnapping and the taking or having my way if you tell me you agree. It must be of your own free will. I will not take another step if you do not love me as I love you or if you would rather another man to husband or none at all.'

'You daft man,' she whispered. 'I have wanted you since I hated you all those years ago. And I have loved you since almost the same time. It just took some time to understand that.'

'You love me?' he asked.

She slid her arms around him again and lifted up on her toes to kiss him. 'Aye.' She smiled at him and laughed. 'And you love me?'

'Aye,' he said. 'Come now, before it gets too late and someone hears us.'

'How does this kidnapping work?'

'We have to get to Wee Dubh, then to the horse I left on the road and, after our escape, I take you to my lair and have my way with you.'

And they did just that.

She thought he was giving up so much to be with her, but Robbie knew the truth of it. He was gaining everything by choosing her love.

Though their movements alerted some of the guards, who gave chase, once they were on Wee's back nothing could stop or catch them. The sound of her laughter behind him warmed his heart and told him this was the right thing.

Rurik was about to call out the order to mount up when the sound echoed back from the road. Connor halted his cousin with a motion of his hand.

Sheena's laughter, a sound he had not heard in years, told him everything he needed to know. She was safe with Robbie. But, more importantly, she loved the man as he did her.

He would tell Jocelyn that he'd been right about the boy who'd lived with them all those years ago. That he had honour and would do his father and his clan proud.

When Robbie had strode into his tent last evening and demanded justice for Sheena even when it meant losing her, Connor recognised the truest love for Sheena lived within his foster son's heart.

So if Sheena wanted him, and the laughter told him she did, Connor would find a way to accept it. For Robbie Cameron had given him his daughter back, and given him a chance to make up for his mistakes.

And that was worth any price a man, a father, could pay.

They rode for a few hours while the second night of the moon's fullness lit their way. After sleeping in the shelter of a large tree for a few hours, wrapped in his plaid and hers, he led them along a road Geordie had spoken of that led to Loch Lochy farther north than Achnacarry. To a small church where a Cameron cousin served as priest in a Celtic order. It would be a wedding that was accepted in this part of the Highlands and more binding than a simple handfast.

The ceremony was quick and simple, they exchanged their vows and, after his cousin's good wishes, they rode south and entered the clearing above the falls from this other direction.

Robbie helped her from Wee's back and tied the horses at the edge of the clearing so the sound of the falls would not frighten them. Taking her hand in his, they walked to the door of the cottage. The surprised expression on her face as she opened the door told him that Tavie and the other women of the village had helped him as he'd asked.

Chapter Twenty-Four

Ⰹⰰⰴⰽⰰⰱ

It was so different inside, Sheena was certain it was not the same cottage above the falls she'd visited before with him. The crashing of the water so near told her it was.

'Tavie and the other women were here,' Robbie said, waiting for her to enter ahead of him.

'You told them of your plan?' Sheena glanced around and smiled. 'They did this for you?'

'Nay, my wee beastie,' he said, pulling her into his arms and kissing her…again. 'They did this for you. For your wedding night.'

''Tis not night.' She nodded at the sunlight streaming into the cottage through not only the open door but the small windows on the other side.

'Are you worried over what will happen between us?' he asked.

'Nay,' she said with a shake of her head that turned into a nod. 'Aye.' She laughed and repeated, 'Aye. Especially about the light of day.'

'But I held you by the river in the light of day,' he reminded her. 'I kissed you.' He kissed her until he stole the breath from her body. 'I touched you.' His hand slid up to cup her breast. As his thumb stroked over the tip of it, she sighed. 'And I touched you here as well.'

He guided her hands onto his shoulders and kicked the door shut behind them. Unlike the time by the river, he used both of his hands to gather the length of her gown and lift it up until she felt the cool breeze in that private place. But that air did not cool the growing heat within her body. Robbie slid one of his hands between her thighs and moved it slowly up until he brushed the curls.

Her core clenched and her legs shook in anticipation of more. Slipping his hand deeper, his fingers dipped into the folds of heated flesh and he stroked. She moaned and began to tumble against him. Wrapping his free arm around her waist, he held her up and tormented her over and over with his intimate caresses.

'Do you remember this, Sheena?' Another moan was her reply for she could not form a word. 'When I touch you here—' he touched her in that place '—you liked it.'

Soon, she was mindless to everything but the movement of his hand and his fingers. As his thumb pressed that place, that throbbing, slick, heated place, and her body tightened and tightened until something spun out of control. Waves of pleasure raced through her blood and tremors shook the whole of her.

'Oh, you are beautiful to watch in your satisfaction.'

Sheena opened the eyes she didn't even realise she'd shut and met his gaze. Her body was being held up by his arm around her, for her legs would no longer hold her. He scooped her up into his arms and carried her to the pallet now in the corner. Pulling a blanket loose, he laid her down and stepped back. When she tried to tug her gown back in place, he stopped her.

'You saw all of me, but I have not seen the rest of you, lass. Take it off for me. Show me all of you.'

She hesitated for a moment and then laughed at her nervousness. He'd given her pleasure twice over and had not sought his own. She had seen him, all of him, as he'd walked from the river. Like an ancient god of the water, the rivulets had rushed over his body, following the contours of his muscles and streaming over his flesh. She'd touched him.

She wanted to touch him again. And bring him pleasure as he had her, if that was possible.

'Will you let me see you?' he repeated softly.

His body trembled and he laughed. The smile he gave her was full of wicked promise. He did not wait for her but tossed his plaid and his jack onto the table. His shirt followed and, quicker than she thought possible, he stood before her, his strength and every bit of him open to her sight. She sighed at his male beauty. His hard flesh jutted out of the nest of dark curls, begging for her touch. When she reached out for him, he grabbed her hand.

'If you touch me now, I will be done.'

She frowned at his words.

'I will spend my seed before I want to.'

Men thought about such things?

'This is the part when I have my way with you, love.' She loved hearing that from him. 'Lie down, but first—' he said, reaching for her gown.

The way his flesh moved as he saw her naked form filled her with some kind of excitement she'd never felt before. He wanted her. He wanted to join with her. Robbie guided her to the pallet and knelt between her legs. Although she clenched her knees together, he eased them apart with his hand on her thighs.

He could see every part of her now and that made her shiver from deep within. As her legs fell open, he leaned over and kissed the sensitive skin on her thighs. Her head tilted back and she moaned. The pleasure, the tension, was building again. He slid his mouth across her thighs and moved closer and closer to that place where every feeling, every sensation centred. The touch of his hot mouth on the folds between her legs sent her careening over an edge she did not know was there.

But her body did.

Her hips arched against his mouth and his tongue and he traced along the folds over and over, faster and deeper until she let go. This time, she could not hold in the scream of pure pleasure as she throbbed against him.

She thought him done, when he pushed himself up and moved into the cradle of her thighs. He rubbed his hardness along her cleft until he found the entrance to that deeper core. Her body was so relaxed and her pleasure so strong that she felt only a brief sting and a few moments of tight stretching as he filled her. Sheena sighed as he paused, allowing her body to adjust to his flesh.

'Sheena, lass, speak to me.' His whisper was filled with worry and it warmed her heart. 'Are you well?'

She did not mean to, but as her inexperienced body reacted to the feeling of being filled with his flesh, she tensed the muscles she was now aware of within her core. The way his hardened flesh flinched and his intake of breath at it told her he liked it. The stinging soon eased and he moved deeper again. Her body eased and readied for him. Stroke after stroke, some deep, some shallow, slow and easy and then fast and hard, and her body wound tight once more and exploded under his. He leaned against her neck, suckling on that sensitive skin as his flesh hardened within her. With a moan of his own, he joined her and they reached that pinnacle of pleasure together.

He stayed within her for some moments and she enjoyed the closeness and the warmth of his body. The exhaustion of the last weeks and last night's journey took its toll and she fell asleep still joined with him.

When she next opened her eyes, the darkness of night surrounded the cottage. Robbie lay draped over and around her, with nothing between them. His flesh rose, pressing against her, and her body reacted to it. Her hips arched against him as though seeking it.

''Tis your wedding night, lass.'

'Aye, 'tis night-time.' She leaned back and turned her head, allowing his kiss. 'How is it different from what we did in the daylight?'

'So much wickedness exists in the dark of the night. Shocking deeds to be done. Pleasures to be had.'

She stretched and shuddered, pressing against him, and sliding along his hard muscles. And, as he caressed her from her shoulders, over her breasts, across her belly to that place that ached the most, her stomach grumbled so loudly that they both laughed.

'Still not eating?' he asked. He eased away and found a basket packed for them with cheese and bread.

'I would have, but someone was kidnapping me and having his way with me.' She sat up and he handed her a piece of the cheese.

'I will take care of you now, Sheena. Always.'

'And I you,' she promised.

That night and for several more, they found pleasure in each other. They returned to Achnacarry to make peace with his family and soon visited her parents, where she found a comfort with them she'd not experienced before in her life.

It took some time for her fears to lessen and to find a way to contribute to their clan, but Robbie was always by her side. As he was for the rest of their lives together.

Through good times and bad. Through joyful times and sad ones. Through peace and times of strife. Through births and deaths. They took care of each other.

Because she'd loved him before she'd hated him and she'd liked him before she loved him again.

And he realised that he'd loved his wee Highland beastie from the moment he'd pushed her in the river… both times.

* * * * *

If you enjoyed this book, why not check out Terri Brisbin's A Highland Feuding miniseries

Stolen by the Highlander
The Highlander's Runaway Bride
Kidnapped by the Highland Rogue
Claiming His Highland Bride
A Healer for the Highlander

And be sure to read her story in the Sons of Sigurd collection

Tempted by Her Viking Enemy

Author Afterword

As you might have realised, my heroine Sheena Mac-Lerie suffered from two medical conditions that would have made her life today challenging at best and terrible at worst. But since she lived in the fourteenth century, those conditions would have been even more frustrating and dangerous for her and her family.

Dyslexia is a language-based learning disorder with a cluster of symptoms which result in difficulties in language skills such as reading, spelling, writing and pronouncing words. To sufferers, letters can seem reversed, or appear scrambled and confusing visually. Even today it can be difficult to recognise, diagnose and treat, since the way it presents varies, and a lifelong approach must be utilised since there is no 'cure' for it.

Panic attacks—or panic disorders—have many variations, from how long they last to the symptoms a person suffers. They're usually brought on suddenly, and can be infrequent, occasional or frequent. The very stress of the fear of having an attack can trigger one. Mostly, they peak and last only a short time—sometimes just minutes—but they can last longer. They are often followed by exhaustion or a feeling of being worn out.

The most common symptoms are a fear of a loss of control, a fear of death, a rapid, pounding heart-rate, sweating, trembling or shaking, shortness of breath or difficulty in breathing, chills, hot flushes, nausea, chest pain, headache, and a feeling of unreality or detachment.

As I said, these conditions are confusing, and people with either or both face huge challenges in their lives.

In medieval times, though, there would have been no rational explanation for these behaviours...so they would have been blamed on the devil, and the sufferer would have been suspected of being under the devil's control or 'possessed'. Such people would have been evaluated by the Church and treated harshly because of their condition. In later times they would most likely have been accused of being witches.

So Sheena would have been both ashamed and terrified by the 'spells' or 'fits' she suffered, as well as distressed by her inability to do even the simple task of learning her words and numbers. And her parents—even a father as powerful as the Beast of the Highlands— would have had few options except to try to keep her from the view of people who would draw the attention of the Church to her.

The descriptions above are very elementary, and don't begin to explain or detail the complexity of either dyslexia or panic attacks/panic disorder. If you suspect you or someone you know or love suffers from panic attacks, you can get more information from your primary care centre or a mental health professional. For information on dyslexia, contact your local school system, learning specialist or paediatrician.